BLOOD SUGAR

BLOOD SUGAR

Sascha Rothchild

G. P. PUTNAM'S SONS
NEW YORK

PUTNAM
— EST. 1838 —

G. P. Putnam's Sons
Publishers Since 1838
An imprint of Penguin Random House LLC
penguinrandomhouse.com

LIBRARY OF CONGRESS CATALOGING-IN-PUBLICATION DATA

Names: Rothchild, Sascha, author.
Title: Blood sugar / Sascha Rothchild.
Description: New York : G. P. Putnam's Sons, [2022]
Identifiers: LCCN 2021051104 (print) | LCCN 2021051105 (ebook) |
ISBN 9780593331545 (hardcover) | ISBN 9780593331552 (ebook)
Subjects: LCGFT: Thrillers (Fiction) | Novels.
Classification: LCC PS3618.O8644 B56 2022 (print) |
LCC PS3618.O8644 (ebook) | DDC 813/.6—dc23
LC record available at https://lccn.loc.gov/2021051104
LC ebook record available at https://lccn.loc.gov/2021051105
International edition ISBN: 9780593541562

Printed in the United States of America
1 3 5 7 9 10 8 6 4 2

Book design by Ashley Tucker

For Matt.
I knew when you first walked into
the room, and I still know.

BLOOD SUGAR

CHAPTER 1

OCEAN

THE WAVES WEREN'T THAT BIG. BUT HE WAS ONLY SEVEN, SO even the smallest of chop towered over his drenched head. "Never turn your back on the ocean" was advice he would never hear. Instead he faced the shore, proudly gesticulating. His father was busy, drinking a sweating can of domestic beer and complaining to his group of friends about the lack of waterfront-zoning laws. His mother was busy looking at the stretch marks drifting across her once flat, smooth stomach. So neither noticed their son waving and smiling at them in the Atlantic Ocean, just thirty feet ahead.

At the moment he was going to give up on making eye contact with his parents and turn toward the blue-on-blue horizon, a crest crumbled and slapped him in the back, pitching him forward, facedown, forcing him to take a big gulp of warm salty water. He coughed. A new wave jostled him before he could regain his natural rhythm of breath, and then another. So panic started to set in. A panic with flailing arms, jerking legs, and lungs fighting against themselves, taking turns both hyperventi-lating and coughing. Soon, all his composure was lost. It seemed like the ocean knew he was in trouble, and was happy to take advantage. Toying with his fifty-four-pound frame.

The rest was easy. Too easy, really. I was a breaker away, watching it all, holding my head high above the water, my neck straining a little so I could see him struggle in the undulating foam. My first instinct was to help him. I was a strong swimmer. I could paddle over and prop him up and call out to an adult to get him safely to shore. Then a second instinct kicked in, if there can be such a thing as a second instinct. A calm resolve filled my chest, followed by a burst of gold-glitter excitement that traveled to the tip of every limb. I dove under the water, eyes open. The sting felt good, a reminder that I was alive.

The ocean was murky, so it was hard to make out details, but I was able to see enough to grab on to one of the boy's slick, thrashing ankles. My hand was too small to get a good hold. He was only seven years old, yes. But I was only five.

Using both my tiny hands, I had just enough grip to pull him down. And hold him down. A calmer boy might have held his breath and kicked free. He was only inches from oxygen. But he wasn't calm. He was sucking in more and more water. Until he wasn't.

When I felt his leg go slack, I held on for ten more seconds. Just to make sure. Counting slowly backward. Like I learned in school. Like I did when I couldn't fall asleep at night because my brain was swirling with too many high-voltage thoughts to power down for the day. When I reached the count of one, I let go of his ankle and swam away. Flipping my back legs together in unison, like a mermaid tail. I wasn't so different from other five-year-old girls; I too loved mermaids.

When my own need for air became unbearable, I finally popped my head up a good distance from him. I searched the water until I saw his lifeless form being pushed closer to the shore, gently swaying with the seaweed. The ocean delivered him onto the sand, not wanting to play with a dead toy.

I didn't even need to scream. His mother was already doing that. Adults raced to him, rushed and frantic, unwilling to accept that time was no longer a factor.

My mother started shrieking for me to come back in, worried that drowning was somehow contagious. As I splashed to shore, I thought about how primitive adults were sometimes. And predictable. All the swimming kids were plucked back to land, held tightly in oversized once-bright tropical-patterned towels, now faded from years of use in the sun. For a brief moment, parents and children alike were not taking anything for granted. We all noticed details like the scratchy, hard corner edges of the towels, the grace of a seagull gliding past the billowing clouds that hinted at the afternoon rain that would be coming, the beauty of the peeling pink and green pastel buildings lining the bright-sanded beach. The warmth of the air was only trumped by the warmth of skin hugging skin and the rise and fall of chests that housed healthy beating, living hearts.

As my mother held me, I waited for guilt to set in. But it never did.

CHAPTER 2

PHOTOGRAPH

TWENTY-FIVE YEARS LATER I SAT IN A SMALL INTERROGATION room inside the Washington Avenue branch of the Miami Beach Police Department. A cup of water was placed on my side of the table. The chair I was told to sit in was metal and flimsy. Light enough to pick up and swing around and throw at someone, but also light enough to not do much damage to property or person, if thrown. The table was also metal, but thicker and heavier and bolted to the concrete floor. There were some long scratches in it, of varying degrees of depth and age. Decades of frenetic doodles and cuts made by the people who had been trusted enough to hold sharp objects while sitting there.

I had my purse with me, which I hung on the back of the tin chair. A nice bag to show I was a professional working woman. But not so nice as to be flashy. And inside it, I had a few pointy items. A purple pen. A house key. Tweezers. A nail file. I also had my wallet in there, with identification confirming I was

Ruby Simon. Miami Beach resident. Thirty years old. Five five. Organ donor. My weight a lie. Brown eyes. Brown hair, because auburn was not an option at the DMV. My hair was a deep pecan color dappled with copper. And so were my eyes. The reddish flecks in my nut-brown irises matched my mane perfectly. And this color coordination was the most striking thing about me, physically, and pulled my otherwise unremarkable face together. I thought about taking out my nail file and idly smoothing a few edges, to show how unconcerned I was about this whole thing. But it felt like it might read as too performative, so I kept my would-be weapons in my purse.

The man who gave me the water was Detective Keith Jackson. He lumbered into the seat on the other side of the table and placed a closed file folder in between us. No doubt a tactic to put me on edge. To make me squirm and worry about what could possibly be inside the folder. I refused to give in to basic interrogation techniques. I didn't squirm, but instead sat still. And looked at the man in front of me. He was handsome and weathered, maybe fifty. His head was completely bald and smooth. He had a nicely shaped skull. Symmetrical. And a small nick on his neck from shaving. As he settled in, I caught a glimpse of his ankle skin, peeking out over his black sock. His pants were a little too short for his well-over-six-foot height.

He slowly opened the folder. Making a real meal of pulling out four pieces of paper, which I could tell from the edges were all photographs. He looked at each one, hidden from my view, and then purposefully placed each facedown on the table, until all four were in a tidy row in front of me. He certainly wasn't concerned with seeming too performative. This felt like more of a game show than a police interview. *Behind photograph number one is either life in prison, or a brand-new living room set!*

Then he turned over the first photo. It faced me. A smiling seven-year-old boy, awkwardly posed, wearing a pressed collared shirt, stared up at me. An unease started gnawing through my ribs. I remembered that very school picture day so well because my big sister, Ellie, couldn't decide what to do with her hair for her own school picture. As I looked at the backs of the other three hidden photos, the gnawing gave way to an educated guess. If they were like the first, they were each of a different person. And I knew these four people had at least two things in common. One, they were all dead. And two, they all died within arm's reach of me.

To be clear, I'm not a sociopath. I've studied myself. I've felt empathy and sympathy. I've had long-lasting friendships and relationships. I've laughed so much so often that my obliques get sore like I've been rowing a boat. And I've cried too. At normal things like breakups, goodbyes, and manipulative commercials about cars with safe airbags. I've felt compassion. For the homeless. For the starving. For the lost. I'm also extremely kind to animals. Even as a young child, I boycotted the evil elephant-using circus every year when it rumbled into town. To put it simply, I respected life. But Keith Jackson didn't know this. He stared me down, wanting to believe the worst of me, waiting for me to break.

After a pause long enough to make most people uncomfortable, the detective laid into me. He started by leaning back, away from the photos, a show of calm strength. He said, "I've been on the force twenty years. Before that I was in the army. And no one has ever died in front of me. Not one person. Soldier. Civilian. Cop. Criminal. Not a one. Sure, I've rushed junkies to the hospital while they overdosed. I've hauled my fair share of people with gunshot wounds into ambulances. And of course, when I'm called in to investigate a homicide, I'll see a corpse or two. But never has anyone had a freak accident and died while in the same room as me. Even my ninety-year-old grandma gracefully passed away when I was out of the house.

"But you. You have four dead people in your midst. At least. That I know about for sure. And one of them is your husband." He punched the word *husband,* to make sure it hit hard, in the air. I felt it. But did not flinch. He leaned forward, his broad shoulders hulking in, just a little. "How do you explain that, Ms. Simon?"

It was a valid question. And as I decided how I might respond to him, my mind raced back and all the details of my life that led me to this exact moment came to the surface. It was like *Remembrance of Things Past,* but instead of waxing poetic about my life while drinking a cup of tea, I had a cup of tap water. Which I was sure was given to me to acquire my DNA and fingerprints without a warrant. Before I answered him, I took a long sip, knowing my DNA and fingerprints were not going to help this homicide detective one way or the other anyway.

CHAPTER 3

ELLIE

THE BOY IN THE PHOTO, THE BOY I MURDERED, WAS NAMED Duncan Reese. He was a bratty only child governed by the assumption that there was a limited amount of happiness in the world. So if some other kid was happy, it zapped Duncan of his own joy. Because of this toxic belief, he took it upon himself to sabotage the merriment of others. Joshua got a new bike. Duncan smashed it with a baseball bat. Vicky was chosen to play a piano solo for the back-to-school assembly. Duncan "mistakenly" broke the school's piano while "horsing around" in the auditorium that morning. To celebrate his birthday, Griffin brought in chocolate chip cupcakes for everyone in his class. Duncan, not in Griffin's class, decided if he couldn't enjoy one, no one should. Claiming it was unfair, he flung the cheery red-and-orange-polka-dotted box into the school hallway, ruining all twelve cupcakes inside.

I was too young to be on Duncan's radar, and although I was energetic and spirited, I rarely exuded actual happiness, so he never tormented me. It was my older sister, Ellie, who was his favorite target. Also seven, she was in his grade. They had known each other since prekindergarten, and each year the systematic bullying got worse. Ellie had ringlets of curly sunset-colored hair and big green eyes. Traits of beauty later in life, but in childhood, fodder for teasing. Lizard Eyes and Snake Head were her usual nicknames. Whatever. She didn't lose sleep over it, especially since even crueler names existed for other kids in school. But Duncan took the teasing and added viciousness. He would often block her path in doorways, trip her on stairs, and drop insects he caught and trapped into her lap in class so she would jump up, screaming, and look like a fool. He constantly threatened that he was going to hold her down and cut off each crimson curl, one by one. Or maybe, if he felt like it, yank them out instead. One day during a fire drill, he made good on his promise and actually ripped out an entire lock, leaving a bloody bald spot on her porcelain scalp.

Duncan swore it was an accident. He got off with a casual warning to play more gently, especially with girls. Victim-blaming starts young. It somehow became my sister's fault for being too delicate. Too breakable.

After that, I started to worry. She was not just my sister; she was also my best friend, my safe place, my idol, and my god. She was my prize possession. Ellie was, and still is, my favorite thing in the whole wide world. I feared Duncan would break her to the point of no repair. Ruin her forever. Because of Duncan, she was ashamed of her fiery hair, she rarely smiled, and she stopped playing dress-up and pretend with me altogether. She started to hate school, looked over her shoulder constantly, refused to use public bathrooms, and now had nightmares. Duncan was infecting even her most private moments. Her dreams. I could hear her through the walls, yelping in her sleep. Our bedrooms were connected by a bathroom that we shared, and her pitiful cries echoed across the black and white Art Deco tiles. Our parents' bedroom was far away, on the other side of the kitchen. So no one but me could hear Ellie's whimpering.

Years of therapy have taught me not to use the word *should*. It's empty and pointless. But fuck it. My parents should have taken more action against the bullying. The teachers should have protected Ellie and stopped it. The principal should have kicked Duncan out of school long before things got so bad. But none of them really saw it the way I did. Like Duncan's parents on the shore, they were all too wrapped up in their own lives to notice Ellie's confidence and sparkle fading away. Because to a great degree Ellie *was* my life, I was the one to clearly notice her descent into wishing to be invisible.

Before Duncan accelerated his engine of persecution, Ellie was vivacious, effervescent, kind, and giving. But not cloyingly sweet or desperate to make friends. She had her own strong opinions, one being that poems should have to rhyme. But she was open to listening to others, and if anyone needed a fourth for box ball, even if she wasn't totally in the mood, she would jump in. She made any room she was in more appealing, always fun yet never frantic. Like a perfectly balanced scented candle. The opposite of Duncan, she believed joy was limitless, not a commodity to be stolen. The more others felt happiness, the more she felt it. So she tried to spread it around, multiply it until it filled the whole world. She smiled at the elderly who were so often ignored; she made nondenominational holiday cards for everyone on our block, including the grumpy divorced lady on the corner. She chatted with the school bus driver so he wouldn't feel left out of the conversations going on in the back.

And unlike most big sisters, she let me play in her room. I had a swing set in the backyard, toys of my own, a box of arts and crafts supplies, and plenty of colored pencils and construction paper to keep me occupied. But despite these distractions, I couldn't keep my hands off Ellie's perfume bottle collection. Each with a different magical shape and hue and smell. The mini crystal sculptures were so pretty all lined up on their little shelf. And, shockingly, even prettier all smashed on the floor.

I didn't mean to knock the biggest one over, causing a catastrophic crash. But once I did, I was mesmerized by the droplets of broken colored glass that smelled like flowers and candy. I reveled in the beauty of the destruction. I was so immersed, I didn't hear Ellie come home and into her room. She found me happily playing in the glassy potpourri. I looked up, embarrassed. I saw the betrayal and fury on her face and she burst into tears. "How could you?!" she screamed at me. I too burst into tears. I explained it was a horrible accident, but it all looked so pretty that I couldn't resist in making the best of it and playing in the aftermath of her perfume bottle massacre.

Ellie noticed my hand was bleeding. A shard of pink perfume bottle glass was lodged in the fleshy heel of my left palm. She removed the sliver and held a towel to the wound to stop the bleeding. She forgave me because she loved me more than she loved the glass bottles. She loved me as much as I loved her. And together we carefully cleaned up the sharp, sweet-smelling, colorful mess.

Unlike Duncan, I would never intentionally destroy anything that brought her joy. And she saw me sobbing, and she knew that. So she grieved for her broken bottles, but didn't hold on to any anger toward me. That's how amazing she was. She could let go of resentment and see the best in people, if they had any best in them. And I did. I had a lot of best in me.

My parents knew Duncan Reese was rotten, and my mother happily predicted that he would end up working at a gas station one day, while my sister would be successful and fabulous. To my mother, it seemed, working at a gas station was the lowest of the low. But that prediction didn't help the situation at the moment. That didn't stop Ellie's scalp from bleeding. It didn't quicken the months and months it took for her curl to grow back and reach a length that suited the other curls. By the time Duncan would be working at said gas station, Ellie would be so beaten down and haunted that she would never bloom into being successful and fabulous. And she would never be happy, a quality my mother left out of the equation.

Both my mother and father, who were contentedly married and more often on the same page than not, believed children were little individuals, capable of making their own decisions. In a new world of "helicopter moms," they could have been best described as "submarine parents." Always there, a giant lumbering presence, but often unseen and too deep to be accessible. They felt more like helpful landlords than parental figures. Each raised in a controlling, unpleasant household, they allowed the pendulum to swing perhaps too far the other way when raising their own offspring. They wanted us kids to work it out on our own. Learn to interact with all kinds, fill our toolboxes with skills, like being social, using negotiation tactics, and problem-solving with guile. They would, however, pop up from the depths from time to time to give advice and guidance. They actually wanted us to talk to strangers. My mother would point out a guy in the park.

"Go say hello."

"To that man in the overcoat?"

"Yup. Give it a shot. Suss out for yourself if you like him or not."

"But . . . why?"

"So you can learn to trust your own gut. If you don't like him, walk away. Or run. But if you never make contact, you'll never have your own barometer."

My parents certainly weren't perfect, but that was a lesson in self-preservation that has served me well. I know what I feel about people. Immediately. What to do with those feelings next is another question.

My parents never expected me or Ellie to rise above it all. We could lash out and complain and talk back, but we were expected ultimately to handle life and all its foibles and unfairness ourselves. So my parents didn't hover. Instead they glided along the deep, and stayed out of the Duncan mess. I could not stay out of it. He was evil and he had to go. I saw an opportunity, and I took it. So that day on the beach, murder became another skill added to my toolbox. And once I saw how effective a tool it was, I kept it handy.

I was born with an inner strength that pushed me to help those who were weaker. In fact, just two weeks before that day in the ocean, I heard a pitiful squawking outside our den. I investigated, and in the grass behind the star fruit tree, I saw a small bird with a broken wing, trapped on the ground, bound by gravity like the rest of us. I gingerly scooped up the warbler and raced inside, hysterical. I yelled, "We have to do something!" My mother, effortlessly stunning, her long, wavy red hair barely tamed by a ribbon, put down the crossword puzzle and retied her thin sarong around her neck, as if to establish she was getting down to business.

"Grab the Yellow Pages," she said. I did what I was told. She found what she was looking for, grabbed the phone, and dialed. After the first ring she handed it over to me, saying, "This is your discovery. Your patient. You should be the one to speak."

I heard two more rings and then, "Bird Sanctuary. This is Benita."

I was nervous. But spoke. "Hi, Benita. I'm Ruby. I found a bird."

Not ten minutes later I was in the car, speeding to South Miami. My mother driving, me in the back seat holding the fluttering little soul gently in my hands.

Benita was about the same age as my mother, forty. But she was plumper and softer. Round and slow and comforting, superficially better suited to work at a panda sanctuary. I handed her the wounded package and she said, "You're a good girl. It takes a kind spirit to understand that even the most common bird deserves a chance at a full and fruitful life." I gulped down the compliment and looked around at the tropical flowers, bright and open, vulnerable to the world but still unafraid. I sensed the lush trees were teeming with so much avian energy that it seemed the trunks themselves could fly away. And I peered into the large well-kept cages filled with hopping rehabbing feathered creatures, beaks stoic yet delicate all at once. This was a good place. The right place. So why were there tears in my eyes?

Benita understood I had bonded with my small ward and didn't want to say goodbye. She pet my head, just like I had pet the bird's minutes before, and said, "Don't worry, you can come back and visit anytime." I nodded and turned to leave, keeping my head held high, to help the pressure of tears lessen against the inside of my eyelids. Then Benita called after me. "Wait! What is your bird's name?"

At that time, I was the youngest kid in first grade and had already been put in the gifted program at my elementary school. The IQ test they had me take seemed like a fun game. "Which shape doesn't fit? Which pattern is interrupted?" I had an inquisitive nature and a natural ability to eavesdrop undetected, so the world seemed an endless orb of intrigue. I had an impressive vocabulary for my age (*encourage* and *fuchsia* being my latest word additions) and a very active imagination. Spinning yarns about princess unicorns who imagine human children are make-believe.

I don't want to be misleading. I was not a genius any more than I was a sociopath. I was not a prodigy. I didn't play the violin or chess, I didn't understand computer code, I didn't learn Japanese. I am smart, above average, but certainly not an anomaly. I was simply very advanced, especially verbally. Probably because I was the youngest in a family of wordsmiths, trying to keep up with everyone else.

But when asked to name the bird, I went blank. All my precociousness and creativity seeped out of me at an alarming rate because I was using up my energy fighting so hard to hold in my tears. After a beat of searching all the corners of my brain, all I could think to say was, "Mr. Bird." My mother looked at me, surprised. Was I being ironic? Benita, not knowing anything about my above-average background, thought this was a totally acceptable name choice from a small child. "Wonderful. We will take very good care of Mr. Bird."

And over time I did visit Mr. Bird. Eventually, once her wing healed, she was released back into the wild, but year after year I bonded with the birds that were forever residents, those who would never survive without human care. And I made that bird sanctuary my own sanctuary. A place to volunteer, to breathe, to take in nature. And also a place to hide one of my dark secrets deep in the trees. Detective Keith Jackson would never find it there. I was sure of it. Especially not now, all these years later.

I relaxed my jaw, to be sure not to show any signs of tension. I picked up the photo of Duncan, held it respectfully, and let out a resigned sigh. I looked at Detective Jackson, making direct eye contact but blinking enough to seem natural. I said, "I knew him. He drowned when we were really little. It was so terrible. Tragic. My whole school was totally freaked out." I put the photo back, right where it had been on the table. And waited for what the clever detective would say next.

CHAPTER 4

CHILDHOOD

IN THE WEEKS AFTER DUNCAN'S DEATH, I LISTENED IN AS the teachers whispered at school. "Such a tragedy." "He will be missed." "Sure, he was a handful, but what a wonderful little boy." "He was so special that God wanted him up there in heaven."

If I had believed in any of that religion stuff, it would have been hell for Duncan Reese. Not heaven. And these were the same teachers who had cringed when they saw him barrel into their classrooms. The same teachers who gave a quiet sigh of relief when he was out sick. The same teachers who gossiped about Duncan's parents and how they were raising a terror. And now that he was dead, he was considered a beloved child taken from this earth way too soon. I was confused.

I asked my mother if there was a word for when people think one thing and say another. Or say one thing but do another. She opened our giant dictionary, forest green and leather-bound, with gold inlay title letters, weighing in at twenty-nine pounds, regally perched on its very own hand-carved wooden podium throne in our dining room. My family usually had debates about words over dinner, so it made sense to house it there.

She turned to the *H* section. She flipped a few pages and pointed to the word *hypocrisy.* I read the definition. "A pretense of having a virtuous character that one does not really possess." My mother helped me sound out the bigger words, and I then needed to look up *pretense* and *virtuous.* But once I got my facts straight, everything crystallized. People are hypocrites!

Maybe not all of them. But a lot of them. Acting one way but expecting others to act a different way. Doling out rules they themselves pretend to follow but don't. At first it seemed the amount of adult-on-child hypocrisy was alarming, until I paid attention to the nuance and realized adult-on-adult hypocrisy ran just as rampant. Hypocrisy is not an ageist disorder.

After Duncan's watery demise, I learned about a common subset of hypocrisy. An agreed-upon artifice that once someone is dead, they magically become perfect in the eyes of the living. Dead children and dead adults alike. They take on a new form. Like in the right light, an oil slick in the ugliest of public parking lots turns into a magical mini rainbow. "Don't speak ill of the dead," people say. But why? It's as good a time as any to be honest. Maybe even the best time.

There was an assembly at the elementary school to talk about grief. A funeral. A makeshift memorial strewn with toys and flowers set up at the beach. The positive state of my mental health was exhibited in that once Duncan was gone, I had no need for continued hate. I didn't ruminate on his past vile deeds. The dangerous feeling of malice didn't linger in my blood, poisoning me; instead it dispersed into the salty sea foam with his gasps.

The other thing I noticed after his death was that no one, aside from members of my own immediate family, used the word *dead*. They used softer words and phrases like *passed away, passed on, left us, went to heaven, met his maker, in a better place now, crossed over, perished, resting in peace, departed, returned home,* and, close but still padded with sensitivity, *deceased*. I asked my mother about this too. "Duncan is dead. He died. But no one will say the *dead* word but us. Why?"

She turned to the *E* section of the wise and heavy dictionary and showed me the definition of *euphemism*. Then she quoted Voltaire: "'One great use of words is to hide our thoughts.'" She explained that people are afraid of death, so they keep themselves safe by hiding the actual word. But that's so dumb, I thought. So immature. The word doesn't cause the thing to happen. Cancer and overdoses and airplane crashes cause the thing to happen. People like me cause the thing to happen.

We looked up *denial* next. And after learning all these words, instead of feeling life was even more out of control and unpredictable, I felt it was within my grasp. I was calmed. There was no word voodoo. There was action and reaction. And I would be the one to act. I made a vow then to never live in denial, to know what I've done. I might lie to others, but I would never lie to myself.

What I told Detective Jackson was a half-truth. The whole school was freaked out, but only briefly. And then, after a few weeks, things returned to normal. Kids started swimming in the ocean again. Teachers started gossiping about other events. The ocean-side memorial disappeared. Ellie's joyful bounce returned, and her night terrors ended. I waited for mine to begin and for the horror of what I'd done to haunt me. But instead I slept soundly, dreaming of flying high over cities, above the clouds, drinking in icy air. Feeling weightless and centered all at once. I learned that guilt is like food poisoning. If you don't feel a pang of sickness and a sour dread fill your core within twenty-four hours, you are safe. Your body will successfully destroy the undercooked chicken, or unspeakable act.

I was not the only one who felt elated in the months after Duncan died. The entire school soon seemed lighter. A curse had been lifted. And the kids who were a few steps shy of being as mean as Duncan didn't take his place as top sadist. Instead they all became kinder, almost understanding an unseen pattern in the world. Hedging their bets that Duncan's death was a karmic trap they certainly did not want to fall into.

And so I grew up. As normal as one can in a city as insane as Miami, in an era as schizophrenic as the 1990s, with parents as emotionally invested as landlords. I had killed one boy, one time. It wasn't like I was an out-of-control homicidal maniac.

CHAPTER 5

COCAINE

WHEN I WAS FIFTEEN, MY BRACES CAME OFF, MY BREASTS settled into a C-cup, and my awkward early teenage phase was over. I landed in a place most would call a "seven." Pretty, nice shape, clear skin, not going to be a model or a movie star.

Ellie left for college in New York that year. And for me the void was traumatic. We talked on the phone every few days and emailed, but I felt listless without her. My usual hobbies of Rollerblading on Ocean Drive, getting frozen yogurt with sprinkles in the bottom of the cup and on the top for equal distribution, and dancing all night to techno music in gay clubs on South Beach didn't protect me from crumbling into the empty space in my chest. So I began to look for an escape. Being a local in a city that had morphed from run-down old-age homes and crack houses to renovated designer Art Deco hotels and red-velvet-roped bars gave me an all-access pass. I knew everyone, from bouncers to valets to bartenders to club promoters, and my age was never a factor. The lawless city of Miami didn't adhere to checking IDs or worrying about underage drinking or drugging. At that time anything less egregious than gunning down tourists in the middle of the streets was mostly ignored by police.

So I was out at three in the morning, buzzed from drinking screwdrivers, hungry from dancing for hours with friends, and looking forward to onion rings and coffee at Denny's. It was harmless and innocent enough. Until real danger that could change the trajectory of my life caught up to me.

My friend's older brother was also there, hanging outside with a group of guys who were sexy in a just-got-released-from-prison kind of way. Neck tattoos, gold teeth, and a posture that dared, *Fuck with me and see what happens.* One of the guys called out to me in a voice so deep it swallowed up all the other sounds in the parking lot.

"Oye, muñeca. Come over here."

He was clearly the oldest of the group. From where I stood, I could see the black scruff on his face and the glint of a chain with a cross nestled in his abundant, dark chest hair. His arms, cut and thick, had the look of months of yard-time workouts and not upscale gym visits. This guy was not a teenage boy. And a tiny bit of familiar gold-glitter excitement swooshed through my inner void.

I sauntered over to the deep voice, trying to command a strong, sexy demeanor. Like a full-grown confident woman might.

"You want a bump?" he asked.

He showed me a little glass vial filled with white powder. And offered me a tiny gold spoon. I hesitated.

"Don't worry so much. It's good stuff."

He did a bump himself, as if to prove to me it wasn't poison. I could see his dark eyes light up for a moment as he swallowed the bitter taste that was dripping down his nasal canal and into his throat. *Fuck it,* I thought, *"The unexamined life is not worth living."* So I took the little spoon, dipped it into the white powder, and held it up to my right nostril. I daintily snorted. The blob of cocaine got stuck halfway up my nose since I didn't inhale forcefully enough. The man laughed. He then gently but purposefully grabbed my face with both his meaty hands and lowered his head. Was he going to kiss me? I wasn't against it. But he bypassed my mouth and instead put his mouth around my right nostril. This gesture felt incredibly intimate, way more so than kissing, which I had done before, a bunch.

Before I could think too much about the bizarre sensation of full lips lined with manly hair pressed against one of my face holes, he blew up my nose. Like Poseidon blowing a ship to or fro in a vast sea, this man had the power to propel the now damp and stubborn powder into my nasal canal.

He leaned back. I breathed in again, nostrils clear, and felt a power surge through me. A crackle of invincibility. I didn't need onion rings. Or coffee. I didn't need anyone or anything. Other than maybe more cocaine.

"Can I do a line?" I asked.

He looked at me with knowing amusement—bumps were for pros—then started to walk away. Had I offended him somehow? Had I asked for too much? But he stopped a few cars down, at a navy blue Infiniti.

"This your car?"

I shook my head, nope. He gave one calm glance around, and then, with an adept thrust of his palm, he popped out one of the Infiniti's side mirrors. He walked back to the Dodge Stealth we had been leaning on and opened the passenger door for me. My insides swooned. What a gentleman! I got in the car and sat, although my heart was thumping and I just wanted to run and run and run. Not out of nerves. But because I was so filled with life and energy I wanted to move, not sit low in the hard bucket seat.

It seemed my one bump was affecting me much more than his however many bumps. He clearly had more practice and a solid eighty pounds on me. I tried to stay still and play it cool, but I squirmed. I couldn't stop my legs from jiggling up and down. I watched as he spilled the powder onto the newly acquired mirror. He pulled out his wallet and used his driver's license to make two thick lines. I saw his name was Carlos Enrique Trujillo. And his license had been expired for over a year. He pulled a hundred-dollar bill from a large stack of hundreds in his wallet and rolled it into a straw. My heart now double thumped with the anticipation of getting more cocaine as well as with the thump of already having had some.

He handed me the "straw" and let me go first. Again, such a gentleman. I leaned down and snorted a whole line effortlessly. Then instinctively looked in his rearview mirror to make sure my nose was clean of white powder. My pupils stretched out, the black almost covering the auburn of my eyes. He did his line and turned the car on. His stereo blasted bass music. Every beat making me sure that my need to move was stronger than my need to stay close to the magical drug.

I turned to him and said, "Thank you." Then I tried to dart out of the car. He grabbed my arm with his giant paw, to keep me from getting out. *Fuck, fuck, fuck.* My instincts told me he was a sketchy, low-life, small-time criminal with sex appeal who was happy to give drugs to a teenage girl, but not a really bad guy. Not a guy who would make me do anything I didn't want to do. Was I wrong?

He said, "What's your name?"

I thought about lying. But at this stage, what was the point? "Ruby."

And then he happily let go of my arm, no aggression intended.

"Cool. See ya around, Ruby."

My instincts were on point. He was a good bad guy. And I ran. Feet gliding over pavement until they were gliding over sand. My high heels getting in the way of the speed I felt I had to attain. My legs wanting to pump in time with my heartbeat. I kicked off my shoes and carried them under one arm, like a football player cradling the ball. My mind raced yet was sharply focused at the same time. I could smell the faintly fishy ocean, see every glimmer of moon bouncing off the lapping waves, hear each distant siren responding to gunfire over the MacArthur Causeway. I was the most brilliant, most beautiful, most talented girl in the whole wide world. I wasn't a seven at all. In that moment I was a ten. And I wanted to stay that way.

So thus began my seen-it-before cautionary tale, an afterschool special, typical teen-on-drugs bender. The way it ended, however, the way I pulled myself out, was anything but typical. And when asked why and how I stopped cold turkey, I could never, ever admit the truth. Because to admit it would have meant I was admitting to another unspeakable truth.

A few weeks after the Denny's night, I lost my virginity to Carlos. A few weeks after that, I lost interest in him. His brutish appeal had worn off. Him stealing that side mirror no longer seemed gallant but instead seemed plain rude. He wasn't curious to learn new words. He didn't want to peruse the giant leather-bound dictionary in the dining room with me. Or to volunteer at the bird sanctuary on weekends. All he wanted was to ply me with delicious powder and have sex with me in parked cars, even though my bedroom was available. He was much more attuned to my being a minor than I was, and kept away from my house.

Carlos was the first person to give me coke, but he certainly wasn't the only person I could get it from. I had savings from babysitting jobs, allowance, a little bit of cash my great-aunt left me when she died. I could easily buy cocaine from other people, so one afternoon, after he shoplifted a Lunchables from a grocery store and offered me a small block of processed cheese, I broke up with him. I knew he had other girlfriends anyway, ones who didn't insist on using a condom every time. So he didn't try and convince me to stay with him.

My new dealer was a security guard at my high school, Miss Duvet. Rumor had it she would deal near the flagpole during lunch. And like most rumors, this one was true. The first time I bought a gram from her, she chased me down through the second wing of the dilapidated beige building. *Fuck,* I thought. *This is all some sort of setup. A sting operation. Now I'll never get into Yale!* But she was chasing me down to return a ten. I had overpaid. Miss Duvet might have been dealing schedule II narcotics to high school children while on the clock to keep them safe, but she was an incredibly honest businesswoman with integrity.

Six months into my cocaine-fueled bender, I was back in the Denny's parking lot, the easiest meeting spot to connect with friends and decide on the plan for the night. I wanted to go to Kremlin, a small gay club with the best techno and most beautiful boy go-go dancers. I felt at home at this club because, with just one bar and one dance floor, it seemed intimate and contained. Everyone in one room dancing to the same music, a way to control an uncontrollable world. And no one there was interested in groping me or leering. It was mostly gay men and the occasional lesbian smart enough to stay away from me because she knew I was way too young to be in there in the first place. The closest I got to anyone flirting with me there was when friendly drag queens would coo over my long, thick auburn hair and matching eyes.

I spent so much time at Kremlin that I actually befriended the woman who manned the coed bathroom all night selling gum, mints, candy, lollipops, spritzes of cologne, and condoms. She was worried about me since I was extremely underaged. She smiled, to let me know I had a friend in this world. And while I waited for a stall, I talked to her. I asked her about her day, her week, her life. Did she even like techno music? Did the bartenders give her free shots? She was happy to chat with me since most people came in and out and barely acknowledged her. Techno was not her favorite, but it was okay. And smelling vomit eight hours a night had definitely ruined her love for alcohol, so she did not partake in her free end-of-shift shot. Her hair was always in a tight bun, showing her beautiful, delicate features. She told me she was from Haiti, her name was Jesula, and she had been in Miami for only a year. She was petite and trim, with high cheekbones and deep-set, friendly brown eyes that seemed wise beyond her thirty years. Her strong, long fingers wiped down the sink after each use, handed people paper towels once they had washed, and kept things tidy and organized. She kept that bathroom so clean I would have done a line off the floor.

But that night my friends, Amy and Erika and Hannah and Sharon, were tired of Kremlin. They wanted to go to the enormous new club, Rox, that had just opened in Coconut Grove and flaunted a different music style on each of the five floors. They wanted to bounce from hip-hop to reggae to emo and be groped by cheesy straight men who would buy them overpriced, poorly muddled mojitos.

I would have been happy enough to go to Kremlin by myself, but something that night allowed me to be swayed. Maybe it was a deep and hidden sense of self-preservation pushing me to stay with my friends. We piled into Hannah's dad's Mazda and made the drive into Miami, over the causeway. As far as I was concerned, leaving South Beach to go to a club in Coconut Grove was like leaving Rome to go eat pasta in Cleveland.

"Don't be such a snob," Sharon said to me.

"She is so not a snob. Have you seen the guys she goes out with?" Hannah was a master at the fuck-you compliment. Building you up yet putting you down at the same time. Like, "Ruby, your French braid actually looks good today!" But I had to laugh at this one. She wasn't wrong. As I did a bump in the back seat, I reviewed my taste in boys. It was often peculiar and always inconsistent.

When we arrived at Club Rox, I realized it was eighteen-and-over night. That was the worst. It meant lots of other fifteen-year-olds would be there, and nothing about the night would feel advanced. Amy and Erika, each only children, blond best friends since kindergarten who pretended to be sisters since they wished they were, headed right to the third floor. I could hear Soft Cell's "Tainted Love" blaring. Hannah, tall and lanky and pale, dyed-black hair in a high ponytail to show off the shaved underside of her head, wanted to go to the fifth floor because she had heard the goth-themed area had an S&M room and she wanted to see if it was true. Sharon, her giant natural boobs pushed up to maximum capacity in her new push-up bra, went straight for the first-floor bar since her immediate objective was to meet a guy and get a free drink.

I had schlepped to this god-awful place to spend time with my friends, so I decided to stick with at least one of them. I worked the bar with Sharon, and we did some shots with a couple University of Miami guys. I looked at their puka-shell necklaces in disgust and wondered why it was that to me a neck tattoo of a spiderweb was sexy but these douchebag adornments were nauseating. Who was I to judge? I did another bump.

We went to the fifth floor to find Hannah. We all watched as a hot chick got spanked and flogged by a guy in cheap pleather pants. I did another bump.

Sharon, Hannah, and I made our way to the eighties-music floor and found Amy and Erika dancing. I gave up on wanting to be too cool for school and joined them. I danced and danced, the movement feeling good for my heart. I was trying to keep up with it, to give it a good reason to be beating so fast. I was having fun. Giggling and jumping and goofing around with my four best friends. Dancing to songs I loved but usually pretended I didn't. It was the closest thing to being a normal teen that I'd experienced in a long time. So I did another bump.

I had started the night with a little over a gram. I wasn't sure how much I had left. Like the ring in Frodo's pocket, the remaining coke seemed to be calling out to me, distracting me from enjoying everything else. I thought, *Maybe I should just do it all now. So I don't think about it anymore. I can snort it up, dance like crazy with my girls, then drink it off before I even head home.* It was a good plan.

Rox was not cool enough to have coed bathrooms. And the line for the women's room on the third floor was way long. So I took the stairs, two at a time, to the fourth floor. Classic rock was playing. It was the Doors. I knew this because Ellie had made it a priority to teach me about what she considered to be good music. She would put on songs and quiz me: "Who . . . is this?" If she paused in a certain way, I knew it was a clue, and the answer was the Who.

The women's bathroom was empty except for one woman. She was old. Like forty-five. But she looked much older. Haggard. Years of baking in the sun unprotected showed on her leathery and splotchy skin. Deep wrinkles around her mouth were evidence of chain-smoking cigarettes. Her gaunt face could have once been plucky but was now hollow. Her legs looked frail, patterned with varicose veins and sunspots. Her cheap, long, bright pink acrylic nails were not helping to detract from her swollen fingers but instead brought attention to them. She was skinny and bloated at the same time.

She hunched over the sink, frantically tapping a vial onto the counter. A few tiny wisps of white powder came out. Not enough to snort. She ran her finger around the rim of the vial and over the area of the counter she'd tapped on, and then pushed her finger into her gums, rubbing above her yellow, nicotine-stained teeth, trying to absorb whatever was left of the magic.

Is this what happens to a person who does too much cocaine? Do the good times run out, like the posters say? Does it have to get too expensive to keep up the habit so you end up frantically licking wisps? Does it destroy your looks and your insides and your future? Is it really a slow death by what seems at first like a fun, fast ride? The woman felt me staring at her and she looked up. Her eyes were bloodshot. And ashamed.

She said, "Ruby?"

And it took me a moment. But then I knew who she was. It was Duncan Reese's mother.

CHAPTER 6

ANGEL

MERE SECONDS AFTER DUNCAN'S BODY WAS DEEMED DEAD on arrival by the medics who had reached the beach, Duncan's mother had started screaming at his father. Blaming him. "Why weren't you watching him?! You should have been watching him!" And the father blamed the mother. "This is on you! You're the one who wanted to work on your goddamn tan and go to the beach! This is your fucking fault!"

No one blamed me.

After that day I only saw Duncan's mom a couple of times. And the last time was years ago, at the bank on Forty-First Street. I was inside on line with my parents when she stumbled in drunk. People whispered as she went to the ATM and clumsily took out cash. She then stumbled back to her car and drove off. I don't know if anyone thought to call the police and report her drinking and driving. Probably not, since she was the sad lady whose son tragically drowned long before. I knew through general eavesdropping that she had gotten a divorce two years after Duncan's death. I also knew her husband sold his cigar business and moved to Tampa. He remarried and had a new son with his new wife. He named him David.

Duncan's mother never remarried, never had more kids, and never moved. Why she stayed in Miami Beach, I can't imagine. Maybe she wanted to be haunted by the life she once had. Maybe for her it felt good to look out onto that spot in the Atlantic, like it somehow feels good to push on a bruise.

I wanted to hate her. To hate the woman who was such a horrible mother that she created and raised a monster like Duncan. A monster I was then tasked with slaying. But as I looked at her in the bathroom, I felt repulsion and pity swirl into one ugly color. I didn't feel hate. She was so broken there was no point in hatred.

"Hi, Mrs. Reese," I said back. I didn't know what else to call her.

And then I had my moment of clarity. I didn't want to be anything like her. Never ever. I wanted to have nothing in common with this damaged lonely woman wilting in the classic-rock-floor bathroom, desperate for relief from her regrets. Without hesitation I handed her my vial of coke. I noticed it was nearly one-quarter full. She looked at it, unsure, wondering if there were strings attached. Wondering if accepting it would dig her deeper into her already stifling hole.

I said, "Take it. It's all yours. Really."

Tears welled on her exhausted face. "Thank you, Ruby. You're an angel."

I walked out of the bathroom without looking back. I would wait in line on one of the other floors. I could hear a loud snort from the bathroom before the door even had a chance to swing closed behind me. I never did cocaine again.

If I had continued, would I have overdosed by senior year? Or ended up murdered in a drug deal gone bad? Or run away to live on the streets? Maybe me killing Duncan, his mother spinning out, and me then seeing her a decade later in that bathroom kept me safe from a lifetime of drugs. Maybe it was all some sort of cosmic plan. Or maybe not. My brain told me it was just a series of events that I was collating and then giving meaning. But it was hard for the cause and effect of the pieces of my life not to play on my spirit at the time.

CHAPTER 7

FLAMINGO

NOTICING MY NEARLY EMPTY CUP, THE DETECTIVE ASKED ME if I would like some more water. Or maybe some coffee? I politely said, "No, thanks," understanding he hoped to keep me there for a while. But I wasn't under arrest. Yet. I could walk out at any time. But I felt I was going to get more information out of him than he was going to get out of me. So I stayed. Curious to continue as a contestant on his game show.

Detective Jackson turned over the second photograph. I had been sitting there long enough to notice that his nails were trim and nicely buffed. He took pride in his appearance, too-short pants notwithstanding. He placed his thick pointer finger in the middle of the photo. This one was a blown-up mugshot of a middle-aged man whose nose bent to the left, like it had been broken and never set correctly. He had long, dark eyelashes, which would have nicely complemented his light brown eyes had they not been bloodshot and puffy and menacing. I recognized this man immediately. Looking at his ugly bloated face made me queasy and instantly brought me back to my high school days.

After that bathroom interaction with Mrs. Reese, I went straight-edge. No drugs or alcohol of any kind. I was clean and sober, and therefore, once I turned sixteen and had my license, I was the perfect designated driver. So I became even more popular with my friends, and their parents, since I could be counted on to always get everyone home safely. For a few years I was like a teenage soccer mom, shuttling friends from pillar to post and party to party. Leading me to another unforeseeable fateful night.

When Halloween rolled around, it was assumed that I would drive all the girls to Star Island for our friend's legendary gala. Silva's father was a famous race car driver from Brazil, and the party theme was always Carnival. Dancers were hired, ice sculptures arranged, European DJs flown in, and five different bar stations and candy stations were set up.

In early October, Sharon, Hannah, Erika, Amy, and I descended on the arts and crafts store on Lincoln Road to start creating our matching costumes. We agreed on being flamingos. Hannah was a goth flamingo with black feathers woven into the pink ones. Sharon was a slutty flamingo. Erika and Amy were pretty flamingos, and I went for as realistic a flamingo as a human could, wearing a pink leotard, fastening pink feathers to giant wire wings, and standing on one leg as much as possible while in public.

As I sipped on cranberry juice and balanced, Hannah and Erika were getting trashed on Jell-O shots and Jägerbombs. I knew puking was in their future, and I was happy we had taken Hannah's dad's car that night instead of my father's. I didn't want puke smell trapped in our back seat until the end of time.

And Hannah's parents were such lushes they probably wouldn't even notice the smell anyway.

We didn't exactly have permission to take the Mazda on Halloween, but Hannah was like, *whatever*, and she grabbed the spare keys with the oversized metal sandcastle keychain charm off the little hook in the kitchen closet.

Sharon and her new boyfriend excitedly called me over to their area of the party. They had found the mother lode of the best Halloween candy! We were all too old to go trick-or-treating, but not too old to be euphoric about baskets and baskets of every kind of choice candy. I ripped open a mini packet of peanut M&M's first. My favorite. Then moved on to mini Snickers. And Tootsie Rolls. And Skittles. And for good measure I threw an extra packet of peanut M&M's into the little pink satin purse I'd rigged up to match my wings.

By midnight Sharon and her guy took off to go have sex somewhere. Amy was dancing with Silva and not about to leave, and Hannah and Erika were taking turns puking behind the pool house. I also felt sick, from too much candy, and it seemed a good time to end the night. Hannah and Erika agreed.

By the time I got them to the car, they were puked out and nearly passed out. I piled them both in the back seat, easier that way with all the wings and feathers and drunken flailing. As I drove over MacArthur Causeway back to Hannah's house, I saw red and blue lights flashing behind me. I was sober, I had a valid license, I was going the speed limit, I hadn't done anything wrong. But my heart leapt into my throat. My palms got sweaty. Because deep inside, I knew I'd killed a boy. And even though I didn't feel guilty about it, it was technically a crime. And there is no statute of limitations on murder. And cops were trained to sniff out illegal activity and committers of felonies. Right? So would this cop somehow know my secret the moment he looked into my eyes?

I pulled over. I turned the car off. I turned the radio low. I rolled the window down. And I put my wings on the steering wheel at ten and two. I tried to breathe steadily. In and out. Silently begging an unknown entity, *Please don't haul me off to prison. I'm a good person.*

Hannah and Erika were giggling because they were drunk. And nervous because they were drunk and underage and a policeman was striding toward us. And the more they tried to suppress the giggles, the more they erupted. The cop walked up and shone his flashlight into the car, assessing the situation. I couldn't see his face well since the light was all on mine.

"License and registration," he said evenly.

I grabbed my license from my tiny pink bag, and opened the glove box to find Hannah's dad's registration.

"This is not my car. It's her dad's car," I explained, and motioned to the back seat. He looked at both girls, and I narrowed it down for him. "The goth flamingo." I found the registration and handed everything over to the cop. He glanced at it and walked back to his car. My mind raced with scenarios. Erika burped. Which made Hannah gag. And we waited.

The cop came back. It took about two minutes, but it felt like twenty. He informed me, "I ran the plates, that's why I pulled you over. This car is registered to a Richard Vale." I nodded—that was Hannah's father. The cop continued, "He has an outstanding warrant for not appearing in court for a DUI." Hannah didn't seem that shocked to hear this news. She mumbled, "Asshole." Then glanced up at the policeman. "Not you. My dad." The policeman understood.

He handed me back my license. "You have a clean record, Ruby Simon, and you are clearly sober, driving your drunk friends around." At that Hannah and Erika waved to him and giggled again. He continued, and with every word my heart thumped, waiting for the bad news that was sure to come. "You are being a conscientious citizen, and an especially responsible teenager. For that you deserve to be rewarded. So I'm not going to impound this car tonight. I want you all to get home safe. But give your friend's father this ticket. Let him know he has a warrant out. It's important." The cop then handed me a court summons for Richard Vale. His flashlight was no longer in my face, so I could see his eyes. He looked into mine. "You are a real angel. Keep up the good work." And with that he walked away, back to his lit-up car.

I breathed. Relief. The police did not have special skills to bore into my brain and uncover the truth. I was even better than innocent. I was an angel! But in a computer system somewhere, deep in the Miami-Dade County police database, my name would forever be connected to Richard Vale's on the night of October 31. At the time, as I rolled back onto the causeway and turned the radio back up, I didn't think this would be an enormous problem in my future.

Of course, as I perched on my thin, uninviting chair in the small beige room with cinder block walls, I knew there was no way for Detective Jackson to read my mind as these Halloween memories passed through. Just as there was no way for the traffic cop to see into the crystal ball of my past. Detective Jackson was just looking to rattle me. To show me photos of dead people to push me into confessing to something. I knew that what he really wanted to hear was that I killed my husband. The rest was trimming. But I continued to sit quietly.

CHAPTER 8

SYLLABI

ALTHOUGH COLLEGES EAT UP APPLICATION ESSAYS ABOUT overachievements and overcoming hardships, I didn't think writing about being a murderer and feeling absolutely no guilt about it was in my best interest, so I wrote my personal essay about my drug use. Debating the difference between a physical and emotional addiction, delving into the pros and cons of the twelve-step program adages "Once an addict, always an addict" and "One is too many, a thousand never enough." I concluded I used cocaine to fill the void Ellie had left when she left. I also concluded I was able to stop cold turkey because I never developed a deep physical addiction. Rather, I used drugs as an escape.

Again, I was lucky. I could have become physically dependent at any moment. Or I could have bought a bad batch and had a heart attack. Or bought an incredibly good batch and had a heart attack. Or irreparably ruined my nasal passageways and then been forced to escalate to smoking crack. Lost my teeth. Lost my resolve to use condoms, gotten AIDS, and ended up dead in a gutter by twenty. But none of these things happened. In my applications, I omitted my true rock-bottom moment of seeing the mother of the boy I had murdered all coked up in a bathroom, and instead wrote about my inherent sense of self-preservation. My essay (titled "Miami Vices: A Teenager on Cocaine"), my impeccable grades, my varied extracurriculars, including a long-standing relationship with the bird sanctuary, and my perfect SAT score on the verbal section got me into Yale.

My freshman year I lived on Old Campus. My roommate, Ameena, was friendly and shy, from India by way of the suburbs of Chicago, her thick, long black hair usually braided and then piled high in a bun. She always slept with two pillows, one under her head and one over her face, a system she developed when she was young and had to share a bedroom with her often loud, fussy infant twin brothers. She was just as neat as I was, making her bed each morning, hanging her clothes up immediately, keeping her little desk free of clutter. We were extremely compatible in that way, but were just different enough in our habits that life together was interesting. I used one pen, a purple-ink Pilot Precise V5 Extra Fine Rolling Ball, until that one pen ran out. And then I started with a new pen. She respected that and never borrowed my one pen, which would have thrown off my entire system. She, however, used pens erratically, several at a time, kept in a little plastic organizer. Not caring about color of ink or thickness of point. What she cared about was symmetry and even numbers. She told me that during sex she either had to have no orgasms or she had to have two. Only having one left her feeling anxious. If her boyfriend wouldn't oblige, due to laziness or drunkenness, she would take care of the second one herself.

I started college with a declared major: psychology. My penchant for eavesdropping and my curiosity about human behavior seemed like a clear path to becoming a therapist. And I thought the training would also lend some insight into my own past. I had heard that all psychiatrists and psychologists are "wounded healers," they themselves fucked up beyond belief. I wasn't sure if I was wounded exactly, but I knew there had to be some baggage in there somewhere. And I liked the notion of healing others.

College suited me because I thrived on the structure and clearly defined expectations. Each semester in each class I was given a syllabus. A list of all the lesson plans, books to read, papers to write, and tests to pass, with dates assigned to each. I hated having anything loom over me. Knowing I had to get something done was far worse than actually getting it done. So I was the opposite of a procrastinator. I would attempt to do it all immediately. This resulted in me finishing my workload about a month before the final paper was due or final test was to be given. I would then petition my professors, asking them to allow me to turn in papers early and take final exams immediately after their last lectures were given. Most professors were delighted to comply, excited to hear from a student who was asking for a reduction in time instead of the usual extension.

This way of doing things gave me weeks of extra vacation between semesters to go back to Miami Beach and frolic in the waves I so desperately missed. At first, Ameena thought I was crazy to rev up syllabus deadlines, but she quickly started to adopt my methods. We got along so well we continued to be roommates all the way until graduation.

Before winter break our freshman year, Ameena's parents found out she was dating a Black guy. They didn't care that he was kind and funny and smart. Premed at Yale. Bound to be successful. All they cared about was that his skin was even darker than Ameena's, and they worried their grandbabies would "look like soot." I could hear Ameena screaming at them on her phone while pacing our dorm hall: "Don't you worry about that since I'm not having babies at all! If you care about grandchildren, especially pale ones, I suggest you put your energy into the twins marrying light-skinned women!"

She threw her phone down, knowing this rant would whip her parents into an even bigger tizzy. And she didn't care. She was fed up and decided she would not be going back to Chicago for the winter holidays. So she followed her syllabi, pushed herself, and finished her schoolwork a solid three weeks before the official end of term. She came home with me and basked in the tropical sun day after day without wearing a hat. Letting her beautiful Indian skin get darker, just to piss her parents off even more.

By now my core group of high school friends who'd sworn to never break apart had, of course, gone in different directions. Time and distance and interests all inch people away from childhood bonds. But Hannah was in town. She was always in town, going to the University of Miami. She still lived at home and commuted to classes. She kept changing her major; schedule and syllabi were meaningless to her. She felt no rush to get anywhere.

Our first day in Miami Beach, Ameena and I grabbed an afternoon drink on Ocean Drive with Hannah, and we caught up. I was still sober, having an iced coffee. It was strange to see Ameena and Hannah chatting, two friends from two different parts of my life. But it felt nice, the space-time continuum coalescing. Hannah's aggressive goth style had softened a little, become more refined. She was now goth chic, or, as she liked to say, "postapocalyptic elegant." And she was passionate about creating a line of clothes for sun-sensitive people that actually looked cool, instead of the usual hideous salmon-colored windbreakers with hoods and special ear flaps.

Hannah and I regaled Ameena with stories from our youth. Boys we had dated. Clubs we had sneaked into. Little did I know then that we were *still* so young. Only eighteen. Still too young to legally get into clubs. We were having so much fun chatting, we decided to make more plans for the week, and Ameena asked what Hannah was up to the following day. Then the tone shifted. Hannah told us it was her father's birthday tomorrow. So she would be going to his grave to visit. She said this grave-visiting part like I should have already expected such a plan.

But it came as a surprise. Because for all my following of my own deadlines and dates, my own life's syllabus, it had never crossed my mind that Richard Vale still had a birthday anyone would care about. But of course Hannah cared. Just because in my mind he was long dead, and rightly so, didn't mean his own daughter didn't think of him, perhaps every single day. Probably other people thought about him too. From time to time. His own parents, if they were still alive. His siblings or cousins. His widow. A first girlfriend who still owns his high school basketball team tank top. A neighbor who once borrowed his lawn mower. As this hit me, I saw a larger, more complete picture. Each life and death seeps out to other people, maybe dozens, if not even hundreds. And the seeping never stops.

Hannah told Ameena about that horrible Halloween. How we all started happily dressed up as flamingos and we ended up awoken by screams. Hannah's mom found Richard's body early that morning. Lying dead in the kitchen, his face mottled and swollen, a gash on his head, plenty of blood on the floor. Ameena was truly sorry to hear about this tragedy, and she kept all her questions at bay in front of Hannah, because she was tactful. But the moment after we hugged Hannah goodbye, Ameena completely freaked. And turned to me.

"You were literally there the night he died?"

"Yes."

"That's horrific! Did you actually see his dead body?"

"Yes."

"Oh my God. Are you okay?"

"Yeah. It was over two years ago."

"But still. That's the kind of thing that can stay with you forever. I mean, I've never seen a dead body. And especially to see someone you know."

I realized I was being too stoic. Too laissez-faire. So I softened. "Yeah. It was a bad time, for sure. Really upsetting. So I guess I sort of blocked it out."

This response put Ameena at ease. But she still had more to say. "I just can't believe you never told me about any of this. I mean, I thought I knew everything about you. 'Cause you know everything about me. About every traumatic experience I've ever had. Even the stupid dead-squirrel-in-the-garage story."

I nodded, accepting her disbelief. And she kept talking. "Do you feel you should go with Hannah to the grave site tomorrow? I can hang back. Chill on the beach. I totally understand if you want to go with her. Or I could go with you, if you need support? While supporting her?"

As Ameena kept going on and on about how sad it must be on your father's birthday after he's dead and maybe she should call her own parents and try and be civil, try to forgive them, make amends while there was still time, even though they were both such jerks, my mind wandered a little. I understood what she was saying, but I personally didn't feel triggered by Richard Vale's death and moot birthday. But maybe that was because I was the only one in the world who knew all the actual details of that night.

CHAPTER 9

VICTIM

THE INTERROGATION ROOM WAS BEGINNING TO FEEL WARM. But I was a native Floridian. I liked warm. And not a dry, thin warm like they always brag about in Arizona. But a humid, thick warm. Maybe Detective Jackson was from Chicago or something. Although I didn't detect any kind of accent. I noticed a tiny bit of sweat starting to form on his shaved head. He pulled a linen handkerchief out of his pocket and dabbed his skull. I could see a small yellow butterfly embroidered on the corner. A woman must have given it to him, I thought. It was not an item a man like him would ever purchase.

"That's lovely."

"What?"

"Your handkerchief. Very dapper and old-timey."

He gave a little grunt. "My sister crochets."

"I think you mean embroiders."

His face changed. He went from smug to grumpy. And I knew then that he was not a man who appreciated being corrected.

Especially by a suspected murderer. I worried for a moment that I had made a misstep. But then I thought, he already has it out for me. I might as well antagonize him since I can't possibly make it any worse.

Detective Jackson thrust his hanky back into his pocket and then pushed the photograph of the mugshot closer to me. I pretended to glance at it again, but really looked at a corner edge. Then another. Around and around like a four-cornered clock. Because if I actually looked at it for too long, I was sure I would smell its putrescence and gag. The detective said, "You got pulled over driving his car. Remember? And lo and behold, then he's dead within six hours."

I looked away from the four corners, and up to the sweaty detective. Richard Vale was dead within one hour. But I wasn't about to make this correction.

It was past midnight when I pulled up to Hannah's house, where we all planned on spending the night. I tried to be quiet while getting the hammered Hannah and Erika out of the car, but as I got out myself and opened the rear door, I noticed a mini bag of peanut M&M's on the floor. It must have fallen out of my little pink purse when I pulled out my license to show it to the cop. And this was seriously bad. Hannah was so allergic to peanuts that even with the bag closed I worried about it being so close to her. Last time she came into contact with peanuts, her throat closed up and she was rushed to the ER just in time. I knew she kept an EpiPen on her, but still. Better to avoid the situation altogether.

I gave up on being quiet and quickly pulled her out, away from the candy, and helped her into the house and up to her bedroom. I flopped her onto the bed, and she started giggling again. I went back down for Erika, but she had managed to walk inside the house all on her own. I nudged her up the stairs and onto Hannah's bed as well, and I removed all their flamingo accoutrements. I left them happily slumped on each other. Hannah's cheery bright yellow smiley-faced bedspread looked extra ironic beneath the passed-out girls who would be deeply regretting so many shots in the morning. I noticed how good Hannah's eye makeup looked, all smudged from sweating and puking. The kind of smoky smudge you can never get just right when you try.

I then went back down to the car to remove the dangerous bag of peanut M&M's, and as I walked into the dark house, I hit a wall of flesh. I looked up to see Hannah's father looming directly in front of me. Richard was wearing only sweatpants, and I could smell whiskey coming from his every pore.

I felt I had done something wrong, and immediately said, "Sorry." Sorry for being too loud. Sorry for waking him up. Sorry for taking the car. Sorry, sorry, sorry. He assured me, nothing to be sorry about. He never minded being woken up by a hot young thing. Fight-or-flight adrenaline began pumping through my glands. Or was I just being overly dramatic, as teen girls are so often accused of being?

I tried to step around him, to race up the stairs and into the safety of Hannah's room, but he grabbed my arms and said, "Why don't you stay down here for a while. Just you and me."

"No offense, but I don't want to."

I could see, even in the darkness of the foyer, that his eyes sparked with a drunken anger and that he was in fact offended.

I thought about screaming, but before a sound could come out, he grabbed me and kissed me. His wet hot mouth sliding onto mine. Making my skin crawl. And my body freeze. As he continued to grope me, my mind raced. What kind of victim was I? One who, like a mouse, goes limp in the snake's grasp? One who tries to survive by turning inward and tuning out and playing possum? Or one who fights with everything she has? Teeth and nails and strength and lungs and fury? I picked fury.

The car keys were still in my hand, and I managed to swing my arm up toward his face. A turret of the sandcastle keychain caught his eyebrow and made a deep gash. Blood dripped down his cheek. He shook his head, like a wet dog, and tiny drops of his blood spattered on the walls, on the floor, and again he pressed his mouth against mine. He grabbed my thrashing hands and held them behind my back, with minimal effort. It registered that trying to fight him off with strength and fury was useless. He was bigger and stronger. I needed to use his own weakness against him. I needed to be a victim who was smarter than her attacker. And use cunning and logic.

As he pressed himself against my pink leotard, I remembered the peanut M&M's. Hannah once told me her father was also deathly allergic to peanuts, and it was possible her growing up in a peanut-free home helped create her own extreme allergy. And the mini bag was still clenched in my hand, which was pinned behind my back. Using the same discipline it took to calmly hold my breath under the turbulent ocean waters, I relaxed my body against Richard's. I leaned into him a little. He sensed a shift and liked it. I shyly whispered that I was a virgin, and if he was going to be my first, I at least wanted to smell pretty. So would it be all right if I popped a mint into my mouth? He grinned, and I saw the glint of his slimy wet teeth. "A virgin?" That was a prize he hadn't expected. I knew he thought all of Hannah's friends were sluts, just like he thought she was.

Once he released my arms, I tore through the mini bag with a hot-pink-painted fingernail, turned my head slightly, and shoved several primary-colored peanut M&M's into my mouth.

I chomped down quickly, breaking up the candy coating, expos-ing and freeing as many peanuts from their hard-shell prison as possible. Then I leaned my face up toward Richard Vale, and this time I put my lips on his. As his vile tongue met mine, I pushed the poisoned cud deep into his mouth.

It took him a moment to comprehend that his taste buds were registering something chocolaty. He didn't want to pull his hands away from my tits, my thighs, my tight young ass, but he was now wheezing. He had no choice but to stop molesting me and to stumble back. His throat began to close up; his face started to swell. He knew what had happened. He fell to his knees and started crawling toward the kitchen, reaching for a cabinet way too high for him to touch from his position on the floor. I knew what he wanted. EpiPens and Benadryl. And for him, as the sec-onds passed, the cabinet seemed increasingly out of reach. He looked at me, beseeching. And I looked back and calmly counted down from ten in my head. Just like I had done in the ocean.

Why should I save this rapist? This man who often called his own daughter a slut? If I let him live, I was sure he would attack some other teenage girl if given the chance. If I let him die, I was avenging all the girls he might have already violated. Richard looked at me, and as the life was draining out of him, he chose to use his last gasp of breath to push out two words, "You bitch." And then it was over. And I felt good about my decision. This man was Duncan Reese all grown up.

I ate the rest of the peanut M&M's and put the empty wrap-per into my purse. I noticed some blood oozing its way down the sandcastle charm on the keychain, so I unhooked it and put the charm inside my purse. I was certain there would be so many things for the rest of the Vale family to worry about in the com-ing months that no one would ever notice a missing keychain charm. I then stepped over Richard Vale's body to hang the spare car key back on the little hook.

I looked around, to make sure all evidence was addressed, and I saw five of my bright pink flamingo feathers were strewn about the foyer, having fallen in the struggle, and they each had specks of Richard's blood on them. I collected all five and quietly headed up the stairs. As I passed the master bedroom, I could hear the deep, uneven drunken snores of Hannah's mother. I crept into Hannah's room, and flopped in between my friends, who were in almost the same exact passed-out position in which I had left them. I had now killed two people. Eleven years apart. That doesn't make a habit or a pattern. Just something I happened to do twice, both times for very good reason. I closed my eyes and I tried to fall sleep. Eventually I did.

I watched Detective Jackson's manicured finger tap on Richard Vale's mugshot. And I told him what I knew. That it was quickly clear to police the next morning what must have happened. With all the buzz of trick-or-treaters the night before, an errant piece of peanut candy had somehow made its way into the house. And later Richard stumbled downstairs to get a midnight snack, and in the dark accidentally ate the very thing that could kill him. The police on the scene of course noted that there seemed to be a cut on the deceased's face as well. The toxicology report later showed his blood alcohol level was extremely high. So they concluded that Richard Vale probably fell due to his drunkenness and hit his head. Possibly as he was searching for his EpiPen, possibly beforehand. But regardless of the timing of events, he didn't manage to grab his medication in time and he died of anaphylaxis.

I knew Detective Jackson must already have all this information, so me repeating back what was in some old police file would be harmless. And instead of waiting for another game show question from him, I decided to ask one of my own. I glanced down at photograph number two. "Is this mugshot from when Mr. Vale was arrested for a DUI? That's why I got pulled over that night, driving his car. He had a warrant out for not appearing in court."

Detective Jackson, still a little annoyed at me about the handkerchief comment, shrugged. "Does it matter?"

It did not matter. I shrugged back and casually lied. "Just making small talk." I was not an expert on the law, or on law enforcement, but I did know a little. One of my best friends in college was pre-law, extremely driven and destined to be a great attorney. He taught me when it came to justice, there was no small talk. Every word was important.

CHAPTER 10

ROMAN

ROMAN MILLER WAS THE ONLY FRESHMAN CAST IN YALE'S production of *A Midsummer Night's Dream*. He played Nick Bottom, the fool. His body was so controlled onstage that his purposeful clumsiness seemed graceful. His voice was confident and booming, his timing impeccable, and his smile enormous. I could see under his costume of old-timey tights and pantaloons were the muscular thighs of a track-and-field star and not of a theater geek. Who was this guy?

I didn't necessarily want to sleep with Roman, or date him. But I knew I wanted to know him. My mother's philosophy about me talking to strangers as a child solidified my belief that we are all just people, trying to make our way, so there is no reason for me to ever be intimidated or shy about sparking a connection, no matter how much charm the other person might exude. So I set a plan in motion.

The program displayed the theater schedule, and I saw the play ran for several more nights. I thought through the best approach. I didn't want to hang around behind the stage door hoping to meet Roman, like some theater groupie. That would make me seem desperate and put him on too much of a pedestal. I also didn't want to stalk him on campus and "accidentally" bump into him since that would make me feel cowardly.

So I wrote a note with my one purple pen on my simple, good-quality lavender card-stock stationery: "I'm a fan. Want to meet for coffee sometime? Find me. Ruby Simon." On closing night, during the fifth act, I sneakily maneuvered my way through the bowels of the theater and slipped the note into his locker backstage. Then I returned to my dorm with the excitement of knowing I was vaguely waiting for something.

Using the school directory, Roman emailed me three days later to set a meeting. I walked into a coffee shop near campus at the appointed time. It was cozy and smelled like snickerdoodle cookies. He was already there. On time, sitting at a little table by the window. Up close he had extremely masculine features and a bit of an underbite. It seemed he was gifted with more testosterone than most. He looked like a handsome bulldog, in the best possible way. His incredible musculature was not only present in his legs; it rose up his six-foot-two-inch frame proportionately.

He pulled off his hoodie and with it accidentally also lifted up his thin white T-shirt underneath. It was then that I first saw his flaring obliques. I also saw that his biceps bulged and all three parts of his triceps were clearly defined. His back and shoulders were broad and cut, and his bare torso looked like a superhero's costume, ribbed abs and V-shape included. But it was his obliques that were most impressive. Like thick ropes traveling up the length of his hips. He was clearly a good-looking guy, with wavy, thick brown hair and dark blue eyes, but it was all very obvious. The kind of obvious that all my high school girlfriends loved.

The kind of obvious that made me an anti-snob when it came to men.

We ordered coffee; he insisted on paying. He said he was intrigued by my note. I had balls. That much was clear. It was also clear from the moment we sat down together that we were going to be just friends. The picture he painted was too overt for me. There was no smoldering angst or secret weird layers or hues hidden under the bold bright colors of his charismatic personality and good looks and perfect body. And, likewise, I was too on the nose for him. I wasn't playing it coy or alluring in the least. I was also a seven, and not his usual nine-slash-ten. We seemed like equals, a perfect match, and therefore had no sexy power dynamics to play with or use for flirting. There was zero sexual tension between us, but a deep understanding that our lives would be intertwined from that moment on.

I assumed because of his talent that Roman was a theater major. Yale had one of the best theater departments in the county. But he informed me acting was only a hobby. I was impressed. It takes a special kind of person to be so good at something that is only considered a hobby. Roman explained he was focused on law school, Yale Law School to be specific, and was double majoring in sociology and history, plus taking pre-law classes. He spoke about "famous" lawyers like other guys talk about rock stars and quarterbacks. Roman idolized litigators, followed trials, and rooted for outcomes not based on the crime or the victim or the accused, but based on who was trying the case.

He was the firstborn of four boys and was given his mother's maiden name. She came from a wealthy family that made millions in textiles during the turn of the twentieth century. His father was a self-made man from Cleveland who went to Yale undergrad and was now the CEO of a large commercial real estate firm. His parents met in line at a taxi stand outside one of the nicer New Haven hotels. He was an undergrad at Yale, and would often sit in the fancy hotel lobby imagining the day when he had the money to sleep in one of the rooms. She was just starting her final year at boarding school in Andover and had just had high tea with a girlfriend. She dropped her glove. He picked it up. Five years later Roman Ramsey Miller was born. He grew up in a mansion in New Canaan, Connecticut.

As I learned about Roman and his family, I remembered something my mother once told me. The upper class could do what they wanted because they were so rich, and the lower class could do what they wanted because no one cared about them. It was only the middle class that was expected to follow societal rules, and I was solidly middle class. Roman was one of the many people I met who seemed to prove my mother's theory correct. Rules didn't apply to him at all, including his take on the law. Roman believed guilt or innocence was irrelevant; it always came down to the lawyers. It was a game, and the attorney who could manipulate the facts best was the attorney who would and should win. And he yearned to be that attorney. After briefly seeing him onstage performing Shakespeare, I had no doubt he would achieve his goals. He could most certainly captivate a courtroom, get the jury or judge on his side, and win his case regardless of right or wrong. And I believed he would sleep just fine at night, regardless of the "truth."

Aside from Ameena, Roman became my closest friend. We were inseparable. Equally intense and extroverted but somehow complementing each other instead of competing and getting in the other's way. I would go to the campus gym with him and slowly walk up and down on the StairMaster as he sculpted his masterpiece of a body. I would call out obscene challenges because I knew he was stubborn enough to try them. "Do twenty pull-ups!" "Throw another ninety pounds on the squat rack!" "Run a mile in four minutes and thirty seconds!" His high school track days (I had called it when I first saw his legs in those tights) made this request not totally outlandish, and he came in with an impressive four minutes and forty-five seconds, but he still beat himself up over that additional fifteen seconds of perceived failure.

In his quiet moments, Roman would memorize Trivial Pursuit questions and answers and look over lists of high-point Scrabble words in case a game was to ever pop up. He felt he could manage life the way my mother felt I could avoid getting HIV. I had control. I didn't have to ever contract the disease, extenuating circumstances aside, if I took certain measures and precautions. Condoms always, always, always. Like I relied on the incredible protection of a thin piece of latex, Roman lived life with his own shield. He believed that if the information existed in the world, why not know it? Why not memorize the answers when they are in front of you, therefore controlling the outcome of the question? Why leave life to chance? Roman wanted to learn everything that was available to him because he believed knowledge was power. And power was control. So he wouldn't leave anything up in the air if he didn't have to. I, however, believed knowing you don't have all the knowledge and not caring about it was even more powerful. In a sense it was freeing. This difference between us ignited endless scintillating debates.

In that same vein, Roman wanted to be known by everyone and wanted to know everyone. I enjoyed being known by people and not knowing them back. This specifically turned our debate into an argument. While walking through campus, many people would say, "Hey, Roman. Hi, Ruby." And Roman would come back with "Hi, Jennifer." "Hey, Tim." "What's up, Dave?" "Love those tights, Alison!" I didn't remember any of these people's names, nor did I care what they were. They weren't my friends. Roman was disgusted by my haughtiness. I was disgusted by his fakeness. He didn't care about those people, so why pretend? Roman felt a comfort in the connectivity, even if it was a facade. He felt special by both being liked and seeming likable. I felt special by not needing to be liked by all, but being loved deeply by a select few.

One day, as usual, Roman was carrying my big bag full of textbooks through campus for me, because he liked the extra arm workout. When I revealed I didn't know "Henry's" name after he passed by, and I didn't care to memorize it, Roman threw my bag down on the newly formed spring grass and stormed off, yelling, "Snobby bitch!"

I yelled back, "Needy douchebag!"

We didn't talk for three days, and time seemed to slow way down. Like the seconds were filled with a thick fog. I missed him. So much so, I began to rethink my philosophy. Maybe he was right; maybe I was haughty. I would always now remember Henry's name, but maybe I should also pay attention to Henry's roommates' names. Henry's girlfriend's name. Her best friend's name. And on and on. Like each life seeping out endlessly. When do the names stop? The fog got so thick I became desperate to see through to the other side again. Maybe I should apologize to Roman, end the feud. Maybe I would tomorrow.

Later, in Abnormal Psych class, I grabbed my enormous textbook. It fell open to a specific page with a thud. There was a note in the spine. "I'm a fan. Want to meet for coffee sometime? Find me. Roman Miller." The page was about narcissists. Nice touch. When did he get that note into my textbook? And how the hell did he pull it off without me knowing? It was frightening how resourceful he was sometimes. I was smiling so big that when the professor asked if there was anything I would like to share with the class, I said, "I just got my best friend back."

I found Roman in the quad, surrounded by a gaggle of girls.

"You're right. I can be a haughty bitch. I'm sorry."

"No, you're right. I'm a needy douche for sure."

We hugged, and that was that. We never fought again.

I immersed myself in my classes and books and syllabi, but I sometimes jonesed for my clubbing days on South Beach. Roman often joined me as I attempted to find some exciting nightlife in New Haven and, when I gave up on that, hopped on a train to New York City. He would throw my ID, fake ID, and cash and dorm key into his pocket so I didn't have to carry anything and ruin the line of my skintight clubbing pants. And we would go dancing. Playing wingman for the other. Roman pretty much landed every girl he set his eyes on. And he helped me get the attention of guys I was eyeing by showering me with attention himself. He was always the most decorative peacock in any room, and if he took notice of me, other men would too. We had our systems down pat.

If free nights were spent dancing together, free days were spent in courtrooms. Roman loved going to watch trials, state and federal. It was like he was going to see a matinee. He would get to the courthouse, see who was "playing," and sit quietly in the back row, observing and learning. During important testimony he watched the jurors' faces like some romantics watch the face of the groom when the bride first steps onto the aisle. He wanted to see if he could tell the moment they believed or didn't believe. The moment they decided, regardless of the facts, if the person was guilty or innocent.

And similar to our searches for fun dance clubs, we would sometimes venture to Boston or New York City or Providence if the court cases in New Haven got stale. The Northeast had no shortage of exciting trials and notable local lawyers. I once asked Roman if he wished he could bring a bag of popcorn into the trial. He looked at me blankly. "Of course not. The chewing might make me miss something important. And when do I ever eat empty carbs?"

I accompanied Roman to the courthouse because it was interesting and helpful for me to note the human experience of being the accused or accuser, judge or jury member, for psychological purposes. I was especially curious about signs of guilt and also wondered why in this country to feel remorse meant a lesser sentence. The crime is still the crime, so why do a criminal's emotions after the fact play into it? Perhaps because judges took remorse as a sign that the criminal would not partake in the illegal activity again. But many statistics show that feelings of guilt or lack of guilt do not affect the likelihood of reoffending. It's as simple as if I ate a cookie, and I feel guilty I cheated on my diet. Fuck it, I'll eat the whole sleeve. We've all been there. Guilt is not an intrinsically helpful emotion for future decision-making. And often the spiral of guilt and shame can lead criminals to remain criminals.

This idea was so intriguing to me, for personal reasons that should already be clear, that I later took it on for my undergraduate senior thesis. My paper, which I turned in six weeks early and for which I received an A, was titled "Remorse and Absolution: Peas in a Pod or Dangerous Bunkmates?"

And while Roman and I made the Northeast our own, I got to know his family. Sometimes we would go to New Canaan for a weekend. The live-in housekeeper would do our laundry and make us yummy sandwiches with goat cheese and sun-dried to-matoes and roasted red peppers. His father found my crazy Miami tales amusing and appreciated my work ethic. He liked having me around because he felt I was a good influence on his son. Not that Roman needed any help marching along his path to legal greatness.

During my first visit to the Miller house, they didn't seem to believe that Roman and I were just friends. One of his middle brothers punched him hard in the arm when he saw me, as if to say, *Good going.* And his youngest brother gave me a few sideways glances, like, *Is my brother doing it with you? Gross!* At first I slept in one of the many guest rooms and he stayed in his childhood bedroom. But by my second visit they all saw what we saw, an unbreakable, fully platonic friendship. It was then that his parents let us share his old room. We would fall asleep side by side in the queen bed with the brown-and-green plaid-patterned comforter, me quizzing him on Trivial Pursuit questions mixed in with practice LSAT exam questions, him quizzing me with questions on neuroanatomy mixed in with what it feels like to do cocaine.

In a way, I became a part of his family. And received the perks. Mr. and Mrs. Miller were much more effusive with their own children than my own parents were, but with that also came a certain pressure to live up to their demands. Roman wore that pressure like heavy armor that sometimes weighed him down, but since I didn't have eighteen years of the helicopter-parent dynamic, I only noticed the protective effects of the praise, without the weight. The Millers were so proud of my constant 4.0 GPA they actually put my report card on their own refrigerator. When I saw it up there, mixed in with a magnet from Turks and Caicos and an old sketch from their youngest boy, I got a little teary. I had accidentally found surrogate parents who nurtured me in a way that my own parents never did. I felt awash in joy with a splash of sadness. Getting something new can trigger a painful realization of what you lacked before.

I was so comfortable with Roman, more so than with Ameena and even with Ellie in some ways, that a few times I almost mentioned Duncan Reese in passing. *Totally, like that one time I drowned that bully in the ocean.* I almost casually referenced slashing Richard Vale in the eyebrow. *Believe me, I know the head can bleed a lot, even when it's just a surface wound.* And as the memories and the thoughts were about to fly from my mouth, I would remember that I could never say these things out loud. These were secrets I had to keep forever. From even my best friends. My closest family. Secrets forced me to keep up a thin wall between me and the people I loved and trusted most. Another thin layer of latex. Some might think this is sad, no way to live, but if you've never had sex without a condom, using condoms feels pretty damn good.

But still, maybe, *if* there was anyone I could tell or would tell someday . . . it would be Roman.

CHAPTER 11

BETRAYAL

ROMAN FELT IT WOULD BE A CRIME TO NOT SHARE HIS beautiful body with the world, so he signed up to be a nude model for several Yale art classes. How he would find the time to stand around naked for the betterment of others while crushing his two majors, studying for the LSAT, and doing two-a-days in the gym was beyond me.

His one concern, however, was that while naked in front of the art class he might make eye contact with a pretty girl. Or have a pornographic thought. Or let a daydream turn into a fantasy. Any of these things could make him get hard. He didn't want to get hard. He wanted to be a muse, to be gazed upon and adored, calm, cool, and collected, like a statue, and didn't want his penis to give away that he hadn't transcended natural bodily functions. So he came up with a plan.

I arrived at his studio apartment—he was now living off campus—with my laptop, a bag full of textbooks, and two giant coffees. His with exactly one and one half pods of cream, mine with two pods of cream and two packets of raw sugar. I handed him his coffee and plopped down in his one comfy chair. He took his pants off. And then his boxer briefs. He looked comical with his T-shirt and socks still on. He realized this and he quickly pulled off his T-shirt. And then bent down and removed his socks. Roman was now fully naked, standing in front of me. He was beautiful.

I had never seen him naked before. And I stared. Because that was part of the plan. I was to stare at him, in all sorts of ways, from all sorts of angles. And he was to stand there and see if being naked in front of a girl would make him hard.

"So?" he asked.

"What do you mean, so? I'm not here to critique your dick."

"I know. I just thought I'd ask anyway."

"This might come as a shock, but most women, me included, don't care so much about the penis. It's weird-looking, and as long as it's in the realm of normal human size, it doesn't really matter."

"Wait. All of them are weird-looking? Or mine specifically is weird-looking?"

"Jesus Christ. All of them are weird-looking! Why do you think male sex symbols are always in tuxedos? Men are at their most attractive when they're covered up as much as possible."

This seemed to really demolish his spirit. He plopped down on his couch, deflated. I felt bad, and sat next to him. I put a hand on his arm. Felt the muscles tense under my touch. I then put my head on his shoulder and side-hugged him, allowing my hand to rest on his protruding left oblique. I felt a thrill shoot up my spine and also down into my pelvis.

"Listen to me, your body is incredible. You know that. We aren't here to debate that. We are here to see if you are going to get hard or not." Roman looked down at his flaccid penis. Then looked at me, then took a sip of his coffee. And we waited.

Roman did not get hard, not in front of me and not in front of any art classes. He was as good at modeling naked as he was at everything else he tried. And our friendship continued to soar through to the beginning of senior year. Which was when I met Jake.

It was my twenty-first birthday, and I was celebrating with friends at New Haven's coolest bar. The place was much stricter with IDing than any place had ever been in Miami, so my fake ID had never been able to cut it. I had to wait until the night of my actual birthday to get in. I hadn't had a drink since that night at Club Rox when I saw Duncan's mom. Her pathetic frazzled image and the phrase *gateway drug* kept me away from alcohol for five years. So I was drinking a club soda with a lime.

Ameena's new boyfriend, a cute Indian guy who, unfortunately for her parents, was a staunch atheist, brought his buddy Jake. As thanks for allowing him to crash my birthday, Jake offered to buy me a drink. Instead of explaining to him that I used to do lines of cocaine off stolen side-view mirrors and then ran into the drug-addled mother of a boy I had killed, which turned me off all mind-altering substances, I said, "Okay. I'd like a glass of Champagne."

Jake, who could best be described as a heartthrob, with perfectly symmetrical features and mischievous eyes, bought a bottle.

I reasoned out that I was now twenty-one, older and wiser, and truly happy. My frontal lobes were fully fused. I could make good decisions, and I didn't need the crutch of drugs to dull the pain of loneliness like I had when Ellie left for college. And my curious side wanted to test the "Once an addict, always an addict" belief. With all that in mind, I confidently took my first sip of Champagne.

It was a delight. Dry and bubbly. Feeling the alcohol hit my bloodstream didn't launch me back into some drug-hungry frenzy. It didn't even inspire me to drink too much. I had only two glasses of the expensive bottle, and that was perfect. I was buzzed, but not drunk. I was also surprised when Jake leaned in and kissed my neck.

"Where's your girlfriend?" I asked. I knew Jake was dating the prettiest girl in our whole class, Melody. A solid ten. Just goes to show that for every beautiful woman out there, there's a guy tired of fucking her.

He said she had a test the following day and was cramming. I smiled, mostly because the idea of "cramming" was so unappealing and foreign to me. I never had to cram. Jake asked, "Where's that guy you're always hanging with?"

"Roman? He's around here somewhere."

"Is he your boyfriend?"

"Nope."

Jake tentatively slid his hand up my leg. I didn't stop him. So his hand got surer, and pressed into my thigh harder.

"Would you stop me if he was your boyfriend?"

"I would. But he's not."

Then Jake said, "You're a better person than I am."

Yup, I'm an angel, I thought to myself ironically. And then it all just sort of happened. Premeditation is considered an aggravating factor when it comes to murder. I like to think it also applies to sleeping with hot guys with girlfriends. And thus began what would become a scandalous romance.

When I first told Roman I had slept with Jake, he literally

gave me a high five. He was proud of me. Jake was a good get. Varsity athlete and in the most popular improv troupe on campus. And gorgeous goes without saying, since he was dating the prettiest girl. They made quite a couple. She had navy eyes and blond hair. He had navy eyes and black hair. They had been together since freshman year, an eternity in college time.

I supposed that if I didn't feel guilty about other things, I certainly wouldn't feel guilty about fooling around with a guy who had a girlfriend. *I* didn't make her any promises. *He* was the one breaking his commitment, not me. So why should I care one way or the other? I wasn't even friends with the girl. I vaguely knew her from around. And it's not like they were married. Or even engaged. We were all still so young, in college, pretending to be grown up. How could I take their relationship that seriously, especially with his hand down my pants? It seemed like pure fun. I certainly had no interest in splitting them up, or causing anyone any pain.

Looking back, I realize Roman was so excited about my conquest because he thought it meant Jake and Melody would be breaking up. Then he would finally have a chance with her. She was the one girl he wanted who had remained outside his grasp our entire college existence. The one girl he could never get since she was solidly committed to Jake. Even though, clearly, since he was sleeping with me, Jake wasn't solidly committed to her. Roman had a class with Melody and took it upon himself to try and talk some sense into her. He told her rumors of Jake's cheating. Plied her with compliments. She was too good to be treated in such a way. Too beautiful to be ignored. Too smart to not sense it happening behind her back. Melody didn't believe Roman. She saw right through his desperate attempts to turn her against

Jake so he could have her for himself. She trusted Jake had never cheated on her, nor would he ever. So she ignored Roman's warnings and whispers of rumors.

Roman didn't plan on betraying me. He didn't plan on selling me out. It just sort of happened, he said. It wasn't premeditated. On Roman's fifth attempt to break Melody free from the shadows of Plato's cave and show her the light that Jake was a no-good two-timer, she demanded a name.

"So who is it then, Roman? If you're so sure. If you have proof. Tell me who it is that Jake is cheating on me with."

In that moment it came down to what Roman wanted and what he knew was right. And what he wanted took precedence. He said, "Ruby. It's Ruby."

It was reported back to me that at that moment Melody's pretty face fell. And her deep blue eyes filled with tears. She knew Roman was my best friend. She knew if he was saying this about me, it must be true. Word spread, and I was vilified, labeled a boyfriend stealer. Melody hated me even more than she hated Jake. Even though he was the one who broke her heart. But such is the way of misplaced anger.

What Roman didn't foresee happening was everyone hating him as well. He delivered a message and ruined a relationship and a friendship in one fell swoop. A message that never needed to get delivered at all. People whispered, "How could he sell out his best friend like that?" "What an asshole." "No loyalty." "Lame douche." All the people Roman loved to be liked by, the people whose names he remembered on the quad, now hated him. They were the ones who broke out of Plato's cave and saw the light, and in that harsh sun, Roman looked like a giant dick.

Jake and his friends wanted to jump him. Melody despised him. And even though she and Jake were now broken up, she would never consider being with Roman after he showed his true character by betraying his best friend, me. Which made him no better than Jake, who was betraying her. Even Roman's parents were furious with him. He threw away his closest friendship for a possible piece of ass. Which in many people's minds made him even worse than Jake.

Ameena saw how crushed I was by what Roman did, and of course was furious with him for throwing me under the bus. She said, "I could kill him for what he did to you!"

It was a curious phrase. *I could kill . . .* One I never used since I actually had killed before. I was a murderer, so for me it lost its hyperbolic quality. But like when you buy a car and then see that specific model everywhere, I noticed whenever anyone idly threw out murderous threats. And it was often. For me they stuck out like neon signs in otherwise dull common colloquialisms. People were always exclaiming, "I could kill you right now!" or "I want to fucking kill her!" or the classic joke, "If I tell you, I'll have to kill you," and on and on and on. I heard something like that said at least once a week, and I nodded and smiled and understood, like a well-adjusted nonhomicidal person.

Roman knew he had made a mistake. And he apologized over and over. But I was too hurt to accept. His atonement didn't take away the pain of his betrayal. How could I ever trust him again? And if I couldn't trust him, how could we ever be friends? His using me as a pawn in his quest to land Melody was second in anguish only to Ellie leaving for college. It threw my perception of the world upside down a little. Roman was my control group in a world of variables. So when he became a variable, it shook me to my core. I shuffled around campus feeling the pain of a phantom limb that had been removed. I didn't eat much. I wasn't hungry. I cried in the shower sometimes. I felt something I had never felt before. Shame. Shame that I had slept with another girl's boyfriend, and shame that my best friend was the one who turned me in.

The great irony was that I had enjoyed my time with Jake because I wasn't emotionally attached. I knew I wouldn't get hurt. But by being with him, I was hurt by the one man I did love. And love is love. It doesn't matter if it's friendship or romance or family love. You are either in love or you aren't. There are no levels. And my heart was broken.

Jake won Melody back by proposing three weeks after the scandal. An emerald-cut canary diamond with a pavé band. They were married in a mansion in Newport, Rhode Island, the following year. I heard the free-flowing Champagne was expensive and the vanilla cake was delicious.

Did Roman deserve to die for what he did to me? No. Did I stay up nights picturing how I would somehow overtake his superhero frame and strangle him to death? No. I stayed up grieving for my dead friendship. And that's when the nightmares started.

CHAPTER 12

SALT

MY HORRIBLE DREAMS WERE ALWAYS THE SAME. A FACELESS person would hold me down and shove handfuls of salt into my mouth. I would struggle and scream and wake myself up spitting and drooling all over my bed. My whimpers were so loud even the pillow over Ameena's face didn't block out the pitiful sounds. By senior year most students had moved off campus, but Ameena and I enjoyed the ease and structure of dorm life. So we stayed together, nestled among the juniors.

But night after night the terrors continued, which woke her up and which gave me a waking phobia of salt. I couldn't eat French fries or potato chips without gagging. I couldn't watch people in the cafeteria sprinkle table salt on their food without feeling panicked. I started trying to remove all salt dispensers from my vicinity. But like the king in *Sleeping Beauty,* who tried to do away with all spinning wheels to protect his baby daughter from a curse, I failed. No matter how many salty things and salt dispensers I removed from my eye line, there were always more on the next table over. I became physically ill at the thought of salt-rimmed margaritas, so I avoided Mexican restaurants. I also couldn't even think about eating fish or anything that tasted of the sea, so that ruled out Japanese. I even started to dislike mermaids, once my favorite fantastical creature.

I had, not surprisingly, finished all my required courses for my psychology major, so as well as working on my thesis, I was branching into neuroscience to learn more about the brain. The professor's assistant in my Macromolecular Structure class, named Max, was tall with a slight frame. He had dark eyes and sandy scruff on his face. He wore V-neck cashmere sweaters and elbow-patched tweed jackets with faded blue jeans. It seemed like he'd read a manual on how to look professorial but only followed half the steps. He spoke to the class sometimes, with a low and soft voice, but mostly he lingered behind the much older professor and organized papers. After weeks of nightmares, Max made his way into my unconscious. In my dream we were making out, squished against a child's elementary school desk. He kissed me deeply. And then, in an instant, his tongue dissolved into salt in my mouth and the salt poured down my throat. I woke up once again, spitting and screaming. Ameena looked over at me in the dark.

"Are you discussing this in therapy?"

"Yeah," I lied. I was not discussing it in therapy. The problem was I already had an idea of what the nightmares were really about, and there was no way I could mention it to anyone. I assumed my recent salt repugnance was linked to the ocean. And the ocean was where I had killed Duncan. And that salt being shoved in my mouth was probably symbolic of him sucking in salt water until he died. Or, possibly, the nocturnal terrors could be symbolic of me shoving peanuts down Richard's throat. Neither an option I could discuss.

I worried these new dreams were an alarm that my guilt-free time was up and a hellish "The Tell-Tale Heart" or *Crime and Punishment* end was inevitable for me. Maybe my unconscious was festering, feeling terrible about what I had done, needing to confess, and it wouldn't let me sleep until my conscious caught up. But my conscious wasn't convinced and my waking state didn't feel guilty at all. About anything.

Many psych professors encouraged psych majors to go to therapy. The reason was twofold. One, how could we be good therapists ourselves without experiencing it from the patient's side? And two, the experience of going to therapy might indicate the branch of psychology to which we were most drawn. I chose Dr. Alisha Goldman to be my therapist because she had recently finished her PhD. She was old enough to know a thing or two but young enough to seem like she could relate to my life in general. I had been seeing her once a month since my sophomore year. Sitting on her dark blue corduroy-upholstered sofa and chatting about this and that. She was lovely and wise and kind. I used my time with her to evaluate her methods as well as to discuss ideas and concepts and emotions. I was open, to a point. But never weepy or hysterical. I knew a murder confession was one of the few reasons a doctor could break patient confidentiality, so I could not broach my salt phobia with her. I had to keep it all to myself, and so the terrible dreams continued, now always starring Max and his tongue.

One afternoon, exhausted from yet another night of barely sleeping, I shuffled into my dorm room. I was shocked to see Ellie sitting on my bed. She took one look at me and leapt up, concerned.

"Oh, Ruby. What happened to you?"

I turned to look at Ameena, who was grabbing her bag to head out and give us sisters some privacy. She said, unapologetically, "I called her." And she left.

Ellie held me by the shoulders, to show how serious she was. And she said, "Just tell me. Are you anorexic? Bulimic? Back on drugs?"

"No!"

"Are you in a cult?"

"What?"

"It happens. Are you in one?"

"No. Ellie, I'm fine."

"You're not fine. I expected greasy unwashed collegiate hair. And dry skin since it's cold as fuck here. But you look like death. The dark circles under your eyes. And your posture. You're all slumped. Like you've given up or something. This is not like you."

I meekly tried to straighten my shoulders, but they were too shrouded in a heavy blanket of exhaustion to perk up. Ellie stayed rooted, and stared at me until I confessed the truth. Since I had not expected this confrontation, I had no plan about what to say.

I blurted out, "I haven't slept in weeks. I'm having horrible nightmares. Okay? Like every single night. About salt! About salt being shoved into my mouth. Over and over. And I can't make them stop."

She looked at me with compassion and understanding. And let go of my shoulders.

"It must be about the slugs."

"What? What are you talking about? What slugs?"

"You don't remember?"

Apparently I didn't. So Ellie told me. "When you were really little, like four, you saw Mom in the garden dumping salt on a bunch of slugs. You had a total meltdown, crying and screaming. I'd never seen you so upset and nothing would calm you down. You watched in horror as the slugs dissolved into nothing." As Ellie recounted this traumatic event, it sort of started to come back to me.

"Oh my God. I was positive I could hear their silent screams of disintegration."

Ellie continued to fill in the blanks for me. "You started pleading with Mom to stop it, but she wouldn't. You asked her why she was killing the slugs and Mom told you it was because they were killing her plants. And you asked her, why did she pick caring about the plants over caring about the slugs? Why were the plants more important? Why were the plants more lovable?"

And then I remembered the scene. I didn't have the words for it at the time, but I couldn't understand how my own mother could make such a callous decision, choosing one life-form over another. As my mind raced back, Ellie kept talking.

"Well, Mom realized it was all too disturbing for you, so after that day she only killed slugs when you weren't home. But I knew you still knew. 'Cause sometimes you would stare at a little streak of slime that led to nowhere on our patio and you would get really sad."

I was so relieved to have a reason for my dreams, a reason I could openly discuss, that I grabbed Ellie in a bear hug and danced around while cheering, "Of course! The slugs! Thank you!" As I put her down, it occurred to me that, only one year after I was disturbed by my mother's choice of the plants over the slugs, I would choose Ellie over Duncan. I understood then that when you love something, there is really no dilemma at all. With age comes the wisdom that choices must be made. It's not callous; it's just life. I then wondered aloud why the dreams had started now, after all this time. Ellie thought it was pretty obvious.

She said, "You don't do well when you feel abandoned. And I think all the Roman stuff is affecting you more than you realize."

Once Ellie hopped on her return train to New York City, I called Alisha for an emergency appointment. She already knew about the Roman stuff. But for the first time I spoke about the recurring dreams and my mother and the slugs. With a series of questions that all amounted to "And how did that make you feel?" I uncovered that I felt scared. Scared that I was more the slug than the plant. Scared that my mother would one day choose another life-form over me. Scared that maybe I too was so disposable and powerless that something as harmless and common as salt could wipe my existence off the face of the earth.

By the end of the session I was sobbing. I tried to catch all my snot and tears into tissues, made readily available in a wooden box on a side table, but a few drips made their way into my mouth. The nasty salty taste made me sob even more. I produced guttural heaves and a pile of balled-up, drenched Kleenex. My display of keening made me embarrassed. I thought, especially since I was a psychology major, here to observe more than to emote, that I could handle everything in a more clinical manner. But Dr. Alisha Goldman said the crying was good. It was needed and cathartic. And that I was having what she would describe as "a breakthrough."

She was right. I slept soundly that night, my eyes heavy and swollen from all the tears. I woke up the next morning with no memory of my dreams at all.

It was a chilly December morning. No snow, but frost clung to every archway and bare tree limb. I put on my favorite tight jeans and a thin kelly green sweater that made the red in my eyes and hair pop. I wrapped my bare neck in a long gray wool scarf and pulled on gray ankle boots. I knew I was going to be freezing during my eleven-minute walk through campus, but I thought the cold might solidify my resolve. I was going to conquer my last fear with immersion therapy.

Someone must have lit a Christmas-scented candle, because the hallway of the psychology building smelled of canned pine trees. I was shivering a little, but quickly warmed up as I walked the two flights of stairs to the department offices. Max the TA was alone, perched on a desk near the printer, reading something that amused him. He glanced up.

"Hi there. Ruby, right? I don't think we've ever actually spoken. I'm Max." He put out his hand to shake. The muscle between his thumb and pointer sexily protruded a little. Maybe he played the drums. He certainly didn't get those hands reading Freud.

I said nothing. I walked three steps toward him, putting myself within inches of his chest. He smelled like crisp no-frills soap. He dropped his outstretched arm. I leaned in, my mouth hovering near his. He wasn't sure what to do and just stayed as he was. I took the scarf off my neck, put it around his, and pulled him toward me. I kissed him, my mouth open. And soon I felt his tongue touch mine. It was perfect human flesh.

After that I became grateful for my salt-phobia phase because it taught me I could conquer anything, rational or not. And my breakthrough with Alisha solidified my resolve to become a therapist. To listen to people's darkest secrets and demons and compulsions and to help them by asking, "And how did that make you feel?" I was excited to get started and be the person across from the blue couch, and not just the person on the blue couch.

CHAPTER 13

ALIBI

MY SALT TERRORS NEVER RETURNED. AND JUST WHEN I WAS finding some normalcy without having Roman in my life, I got a call at eight a.m. on an otherwise unnoteworthy Wednesday morning. Ameena slept through the ringing, her pillow still snug over her face. I answered, groggy. It was the office of the dean of students. I was to report there immediately. The elderly voice on the other end assured me she would let my ten a.m. Clinical Neuroscience professor know I would be missing class and that my absence was sanctioned.

What the fuck was going on?

Twenty minutes later I sat in an office with the dean of students, the academic chair of the history department, and a Professor Barnes, who taught Eurasian Encounters. I was reminded by the dean that Yale had a zero-tolerance policy on cheating and academic dishonesty. I had absolutely no idea where he was going with all this. He then said, "And any student who might help another student cheat is just as culpable, resulting in immediate expulsion." I still had no idea what was happening.

The dean then softened, and said I had an impeccable record and was well-liked by all of my professors and the rest of the faculty. He continued to glance over what appeared to be my file, and said he was proud of the undergraduate work I had done, and was looking forward to personally reading my senior thesis on remorse and absolution.

"Thanks," I said, uneasy.

It was then that the chair of the history department took over the conversation.

"A student broke into Professor Barnes's office last night, rif-fled through her papers, read what was to be the upcoming final exam, and placed everything back as though it had been un-touched. This would have been a very clever way to cheat on the test, the professor never the wiser, but what this student didn't realize was there was a hidden camera set up in her office."

Before thinking, I blurted out, "Really? Why was there a camera set up?"

Professor Barnes, clearly stressed out, a little disheveled, and a lot defensive, quickly started trying to explain. "Listen, I'm a libertarian. I hate Big Brother. But I suspected someone on the janitorial staff was—"

The chair interrupted. "Sheryl, you don't have to explain yourself. Not to her." The chair then handed me a photo, clearly a freeze-frame printout of an image caught on Sheryl Barnes's office camera. It was grainy. The man in the photo was covered top to bottom in black sweats and a black ski mask. But even then, I could make out the musculature, the definition of the broad shoulders, the height, the stance. I knew exactly who this man was. And it then dawned on me why I was in a meeting with the dean and two history department professors, none of whom I had ever met before.

As I looked at the picture and concentrated on relaxing my face and body, not allowing myself to give anything away until I decided what I wanted to give away, the dean spoke about the gravity of this offense. Not only was it cheating, it was trespassing and breaking and entering.

I said, "I understand. But why am I here?"

The dean leaned back. Professor Barnes leaned forward. And squeaked out, "You're here because the only man that fits this guy's height and build that would benefit from seeing the Eurasian Encounters final before it was given is Roman Miller."

Ah, I thought. These people were not so dumb. They were professors at Yale, after all. They too knew exactly who the guy in the video was. So why did they need me?

I hadn't spoken to Roman in months. I had heard through the grapevine that he scored a 175 out of 180 on his LSAT. He had been accepted into Yale Law School, of course, and was well on his way to becoming exactly what he always wanted to become.

As I stared at the photo, unsure where else to safely look, I realized that now Roman's whole future hung in the balance. His belief that information should be taken if available was not serving him so well in this instance. I was sure he would have done just fine taking the test the fair way, but I understood him. His desire not to waste time with blanks and maybes, his need for guaranteed success, when the correct answers were simply waiting in a desk drawer, took precedence over good judgment. And now breaking the rules was catching up with him. If he got expelled from Yale undergrad, he wouldn't get his degree, his acceptance to law school would be overturned, his record would be forever compromised, and he would be nowhere.

I had learned in my many psychology classes that silence is often the thing that makes people most uncomfortable. The majority of us would rather be yelled at than ignored. So I decided to remain silent, and let one of the three adults around me break first and tell me more.

After a few awkward moments, Professor Barnes filled in the blanks. Roman had already been accused and brought in for questioning earlier that morning. He agreed the man on the video could have been him, but it wasn't. He proposed that maybe another student who would be taking the final hired someone outside of Yale to break in? Someone who coincidentally had his same build? Or maybe it was a prank pulled by someone outside the history department altogether? Maybe a student knew there was a camera in there all along and did this to prove some sort of point about privacy on campus? Roman had a lot of theories. And all the professors had was circumstantial evidence. But I knew him well enough to know that beneath his bluster that I was hearing about, he was gravely worried that the video was compelling enough to destroy the future he so desperately wanted. So Roman created one last ruse that would irrevocably clear his name of this dastardly crime. He had an alibi.

It was then that the dean spoke up again. He looked right at me. Not taking his eyes off my eyes. Summoning his thirty-odd years of experience dealing with college students and their lies in order to suss out the truth of this matter. The dean said, "Roman Miller claims that he was with you last night. Something about an art project? Therefore he couldn't possibly be the one on the video. And so, Ms. Simon, we've brought you in here to ask, is this true?"

And there it was. Roman had used me as his alibi. He was probably sequestered in some office, unable to warn me that when backed into a corner he chose to put his life in my hands. He believed that even though he had betrayed my trust by ratting me out to Melody, our bond was so strong that I would lie for him, to preserve his future. He picked me above any other friend because by lying for him I was putting my own future in jeopardy. And who else would even consider doing such a thing? Who else loved him that much?

He had a lot of nerve. He once said when we first met that I had balls, but he had balls. How dare he put me in this position? How dare he use me in this way? Especially after breaking my friendship heart.

The dean then said, "Well? Were you with him last night?"

This specific mentioning of an art project could only mean one thing. The dean had cleverly left it vague, but I knew Roman must have wanted me to tell the story of coming over and hanging out while he sat around naked to make sure he didn't get an erection in preparation for him posing nude. A story so specific and preposterous it couldn't be a lie. All I had to do was say this happened last night instead of two years ago. My stellar record at Yale plus this outlandish story would exonerate Roman. The dean, the chair, and Professor Barnes all waited for me to answer as I contemplated my two options. I could ruin Roman, or I could save him.

CHAPTER 14

CAT

THERE WAS A LOUD, QUICK KNOCK ON THE INTERROGATION room door. It startled me and I jerked a tiny bit, rattling my flimsy metal chair. This seemed to please Detective Jackson. "Come in," he said toward the still-closed door. A stout twenty-something man with his arm in a sling popped his head in. He ignored me and only spoke to the detective. "There's a call for you. He says it's important." I assumed this messenger was on some sort of desk duty because of his injury. Based on his build and his tan lines, I would guess he did not hurt himself in the line of duty but on a wakeboard. I was not in a position to ask him. Detective Jackson now seemed annoyed by the interruption.

"Well, who is it?"

"A Dr. Hamilton. He says you called him."

Once the man said that name, I knew this was not an unplanned interruption. This was a clumsy attempt to put me even more on tilt. And it worked. Why did the detective know who my veterinarian was? Why was he talking to him? How much did he already know about my life?

Detective Jackson waved the sling guy away. "I'll call him back later." The guy was about to shut the door when the detective stood up abruptly. This time I did not jerk. It only took him a quarter of a stride to get from the table to the door. He whispered something to the guy. I wished I could hear it, I tried to will the words to float my way, but they never made it into my ears. The detective sat back down and looked across the table at me as if nothing had happened. As if Dr. Hamilton's name was never mentioned. And my mind raced to put the pieces of my past together. So I would know what the detective's next move could be.

Right after college graduation, I decided that I would move back to my beloved Miami Beach, get my doctorate degree at the University of Miami, and warm my chilled bones. One exceptionally hot day I was heading to my car from the office I shared with my supervisor, Dr. Don, a laid-back, snarky man in his sixties. We worked in a nice new medical complex on Forty-First Street, just five blocks from the Atlantic Ocean. I usually parked in the employee lot behind the building, but today I had a large unwieldy lamp to carry in, and I had seen a parking meter right out front, so I took the spot. As I got back into my car, I heard a sad, muffled mew. I looked around and noticed a garbage can at a bus stop a few feet away. I walked over and the mew got louder. I looked inside, and saw the saddest thing I had ever seen in my entire life. A kitten was tossed on top of the trash, and it was tightly wrapped in duct tape. I scooped the little guy up, glanced down to make sure there weren't any more animals thrown inside, and raced to the nearest veterinary hospital. Sour bile moved up my throat when I dwelled on the evil of man, so I forced myself to focus on saving the kitten, and not focus on the monster that had done this to him.

After assessing the situation, the veterinarian, Dr. Hamilton, decided it would be best to sedate the kitten and shave off all his fur to remove the tape with minimal skin damage. An hour later, once the kitten's torturous restraints were gone, the tall, dark, and handsome vet would give the two-month-old tuxedo cat a full checkup, all necessary shots, and a later appointment for neutering. While I waited, the receptionist at the front desk put all my information into the computer and asked me, "What are you going to name him?" I didn't have to think. The answer, of course, was Mr. Cat. She looked up at me and said, "Whoa. Meta."

That evening I went home with my first pet. I lived in a cute one-bedroom third-story apartment a few blocks away from Española Way on South Beach. About a mile from the house where I grew up, which my parents still inhabited, and a forty-five-minute drive to my classes at UM. My apartment building was classic Art Deco and had been refurbished, leaving all its old-timey charm but with updated amenities. It was bright and clean and painted a joyous lavender.

Mr. Cat and I soon had a routine. In the mornings I would have two cups of coffee on the little balcony off the kitchen. Mr. Cat would prance around out there, eyeing birds that he could watch but would never catch. Then I would leave for my classes, or my internship with Dr. Don, and while I was out of the apartment, Mr. Cat would sleep on the couch near the living room windowsill. He seemed content to flop over the arm, look out the window, and sun himself in slats of light that showed through the pastel linen curtains.

In the evenings, when it was time for me to go to bed, Mr. Cat would truly come alive. Since he had been sleeping on the arm of the couch all day—and to be fair, cats are nocturnal—of course he had plenty of energy. All night long he would scamper full speed across the apartment, patrol the perimeter walls, open every cabinet he could get his little paws into, and knock things over while he jumped onto tables and shelves with the whip of his furry black-and-white tail. He would hop up on the bathroom counter and meow at the sink faucet at three in the morning, demanding I turn it on. And I would. He loved running water. He would drink, lapping up the stream with his rough pink tongue. And it was adorable.

Mr. Cat would also leap onto my head while I was sleeping and snuggle into my hair. And his front paws would push push push into my chest in a rhythm. I would call this "making muffins." I learned from Dr. Hamilton that it is a kneading motion all kittens do while suckling, to help get more of momma cat's milk flowing. If a kitten is taken away from its mother too soon, it's a motion it will make for the rest of its life. A built-in survival mechanism.

I watched Mr. Cat as he pushed on my chest, and thought about the complexity of humans, and how we each deal with loss differently. Duncan's father rebuilt his life. Duncan's mother gave up on hers. Hannah connected to her dead father on important dates, even though she thrived way more without him in her life. Humans, unlike cats, don't all knead or need in the same way.

I looked at Detective Jackson, and for the first time sitting in that room, I started to really tense up and lose my cool. My temples throbbed and I dug my nails into my palms. This game show was turning into a haunted house, and I did not like the looks of the funny mirrors. It was one thing to guess what the four photos were, since I knew the four people who were dead. It was another to have the names of living people in my orbit tossed around to manipulate me.

I asked myself, if I had known in those simple, happy routine-filled months eight years ago that the handsome veterinarian, Dr. Hamilton, and my cute kitten, Mr. Cat, would later be used by this detective to implicate me in one of the four murders, the one that would become most public and rip my life to shreds, would I still have picked the taped-up furball out of that trash can and saved him? Yes, I would have. Because it was the right thing to do. And I was about to say that to Detective Jackson. Give him a lesson on right and wrong. I was about to show way too many cards and fold. Then, as I opened my mouth to speak, I heard the sound of the air-conditioning in the room click on.

Suddenly I knew without a doubt that was what he had whispered to the desk-duty guy. Not some secret about me, not some damning proof that I was a killer, but that he was burning up in there. And he asked the guy to please, dear God, turn the air on high, make it cooler in this blasted room. Detective Jackson was not some mastermind; he was just a sweaty man trying to get through his workday comfortably. I unclenched my fists. I was calm again. And determined to beat him at this game.

CHAPTER 15

MIAMI

THE CHILLED AIR RATTLED INTO THE ROOM AND DETECTIVE Jackson refocused on the photos, like there were just so many to keep track of. "Where were we? Right. Richard Vale." He glanced at me, to make sure he still had my full attention. "You asked me if this was his mugshot from his DUI. It was not. It's from when he was arrested for a sexual assault, at a bar in Surfside. The victim ended up dropping the charges."

I waited.

"I'm not going to pretend Mr. Vale was a great guy. I can see his record. So, if he assaulted you that night. If he made you scared, or put his hands on you in any way, you had every right to defend yourself. You were a minor. A kid. If you were a victim, I won't fault you for whatever went down next. I just want to hear the truth."

I knew this ploy and I abhorred it. Others using my perceived victimhood to push their agendas. Even if I told the detective that Richard tried to rape me, that I was in fact a victim and I chose to be a calm methodical one who let him die, it would not be self-defense at all. I didn't call out for help. Or try to save him once he was unable to further harm me. It was murder.

When I started graduate school, I found out I could apply the hours of my own therapy to the three thousand supervised practicing hours I had to accrue before being eligible to take the licensing exam. So I briefly saw a therapist who also tried to force the victim card on me. She worked out of a guesthouse behind her McMansion on North Bay Road. Walking past the glossy nouveau riche driveway lined with luxury sports cars made the therapy bungalow in the back seem like someone's silly little project, like this was a scrapbooking room and not a serious, professional office.

But the tacky surroundings were not the problem. The problem was that we somehow got on the topic of virginity, and Gloria insisted that I had been repeatedly raped by Carlos. She screeched, "Until you acknowledge that you were a victim of rape, I'm not sure you'll be able to find peace. Ever." I thought about storming out, but I was already there, sitting on her white leather couch that didn't lend itself to being comforting or cozy. And certainly learning how not to be a bad therapist was going to be just as important as learning how to be a good one. So I stayed.

I said, "First of all, Gloria, it wasn't rape. I know because I was there. And extremely willing. And I enjoyed it."

"Fine. Statutory rape. You can't debate that. It's the law."

"The law is debated all the time. By thousands of people called lawyers."

"He should not have touched you. You were a child. You didn't have the ability to make a decision like that, especially when being pressured by an adult man."

"He didn't pressure me."

"There is no shame in being a victim."

"I know that. But in this case, I wasn't a victim. And I'm not ashamed. And I think I should tell you that I was much smarter than Carlos. Higher IQ. Better educated. With more societal advantages. I was actually the one in control. So perhaps I'm the one who raped him? Repeatedly. Maybe he's the victim."

Gloria was too miffed to respond. And I could see then that having Dr. Alisha Goldman as my first therapist in New Haven was like winning money the first time you go to Vegas. You think, *Great! This is how it goes! Cozy blue corduroy couch, insightful clear-minded therapist who gets to the heart of the matter in minutes!* Then you keep going back to different slot machines and roulette tables expecting the same advantageous lucrative outcome, only to lose over and over again, finding therapists like Gloria. And you learn that first time was the exception and not the rule.

I missed seeing Alisha, and finding her equal would be nearly impossible. So, I made a decision and I called her. Phone sessions weren't ideal, but they would still count toward my hours. We had a shorthand, and I hoped we could jump back in like no time at all had passed. But time had passed, two years, and when I called her office, I got a robotic voice telling me the line was disconnected. I remembered the names of the other therapists in her wing, since I saw them listed whenever I flipped the little light switch on to let her know I was there waiting in the lobby. I got hold of one of them and he was happy to give me her forwarding number. And as he enunciated the digits, my stomach did a flip. Her new number started with a 305 area code. That was Miami.

"And how does that make you feel?" Alisha asked.

I sat on a new, sea green couch with soft yet supportive cushions. "Hurt."

"I understand. Let's talk about that."

"Why didn't you tell me you were here?"

Alisha answered this one carefully. "You had stopped seeing me once you graduated. So when I decided to move here, it seemed unprofessional for me to try and find you and reach out. I didn't want to assume you still wanted or needed to be in therapy. I didn't want my move here to influence your decisions or put pressure on you to continue to see me."

Humph, was all I could think.

"So, why *did* you move here?" I asked.

This was the question she seemed to have been dreading.

"I will be honest with you, Ruby, because I think you can hear this and not run wild with its possible implications. I moved because I was ready for a change. I moved here because in our sessions together, you made Miami seem so magical."

I grinned, ear to ear. No, my mind wouldn't run wild with ideas that Alisha moved here because she was secretly in love with me, or obsessed with me, or stalking me this whole time. I would settle on the truth: I made a big enough impression on this woman that she moved to my hometown. The hurt was replaced with swelling pride.

I asked, excitedly, "So? Do you like it here?"

It was Alisha's turn to grin. "I love it. I absolutely love it! The eclectic people, the vibrancy, the warmth."

"Yeah, once you get used to the warmth, you'll never want to tackle a Northeast winter again. Below seventy is coat weather here. And you'll understand why tropical fruit is not supposed to be refrigerated. I like to think, if it's too cold for a banana, it's too cold for me."

As the seconds ticked on, the interrogation room became way too cold for a banana. It was air-conditioned to the gills, and I could feel the temperature continue to drop. Even a hearty mango would shrink with chill. I wrapped my arms around my shivering shoulders to hold in some of my body heat. I said, "I was upstairs, asleep with my friends, when Mr. Vale died. That's all I know." Detective Jackson took this as a definitive end of this round, moving on to the next. And he started to fidget with the third photo in the lineup.

CHAPTER 16

WITCH

WHEN I STARTED WITH DR. DON, I NOTICED THE LIGHTING in his office was off-center, creating a gloomy feel. I think I picked up a little of the symmetry bug from Ameena because I felt there should be two big lamps, one on each side of the couch. He didn't care one way or the other, so I brought in a giant ceramic gold-painted 1970s-style table lamp that I had had since childhood. I had looked at it so often for so long, it never occurred to me that it was hideous. It just was what it was. My mother was happy to dole out my old bedroom belongings since they no longer fit her needs or decor. So I took the lamp to Dr. Don's office. The very lamp that gave me reason to park at a meter right out front instead of around back, therefore leading me to find Mr. Cat in the garbage. So the lamp took on a great deal of importance to me. A sign of destiny.

After a few years of my happy internship, Dr. Don got a new client, or patient (I had noticed different psychologists preferred one term to the other), named Evelyn W. I had not yet decided if

I liked calling the people I met with in session clients or patients. It seemed the word *client* made them in charge, and the word *patient* made me in charge. And each individual case warranted a different title. In the case of Evelyn W., she was so awful I called her neither and instead called her the Witch.

The Witch was forced into therapy because of a court-ordered mandate. She never would have sought out self-reflection and personal betterment on her own. She slapped a crying child in line at the grocery store to make her "shut the fuck up." The mother of the child pressed charges, and since the Witch had no kids of her own to take away because of possible abuse and she had no priors, the judge sentenced her to pay a fine and seek help for her anger-management issues. No jail time. So Evelyn W. booked her twenty mandated sessions.

The Witch was in her mid-thirties, tall, and rail thin. Her bony elbows and knees looked like weapons. Her nose was long and pointy and so ugly it shocked me that she had never had it fixed, since she seemed so vain otherwise. Her hair was dull brown and flat, hanging lankily around her long face. She was mean. I could hear her on her cell phone, always on her cell phone, berating her employees. Calling them stupid and lazy. Screaming. Throwing fits. The sessions didn't seem to be helping with her anger problem because she wasn't really present; she wasn't meeting Dr. Don halfway, if at all. She just sat there staring at her cell, scrolling through emails, typing and clicking and swiping and pushing. If she showed up for the fifty minutes, she got credit for the session, even though she didn't investigate her behavior or feelings or learn anything about herself or why she was such a wretched person.

Since she was a lost cause and had exactly zero rapport with Dr. Don, he had me take over her last seven sessions. She usually paced around the room, staring at her phone. The only time she spoke was to mutter to herself and sort of to me about her "idiot employees" and "waste-of-space maid who forgot to lock the side door again" and "libtard dermatologist who didn't call in her retinol prescription." During one session, as I continued to desperately try to dig out a kernel of good in the Witch, she got some sort of email. She flew into a rage. It was from her ex-husband. How she ever got anyone to marry her in the first place was a mystery to me.

"Motherfucking asshole!" She started to kick the side table near the couch.

"Evelyn, take a deep breath."

"Don't tell me what to do, cunt!"

Cunt? I had been nothing but nice to this Witch. She then kicked the side table again, this time hard enough for my giant, heavy gold lamp to tip over and crash onto the floor. The shade crumpled, the light bulb shattered, the metal neck bent, and worst of all, the ceramic base cracked.

The crash of the lamp snapped her out of her rage. She turned and faced me, curious to see what would happen next. I looked at her, a hate growing inside me. I wanted to snap off her bony arm like a twig from a tree, and then shove it down her throat, silencing her malignance. It was the most horrific thought I had ever had, but I couldn't stop the image from cycling in my brain. It made me momentarily happy to replay in my mind.

"Get out," I said coolly.

"Fine by me. And that lamp was ugly anyway."

Before I picked up the pieces of my beloved possession, I seethed and watched the Witch from the office window. She walked to the corner, staring at her phone, as always, waiting for the light to change.

Forty-First Street is a busy thoroughfare because it turns into the I-195, one of the three major causeways that connect Miami Beach to Miami. Incidentally, it's the causeway that Amy, Erika, Sharon, Hannah, and I always used to get to Coconut Grove, where Club Rox lived. Because it connected Miami to the beach, large trucks, big rigs, school buses, and delivery vans traveled on the street constantly.

A group of other people joined the Witch, waiting for the light to change. A young mother holding her little boy's squirming hand, two teenagers on skateboards, a businessman looking dapper but too warm in a suit, and two bikini-clad beachgoers. The light changed, the cars and trucks rumbled to a stop, and the motley group crossed the street. The Witch joined them, never even looking up from her cell phone, simply following the movement of the crowd. It was a wonder she wasn't hit by a truck.

Later I told Alisha about my arm-snapping fantasy. It was troubling me that I could think about something so atrocious, and I had to get it off my chest and talk it through. "Am I a monster?" I asked. Alisha put her little notepad down and looked at me. "Ruby, you are not a monster. The mere fact that you are concerned with being a monster means you're not one, and you'll never be one. You are a good person." As she said this, a similar phrase, *You are an angel,* spoken by Duncan's mom and the friendly traffic cop, quietly echoed through my head.

Alisha mentioned that new mothers, loving mothers, often picture themselves hurting their babies, slamming them against walls, or breaking their little necks. Other people are afraid of heights not because they might fall, but because they might have an urge to fling themselves over the edge. These people aren't actually suicidal; they just have a vision they can't control. Which is very different from an impulse they can't control. A daydream is harmless. These fantasies, as horrible as they sound, are normal. The mind computes thoughts and feelings and emotions in ways that aren't always linear or logical or acceptable. But that's okay as long as we keep them where they belong, as fleeting thoughts that serve to get us from one emotion to the next.

She asked me, in earnest, "Do you think you will actually try to rip off her arm and choke her with it?"

"Of course not! . . . And I don't even think that it would be physically possible, anyway."

"Exactly. It's a cartoonish demonstration of the hatred you feel. So let's talk about that. Why do you hate this woman so much?"

"She broke my lamp."

"Yes. And I'm very sorry that happened. But it seems you disliked her even before the lamp incident. So what about *her* triggers this intense anger in *you*?"

"She's a vile, mean, rage-filled bigot who doesn't deserve to be on this earth, when there are so many other good, decent people out there who are desperate for therapy. Desperate for help. And the Witch will not be helped."

And there was the trigger. Other than the obvious, that she was a hideous person, she made me feel ineffectual, which was one of my own worst fears. I was invisible to the Witch, unable to perform an important task, leaving me worthless. Leaving me like a useless slug, vulnerable to being dissolved by salt.

By the end of the session with Alisha, I had decided two things. One, I would offset my anger toward the Witch and spend even more time helping others by volunteering at a nonprofit mental health organization. And two, I would get my lamp fixed.

CHAPTER 17

LAMP

I HAULED MY BROKEN AND BATTERED LAMP INTO A LAMP-repair shop in Bal Harbour. It had been open since the 1950s and seemed unchanged since then. Headshots of long-forgotten and dead movie stars lined one wall, newer headshots of hopeful Miami models lined another, and faded floral curtains with little lace frills on the edges hung on to their rods by threads. Even the dust was old. It was the kind of place you can't believe still exists in this modern world, until you realize everyone has lamps, and sometimes they break, and therefore a lamp-repair shop makes perfect sense.

The ancient man behind the counter examined my lamp with his gnarled hands, and he said in a thick Russian accent that he could fix, thirty dollars, but it would not be perfect. I said that was all right by me.

The door chime jingled and I instinctively looked back to see who was coming in. A man, maybe late twenties, wearing cargo shorts, Vans sneakers, and a blue T-shirt that made his eyes pop, walked in sheepishly carrying a small green lamp in the shape of a frog. He smiled at me. He had perfect white teeth. I smiled back.

"Nice frog."

"Thanks. It's not mine."

"That's what they all say."

He laughed. An easy, comfortable laugh. He had a lovely hint of a Southern drawl and explained that his mother collected all frog-related items and he spotted this at a garage sale and thought it would be a good gift for Mother's Day. I pointed out that Mother's Day wasn't for months. But he said he liked to think ahead. Wow, a guy who cared about his mom and bought thoughtful presents well ahead of time—and he was cute, at least five eleven, and not wearing a wedding ring.

The Russian man said, "Frog just needs to be rewired. Ten dollars. Will take three days." I asked how long mine would take. "Longer. Three weeks."

The frog guy and I walked out at the same time, leaving our lamps behind. We paused outside, waiting to see if our moment would amount to anything further.

"I'm Jason."

"I'm Ruby."

The Russian lamp fixer hurried out with an old camera. He said he liked photographs. That's why he kept old ones up in the shop. But he liked new ones too. Of customers. And we made such a nice couple. Could he?

Neither Jason nor I had an issue with being photographed. A good sign that neither of us had any reason to not be seen in the same frame. We stood together, under the lamp store sign, like two strangers who might want to get to know each other a bit more. Jason smiled and squinted a little in the sun, and the man snapped a photo.

It was a copy of this very photo that was third in line on the table, the one that Detective Keith Jackson was fidgeting with. He flipped it over and placed it directly in front of me, in a pat manner. I was aware that he was watching my every expression, micro and macro. I had known a photo of Jason was coming, since he was now dead and the detective certainly thought I murdered him. That was what started this whole chat at the police station in the first place. So I should have been more prepared to see Jason's smiling face. But the choice of this photo in particular felt like a gut punch. A photo from the very first day I met him four and a half years ago. A photo I was also in, when life was wide open to a happily-ever-after.

I picked it up and felt the edges. Flimsy and thin. And the colors were dull. Jason's eyes were much bluer in real life. This copy was clearly printed off of a cheap all-purpose office printer. Jason had died sixteen days ago. But seeing the photo felt like it was happening all over again in real time. My body got even colder because all my blood was rushing to my organs, to help them continue on even while my icy sorrow washed through me. The photo was still in my hand. If I put it back down on the table, it would be like I was letting Jason go all over again. But if I held on to it for too long, it would seem like I was merely playing the role of the grieving widow.

CHAPTER 18

SUGAR

WHEN JASON CALLED ME TWO DAYS AFTER I HAD MET HIM at the lamp store, to make a date, I suggested we meet at a café near me on Española Way that had great sangria. He said he couldn't drink sangria. I assumed that meant he was in recovery. I was open to dating someone sober, but I knew with it came a lot of added baggage. If he didn't drink, did it mean going to bars was off-limits entirely? How about clubs or parties? Could I have a glass of wine in front of him? Was he a violent drunk? Was that why he stopped drinking? And how many times had he relapsed? Was he the child of an alcoholic haunted by an abusive past? My mind spun with problems, almost ending the relationship before it even had a chance to begin.

As we continued to chat on the phone, I soon learned Jason wasn't sober at all. Hooray! He was a type 1 diabetic, and he couldn't drink sangria not because he was a recovering alcoholic, but because there was way too much sugar in the fruit-filled wine. He stuck to dirty vodka martinis with olives. The fat in the olives, he explained, helped to slow down the absorption of the sugar in the vodka, which was low in comparison to wine, beer, and the brown liquors. "Huh," I said. "Okay. How about the Delano? They make great martinis."

I knew nothing about diabetes, other than some vague facts I picked up from barely paying attention to the pharma commercials constantly running, and action movies that sometimes had a diabetic hostage who was going to die if he didn't get insulin! I did know that people with diabetes needed to check their blood by pricking their finger, and that people with type 2 diabetes were often overweight. And that was the extent of my knowledge on the matter.

Jason's relationship with sugar was even more complicated than my past relationship with salt. Sugar could kill him slowly but was needed to keep him alive in the moment. Sugar was constantly on his mind and in his pocket. And those action movies usually got it all wrong. A low blood sugar could lead to death in minutes. That's when the diabetic needs sugar immediately. A soda. Fruit juice. Jelly beans. Gummy bears. Candy bars and cookies are not ideal, because the fat in them slows down the absorption of the sugar so desperately and urgently needed. A high blood sugar wreaks havoc on the body and can lead to death, but it can take weeks or even months to fully shut down. That is when the type 1 diabetic needs insulin, since his or her own pancreas is broken and unable to produce any. But that need for insulin isn't life or death in the moment, like the movies would have you believe.

It's a constant balancing act. Every flight of stairs, every common cold, every extra bite of mashed potatoes has to be accounted for to keep a type 1's blood sugar at a healthy level.

Around 150, let's say. A healthy nondiabetic hovers around 90 before eating. Little did I realize on my very first date with Jason that his chronic disease was far more complicated, time-consuming, and frightening than him being a recovering alcoholic ever would have been.

CHAPTER 19

PSYCHOPATHS

THERE WAS A GREAT NEED FOR MENTAL HEALTH PROFES-
sionals in the public sector, so I had several options as a volunteer
psych intern. After review, I picked the Miami Dade Juvenile
Detention Center. Always fascinated by my own young brain, I
had taken several advanced classes in childhood development
and was excited to work with delinquent teens.

I knew that the teenage brain is not fully formed, the frontal
lobes not yet connected. Therefore a clear understanding between cause and effect cannot be wholly processed by a teenager,
which can make their behavior seem reckless and erratic. That's
why teens so often drag race, or shoplift, or experiment with cocaine in a Denny's parking lot. Teens are also driven by their own
impulsive wants and needs, which translates back to them as basic survival instinct. Stealing that lip gloss you covet feels like a
matter of life or death. Having sex with that girl and never calling her again is part of the survival-of-the-species imperative.
This basic misguided survival instinct coupled with most teens

seeing the world around them through the narrow lens of their own limited experience makes it harder for them to be compassionate. In essence, teenagers are like little psychopaths. Running around, making bad decisions, without a thought of how those decisions will affect themselves or others.

Knowing this about the brain brings up interesting dilemmas when it comes to teens being tried as adults in a court of law. How can they be held accountable if their own brains aren't finished growing? But how can they not be, if they coldly gun down an entire family just to steal a Rolex watch and Fendi purse?

My new supervisor, Joyce Brody, strongly felt teens should never be tried as adults, no matter the severity of their crimes. *She* certainly would not have blamed me for shoving a peanut down Richard Vale's throat. She fervently believed teenagers should be rehabilitated, not demonized, which was why she devoted all her time to working at the juvenile detention center. Joyce was the kind of woman who usually had more than one pencil stuck in the messy gray nest-like bun on top of her head. She was frazzled and overworked and so dedicated one had to wonder what in her own life she was running from. I couldn't believe that she wasn't already burned out and retired, perhaps running an artisanal yarn shop in Vermont.

I knew I would learn a lot from Joyce, but I didn't want to emulate her. I wanted to do good, but I did not want all children to feel like my own children. At that time, Mr. Cat was plenty. Investing as much as she did in everyone else was an ulcer or heart attack or thinning hair waiting to happen. Living like that would suck the identity out of you until all you had was the impossible yet endless need to make others whole.

Some of the teenagers I counseled were already so hardened, I feared there was little I could do. Others were nice kids put in bad situations. I had hope for them. The saddest cases for me, the ones most difficult to put down at night when I was trying to fall asleep while Mr. Cat meowed at the faucet, were the kids who had made one or two mistakes and felt they had already ruined their lives, so they thought, why even try? These were the kids who for me proved the hypothesis of my senior thesis. That guilt begets more bad deeds. These kids weren't evil. They were defeated.

Since I used cookies in my thesis analogy, I stayed on that track and used ice cream as an example with them. And brought in ice cream bars to make the lesson more fun. These good kids who had made one or two mistakes felt exactly like a person on a diet might feel when they cheat and eat a little ice cream. They've fucked it all up so irrevocably that they might as well eat the whole carton. It was these kids who I tried to connect with the most. I tried to break through to them, wanting them to know that life was long, hopefully. And doing one bad thing didn't mean they had to continue to do many bad things. And it certainly didn't mean they should hate themselves. I would urge them and coach them to "forgive yourself, believe in yourself, and move forward." I felt extremely qualified to give this advice, and my earnestness and lack of condescension seemed to seep through and reach a few of the kids. I was more convinced than ever that feeling guilty solved nothing. And self-hatred was never the answer.

I was loving my new internship—it was rewarding, and I was truly helping others—and so it was fitting that while there I got the good news. Dr. Don called me. After her final mandated session, the Witch had obnoxiously marched out of Dr. Don's office, crossed the street to the parking garage, and, as usual, wasn't paying attention to the road. She was hit by a truck and killed on impact.

In our next session, Alisha, having heard all about Evelyn W.'s demise, asked me if I felt guilty at all, because I had harbored bad feelings toward her, and now she was actually dead. I thought about the hypocrisy of the posthumous Duncan Reese chatter. And I said no. I had nothing to feel guilty about. Alisha was happy to hear it, and agreed. We talked about Evelyn W. for a while that day, and I expressed my feelings. She was a cruel person who blamed others for her unhappiness. She had no interest in taking any responsibility for her behavior, and she sucked the joy from people, rather than adding anything positive to society. She would not be missed, and her death might just make the world a slightly better place. Alisha listened and mused that sometimes karma had a way of working things out. "Yes," I said. "Karma."

CHAPTER 20

JASON

JASON WAS TWENTY-EIGHT, FROM A SMALL TOWN RIGHT outside of Atlanta, had divorced parents, was an only child, a Falcons fan (couldn't get behind the Braves because of their offensive use of Native American culture), and a cameraman for ABC's local news affiliate. He had started in the field driving around in the van with the reporters, shooting exterior shots and on-the-fly interviews, but was now in the studio, which he much preferred. I learned none of this on our first date.

We met in the Delano hotel lobby. Jason asked if we could have dinner instead of just drinks. He got off work later than expected and had to eat. A healthy blood sugar depended on it. I made a little joke that he was upping the ante. Turning our first date from a casual drinks situation to a whole formal dinner. He said if dinner went horribly wrong, we could each make an excuse to not go for drinks. I liked it. Our date was already becoming self-referential. Meta, as the receptionist at the vet's office might say.

I told him my excuse for canceling drinks and cutting our date short was going to be not feeling well, food poisoning of some sort. He said since he had real medical issues he didn't like to lie about that kind of stuff and test the fates, so he decided his excuse would be a friend calling with some sort of locked-out-of-the-house emergency so he would have to leave to save the day. We shook on it. He had a nice firm grip, but I could tell he was being gentlemanly about it, not giving me the full extent of his squeeze potential. We headed out to the poolside restaurant.

I wasn't worried about not having a reservation since I knew everyone in town, Miami Beach was small, and locals always took care of one another. I was sure I could finagle a last-minute table. But at the hostess stand it was clear that my date had called ahead and had a table for two reserved under the name Jason Hollander. So now I knew his last name. I liked it. It sounded handsome without being too soap-opera-y. And I also now knew he took the step of making a dinner reservation before asking me if dinner was even okay. I liked that too. He was both confident and prepared. But not pushy.

Jason and I fell into an easy rhythm of people watching and talking about what was happening around us.

"Is that her father or her date?" I asked about the slinky blonde at the corner table sitting next to a liver-spotted man.

"Oh, wow. He's way too old to be her father. So he must be her date."

We laughed and moved on to another table. A group of sunburnt men in their thirties smoking cigars. Jason asked me, "Corporate retreat?" I looked the men over, sensing a frantic time-is-ticking vibe.

"Bachelor party. For sure. On Monday they all have to go back to their lives, which they're dreading." Jason wasn't convinced, so I called over to the table, "Hey, which one of you guys is getting married?" The most sunburnt of them all raised his hand, like a good pupil. The others punched his arms in camaraderie. "Congrats!" I said.

Jason was impressed that I had guessed correctly. I wanted to tell him it was my job to study people and assess their situations, but I didn't. Because he didn't ask me any of the usual first-date questions, like "What do you do?" "Where are you from originally?" "Do you have any siblings?" "Where did you go to college?" And, of course, "What year did you graduate?" which was the polite way of asking, "How old are you?"

And since he didn't ask me any of those questions, I didn't ask him. It was like a game of chicken. So by the end of the date I felt I knew him as a person, without any of the details and facts that usually make up a person. I knew he was patient with the waitress, but not overly chatty. He was curious about others, but not judgmental. We told little stories and anecdotes, but didn't delve into our stats. If someone had listened in to our entire date, they would have thought we had been together for months. I say months and not years because our physical attraction to each other simmered and popped like hot oil, in a way that years tend to cool.

It was one of the oddest first dates I had ever been on, since the predictable first-date script was never recited. I wanted him to know how old I was. That I had an older sister. That my parents lived just down the road. That I had gone to Yale for undergrad and was finishing up my doctorate in psychology at UM. But why? Why did I want him to know these things? Maybe it was because I didn't know who I was without them.

We each had two drinks at dinner, and once the check came (Jason paid, although I of course reached for my purse to offer to split it), neither of us gave our predetermined excuse as to why we couldn't possibly now have drinks. So we walked over to the lobby bar and settled in. He had another martini with three olives, and I had a glass of Champagne. He asked why Champagne, and I explained the bubbles made it impossible to drink too fast, it was light and not too sweet and left me feeling buzzed and happy but never hammered, it didn't give me a hangover, and it made me feel fancy.

Plenty of men had asked me what I wanted to drink, but he was the first to ask why I wanted to drink it. He was getting to know me in a different way from anyone else. It was exhilarating and uncomfortable all at the same time. I clinked his martini glass and made a toast to broken lamps. And we talked for hours.

It's nearly impossible to close down a bar in Miami since bars never seem to close. But at two a.m. we both called it quits. Work the next morning, et cetera. I thought Jason could be a thing, a real thing, and didn't want to muddy the waters with sex too soon. I did, however, expect a kiss, but he didn't even try. Instead he put me in a cab in front of the hotel and watched as I was driven off.

When Jason first met me at the lamp store, I was wearing work clothes. As a therapist I want my attire to portray me as professional yet comfortable, competent yet relaxed, simple but thoughtful, nonsexual yet feminine. That usually amounted to a muted structured but not-too-tight top, dark jeans, and a fun-colored flat shoe. Since he'd already seen me in that type of outfit, for our first date I wanted to show Jason that I was stylish without needing to try too hard. So I wore a thin off-the-shoulder gray sweatshirt à la *Flashdance*, tight jeans, and extremely high heels.

After the fact, when I got home and called Ellie and gave her a play-by-play of our date, she was horrified to learn I had worn a sweatshirt.

"But it's a cute one! Off the shoulder!"

"No, Ruby. Just no. That's not okay for a first date! That's for a tenth date when you stay in and order pizza in the middle of your sex marathon."

I turned on the faucet for Mr. Cat and listened to Ellie berate me. And after listening to her, I decided perhaps I had given Jason the wrong impression with my sweatshirt choice. Maybe he thought I wasn't truly interested. Maybe that's why he didn't kiss me.

So for our second date I decided to go in an opposite direction. I wore a tiny black wraparound dress that had a plunging neckline. My breasts were perky enough that I didn't need a bra, and it was clear by the way the dress clung to me that I wasn't wearing one. I threw on some flats to offset the sexiness of the dress. A similar approach to putting on high heels to offset the sweatshirt.

Jason and I spent the afternoon looking at art galleries in the Design District. He didn't comment on my tiny black dress. I didn't comment on the third blue shirt I had seen him wear. Clearly someone told him long ago blue was his color. It was another odd date, filled with chatting about our opinions on everything from Colombian folk paintings to water fountain germs, but little about our personal backgrounds. He enjoyed lingering on each piece of art, slowly taking it in. I did not. I liked to breeze through, only stopping when something truly caught my eye.

I did learn, as I searched for a café Cubano stand, that he did not drink coffee. Instead he drank diet soda. Even in the morning. Jason gave me a hint into his past and explained that where he grew up they mostly drank sweet tea, and since he was diabetic, it was diet soda for him. I listened to his words and watched his well-proportioned lips as he drawled in his slight Southern accent. But I wasn't able to figure him out. He was so hard to read, I couldn't decide if he liked my personality but wasn't attracted to me physically. Or the other way around. Maybe he just wanted to be friends? Maybe he was gay but not out? Maybe he had an STD he wasn't ready to tell me about so was keeping his distance? Maybe he was secretly married? Maybe maybe maybe. The date again ended without a kiss.

By the middle of our third date I was feeling a little frantic. Jason still didn't know how old I was. Or where I went to college. Or that I broke my wrist roller-skating on a basketball court with Ellie when I was ten. He didn't know anything about me, and yet he was more tuned in to me than any guy I had ever been with before. He was like an alien, highly emotionally developed, educated about the human race and condition, but not able to play the role of human casually.

We went bowling, something I am convinced is a thing one only does on third dates and then never does again. The entire concept of a bowling alley lends itself to being an enterprise for new couples who want to seem adventurous and spirited, since dinners at nice restaurants only go so far. And bowling is a fun, active endeavor that doesn't require one to be too athletically skilled yet allows for asses to be checked out, stamina to be assessed, and close access to be granted when teaching each other good form and technique. There's also always a bar, so alcohol can be blamed for the terrible rolls. And alcohol can be credited for the ease of flirtation. I think bowling alleys have survived the test of time because of third dates alone, and the ubiquitous lame last-minute birthday party.

Not surprisingly they didn't serve Champagne, or any sparkling wine option, at the bowling alley. So I was drinking vodka and soda, which was mostly vodka. I was drunk, really drunk, and my thoughts and fears boiled to the surface. Maybe Jason thought I was crazy? I did wear a sweatshirt to a first date, barely a dress on our second, and now was back in my conservative work clothes. Maybe he thought I was bipolar since visually I was giving off such disparate signals? But if he thought I was insane, why go out with me a third time? That would make him insane! And I was a professional psychologist, so wouldn't I be able to tell if he was insane? Or maybe he was normal but had had a string of unhinged girlfriends and that was why he was taking it slow? And why was I in such a hurry anyway? This ruminating was not like me. I barely gave a second thought to murdering people, and here I was overthinking Jason's every mannerism. I enjoyed analyzing human behavior, sure, but obsessing about dating, no way. Not me.

After another disastrous attempt at hitting the pins, I drunkenly turned to Jason. I shrieked out, "You don't even know how old I am!"

"Does it matter?"

"Of course it matters!"

"Why?"

Hmmmmm. That was a good question. Why did it matter? When I was fifteen, I believed age was just a number, and I told Carlos so because I wanted to seem older. But at the same time I enjoyed people's shock when they learned how young I actually was: "You're so mature, and what an advanced vocabulary!" But now that I was twenty-five, my age not impressive one way or the other, it seemed like more than just a number. It seemed like the code to a safe that needed to be unlocked.

I answered Jason, "Well, what if I was forty? And you wanted kids. And I was too old to have them?"

Why was I talking about kids on a third date? What was

wrong with me!? If he didn't think I was crazy before, he defi-nitely would now. I blamed the vodka but knew somewhere un-der the drunkenness I was falling in love with this guy. Maybe that scared me and I was trying to sabotage what could be a wonderful relationship. Or maybe I wasn't trying to sabotage it at all, but came across as grasping and neurotic because I was scared the love of my life was slipping away.

Jason looked me over. "Are you forty?"

This question was an outrageous affront. So I yelled, getting the attention of the third-date couples on either side of our lane. "No, I'm not forty!"

"Well then, we don't have to worry about your fertility, do we?"

I plopped down on a hard plastic turquoise-and-yellow swiv-eling bowling alley seat. And pouted.

Jason asked, "Do you want to tell me how old you are?"

"I'm twenty-five."

"Okay. I'm twenty-eight."

"Fine."

"Fine."

Jason took his turn, hitting a strike. He gave a congratulatory hoot, but the vibe of our date was now tense. My franticness was turning into resentment. A pressure behind my eyes. I didn't know where I stood with him, and it wasn't like a fun cat-and-mouse game. It was frustrating, especially since I cared so much about him so quickly. I knew he felt something for me too, but I couldn't quite capture it.

Jason won the game by a ton of points, or pins, or what-ever. And he thought I was too drunk to drive. I agreed. He lived close by, walking distance, and suggested I sober up at his apart-ment. Now we were getting somewhere, I thought. But when we arrived, he put a giant glass of water in my hand. He really did want me to sober up—this was not some ploy to get me back to his place and in bed. Jason had a two-bedroom, two-bathroom condo. He bought it three years ago, he said, only giving me this information because I asked direct questions about the building. He didn't need so much space, but resale value on two-bedrooms was much higher than on one-bedrooms, so he went for the more promising investment. He was a real grown-up.

I sat on his couch, black leather, very masculine, and looked around. He was messy but not a slob. He had some framed concert posters, some cheesy art of waves, lots of camera equipment in black boxes that I would learn were called Pelican cases, and some meditation pillows in the corner. I could see a few beach towels lying around, and sand near his pile of shoes, which he seemed to kick off his feet right at his front door.

Based on his condo, sand and waves and all, he clearly loved the ocean. We had that in common. His frog lamp, now rewired, sat on his dining room table snug in bubble wrap, waiting to be given to his mother. Everything smelled like tangerine, in a good way. I recognized it from spending so much time at the beach. It was a type of surf wax. I then noticed a long surfboard leaning against a wall in one of the bedrooms.

Jason had still not tried to kiss me. I wasn't the sort of girl who needed the guy to always make the first move, but with him I felt there was a wall. And I didn't want to throw myself against it.

I finished my water and walked into the kitchen. His counters were cluttered but organized. There were jars of sugary goo packets, containers of glucose tablets, electrolyte powders, and large plastic vats of protein power. I knew what everything was because it was labeled. It seemed like the kitchen of a professional athlete.

I realized, with a bit of sadness for Jason, that being a healthy type 1 diabetic took the same willpower, control, and maintenance as being a professional athlete does, but just to be average. I put my glass in his sink.

"I think I'm fine to drive now."

"You sure?"

"Yeah."

"I'll walk you back to your car."

"Nah. I'm good. I grew up on these streets."

I knew I sounded ridiculous. Growing up in Miami Beach didn't protect me from being mugged, molested, or murdered. But in that moment I felt safer being out there with crack-smoking, gun-wielding criminals than in here, balancing on the sharp edge of rejection.

I started to walk out. Things felt unresolved. But why? I had met Jason at the lamp-repair store only a few weeks earlier. Sure, we had chatted on the phone, and texted, and had three dates, but it wasn't like we were lifelong friends. Or connected in any external way. It wasn't like I was desperate to have a boyfriend. So why was I so intrigued by him? Why was I unwilling to just walk away and chalk it up to a non-thing when I'd been willing to do that plenty of other times with plenty of other men? Did love at first sight really exist? Or love at three dates? One does hear stories of couples meeting and knowing and getting married that same week and being together for sixty years of connected bliss.

I lingered in the doorway. And looked at him and his white teeth. Half sure I should walk out and never look back. Half sure I should turn around and say one last thing.

CHAPTER 21

SEX

SINCE MOST PEOPLE LIE, EVEN IN THERAPY, EVEN IN BLIND studies, even to themselves, it's nearly impossible to know true average number of sexual partners. But I'm certain growing up in Miami skews what might seem outrageous in other parts of America as totally within reason. Miami is hot and steamy, filled with attractive people wearing tiny clothes, drinking rum, dancing to sultry salsa music all night long, gay and straight and every tick of the pendulum in between. There is no slut shaming in Miami. Instead sex is openly celebrated. It's the prudes who feel uncomfortable and unwelcome.

However, I did develop my own sex rule. I would not sleep with more men than my current age. There was Carlos first. Then Mikey the water polo player, Kevin the vegan. Max the professor's assistant. Plus Jake, Melody's boyfriend. And a few more over the years. When I write all their names on a list, it seems like a lot of men. But then when I step back to do the math, it doesn't. I've been sexually active since I was fifteen, so by my mid-twenties, having dated on average one to three men every year, that adds up to sleeping with over twenty men. When I think about it that way, my list doesn't seem so long at all.

But that's why I created my rule of never sleeping with more men than my age. Not to make myself frigid or ashamed or to deny myself pleasure and fun, but to make myself a little more thoughtful about sex. More aware that it doesn't have to be a given with everyone I might date a few times. My rule also made me pause before going from one short relationship right into the next, allowing me to spend some alone time reflecting. Mr. Cat had his opinions too. Some men he liked, some he didn't, and a few times while a gentleman caller was spending the night, he showed his disdain by pooping not in his kitty litter, but in the bathtub. His way of saying, *Try and be romantic now, dickwad.*

At the time of my bowling alley date with Jason, my ex Seth had been my longest and most serious relationship. We started dating my first year in graduate school, and we were together for a full year. He could quote Goethe's *Faust* and John Hughes's *Pretty in Pink*. His well-roundedness was very attractive. He was the first man I ever said "I love you" to in a romantic sense. Roman and I used to say it to each other all the time, with the ease of friends who aren't physically connected.

I thought for sure Seth would be the one to say it to me first, since he was good at emoting, but I was caught off guard two months into dating, usually around the time I start to get antsy and have the distinct feeling I'd rather be somewhere else with someone else. One morning I watched Seth put on his sock and then his other sock and then his shoe and his other shoe. Something about the way he did it—rather than sock, shoe, sock, shoe—made me content. Instead of wanting to be somewhere else with someone else, I knew it didn't matter where I was as

long as I was with him. And I knew that was love. When he finished tying his laces, he looked up at me, caught me staring
at him.

"What?" he asked.

It came out slow and awkward but deliberate, like a baby bird
pecking through its eggshell and crawling out for the first time.
"Nothing," I said. "Just. I love you."

He smiled an easy smile. "That's good news. Because I love
you too."

That was three years before I met Jason. I had been twenty-
two at the time. And since being with Seth, I had slept with a
couple others, putting my number dangerously close to my age.
Twenty-four partners. That meant if I had sex with Jason and
things didn't work out, I would have to take a sabbatical from sex
for a while to let my age overtake my sex number. A lot was rid-
ing on this Jason decision since I would under no circumstances
break my sex rule. Since I didn't always follow other people's
rules, the laws of man, and some might even say the laws of God,
if I started breaking my own rules, life would seem dauntingly
limitless in its possibilities. Without my own personal self-
imposed syllabi and code, I would have crumbled under the
weight of an existence without any meaning or structure.

But standing in that doorway, I believed in me and Jason. I
thought maybe I was pushing it. Moving too fast. Maybe a different approach. So I said, "You know, we can just be friends."

I saw a trace of hurt in his eyes. But I got too angry to care
about his hurt. And said, "Actually, forget that. I take it back. I
have plenty of friends. I don't want to be your friend. I want to
date you. I don't quite understand you, but I like that. And I like
you. A lot. And if you don't feel the same, okay. But I won't be
your friend."

Before I could shut the door on him forever, Jason strode over to me, grabbed me around the waist, pulled me in, and kissed me. And that night he became my number twenty-five. He was more defined than his blue T-shirts had led on. Each muscle in his shoulders and back twitched as he pulled his shirt off. When he reached for me, I could picture him paddling out through the water, on his surfboard, his arms and core well attuned to working together. As I pressed against him, I thought we could be that sixty-years-of-bliss couple. I was wrong.

CHAPTER 22

FLOWERS

THE MORNING AFTER OUR THIRD DATE, JASON ADMITTED he was in fact giving me mixed messages. Not on purpose to play games, but because he really wasn't sure about me. It wasn't until I told him I didn't want to be friends that he clicked in. As he sipped on his Diet Coke, he said there was a rare honesty and integrity to my outburst, so he was willing to let his guard down. What would scare most men away even more made the alien in him dive into the deep end with me.

When my supervised internship hours were complete, my classes were finished, and my thesis on sociopaths and narcissists being like first cousins once removed was turned in and getting rave reviews from my professors and advisers, I officially graduated with my doctorate degree.

Immediately after graduation—because why would I start procrastinating now?—I took the Examination for Professional Practice in Psychology, EPPP for short. I studied for it using the old-school cue card method, and missed Roman so much at these times. The nostalgia came in waves, sometimes so strong I felt almost pushed overboard. But I hung on, breathed in through my nose and out through my mouth, and remained focused.

Like the IQ tests I used to enjoy as a child, I reveled in the 225 multiple-choice-question test focusing on core areas of psychology, such as assessment and diagnosis, and social and biological bases of behavior. Fun! There was a right and wrong to every question. Nothing open-ended, nothing left to chance.

I passed and was officially a licensed psychologist. Ready to go into the world unsupervised, delve into the trauma and darkest places of others, and do my best to make their lives better. To use my strengths to help those weakened by life.

To celebrate this achievement, Jason arrived at my apartment with a bottle of my favorite Champagne and a beautiful bursting bouquet of several different types of purple flowers. He made sure that all the varietals were nontoxic to cats, since sometimes Mr. Cat would nibble on the petals and harmlessly puke up his own bouquet. Jason was always so conscientious like this. And wonderful and kind and supportive. He brought out the best in me. So why was I being questioned about his death?

Goose bumps crept up my legs because the metal chair I was sitting on had itself succumbed to the cold air and become a conduit for shivers. Detective Jackson now looked at me with kindness. His face was open and patient. He was playing both good cop and bad cop all on his own. As I held the flimsy photo of me and Jason at the lamp store, I asked myself a very important question. If I could think of no reason to kill him, why on earth would anyone else think I killed him? As I put the photo back down on the table, I thought about all the flowers he had given

me over the years. How there is always an end to things. No matter how long the flowers stayed fresh, they always seemed to die
too soon. I suppose the moment they were cut from their stems
they were already dead and, like me in happier times, were just
reveling in the beauty of their slow decay.

CHAPTER 23

CAKE

JASON SPOKE TO HIS MOTHER ON THE PHONE AT LEAST three times a day. He filled her in on his minutiae, asked her for advice constantly, and rarely made a decision without her input. If he had a major flaw, it would be this. It seemed a tad codependent to me, but I murdered a little boy to protect my sister, so who was I to judge?

After we'd been dating for several months, Gertrude wanted to meet me. Jason's twenty-ninth birthday was coming up, so it was the perfect opportunity. He said that way it would be a big group and not too much pressure, but I didn't feel any pressure. Meeting parents had never caused me anxiety. Parents usually loved me. And because I was a psychologist, I was great at asking other people questions and either really listening to their answers or pretending very well to really listen. Most people like talking about themselves, so if you walk away from an interaction feeling you've been heard, you usually like the person who you believe was listening. I kept reassuring Jason that it would all be great, his mom and I would be fast friends, or at the very least cordial acquaintances. How could we not get along when we both clearly cared about him so much? But looking back, I now see he was trying to shield me from something. Something he wasn't able to communicate at that time but subconsciously knew was a danger.

Jason decided to have his party by the pool of the landmark hotel the Fontainebleau. It was the place to be seen in the 1950s, all glitz and glamour, kitten heels and cat eyes. By the eighties it was a punch line. Sunburnt, overweight tourists and discounted frozen daiquiris. But like so many old ladies on Miami Beach, it got a face-lift and a makeover and a rebrand and was forcing its way into a comeback. New owners! New lobby! New guest rooms! But the same classic chandeliers and pizzazz of yester-year. Jason reserved several of their cabanas and planned a lunch of burgers, veggie skewers, and an open bar.

He invited lots of his coworkers from the news station, both on-camera talent and fellow behind-the-scenes employees, and many of his surfer friends who saw him at sunrise most morn-ings. Because he grew up in Georgia, he didn't have any child-hood friends in town. But several of his college friends from Florida State University were in Miami and also attending.

So not only was I going to be meeting his mom for the first time, I was going to be meeting almost everyone else from Ja-son's world for the first time as well. And I wanted to be liked. I wanted his friends to give him a knowing smile, like, *Hey, you got yourself a keeper. She's smart, yet easygoing, yet keeps you on your toes. She's pretty, but not in an intimidating or trashy South Beach way. She's a great match for you, Jason. Don't fuck it up!*

It mattered to me that all his friends thought this because it's normal to want to be liked and accepted, and although I might be a murderer, I was still just like everyone else. And as far as platitudes go, "There's never a second chance to make a good first impression" is at the top of my list. Because it's true. There's been plenty of times I've met someone, liked them at first, and then learned I didn't like them one bit. But I can't think of a time I met someone, didn't like them, then learned to like them.

Jason wanted a new outfit of his own to wear to his party and thought we should have some fun and go shopping together. Many guys I knew dreaded going clothes shopping and sitting in the man-chair in the center of the store while pretending to care and doling out phrases like, "You look hot, babe" and, "Whichever one you like better" and, of course, "Stop it, you don't look fat." But Jason actually loved shopping. Again, total alien. Going into stores with him was like a movie montage of trying on fun hats and silly pants and laughing and telling each other the truth about outfits.

There was one place in particular I knew Jason and I had to go—Hannah Vale's thriving boutique on South Beach. And after the awkwardness of Ameena coming to visit me in Miami and learning about a big event I had kept to myself, I made sure to fill Jason in on the major details of Richard's tragic death. But, of course, omitting a few minor details that in my mind were unnecessary to ever share with anyone. Including the man with whom I might be falling in love.

Hannah gave me a huge hug when I walked into the store. We actually hadn't seen each other in a long time; work, stuff, life got in the way. I introduced her to Jason, told her we needed birthday party outfits, and let her start whipping things off racks. After finally getting her bachelor's degree in marketing, she got a small-business loan and opened up her store. She still had her own princess-of-darkness vibe going, but she had the insight to curate her boutique with the best of all styles for men and women.

She also had a small section where she sold her own designs, a line called Vampire in the Sun, which consisted of long-sleeve black shirts and long, tight black maxi skirts in breathable material that looked like sexy Elvira-goes-to-brunch outfits but had a sunscreen woven into the fabrics. It was a clever idea, cool clothes for goth, punk, and emo sun-sensitive people. It hadn't taken off yet, but I was proud of her for pursuing her dream.

She handed Jason a pair of white linen pants. He looked at her, then at me.

"You sure I can pull these off?"

Hannah said, "No. That's why you're going to try them on."

He took them into the dressing room and she gave me a knowing smile, as if to say, *Hey, you got yourself a keeper. He's smart, yet easygoing, yet keeps you on your toes. He's handsome, but not in a trashy South Beach way. He's a great match for you, Ruby. Don't fuck it up!*

Jason walked out of the dressing room, and yes, he pulled off those pants perfectly. Hannah had me try on a Greek-goddess-esque white-and-gold sundress that looked amazing over the gold bikini she was also about to sell me. And Jason bought a thin cotton light blue button-down to go with his new white linen pants. Hannah was happy and deemed us complementary without being too matchy. She sent us on our way, bags full of new clothes and hearts full of love.

Jason planned his party mostly by himself, and I knew he wouldn't have a cake since it was way too sugary and carb-heavy. As I watched Jason make his morning protein shakes and measure out his berries, I wanted so much for him to be able to blow out twenty-nine candles and eat a piece of cake like a person with a normal pancreas gets to do on his birthday. So I thought it would be a nice surprise if I hired a baker to make some sort of special low-glycemic-index sugar-free dessert. But since he stayed away from all desserts all the time, I didn't even know what type of cake he would most enjoy. And I didn't want to casually ask him, fearing it would ruin the surprise. I was good at keeping things close to the vest, but he was good at seeing right through me. Which made being with him make me feel more alive than stinging salt water on my eyeballs or pounding dance club music or cocaine or even oxygen ever could.

The person who would know what kind of cake he liked when he could eat that sort of thing, before he was diagnosed with type 1 diabetes, which he told me happened when he collapsed on the playground when he was seven years old, feeling parched, begging someone, anyone, for a sip of water, was the person who he spoke with three times a day. The person who meant the most to him in the whole wide world, the person who knew him best. His mother. So one day, when he was in the shower, I grabbed her phone number off his cell. I called Gertrude the next day.

That was my first mistake.

CHAPTER 24

COBRA

GERTRUDE ANSWERED HER PHONE WITH A NEUTRAL "HELLO." I used my chipper voice and introduced myself: "Hi! It's Ruby, Jason's girlfriend. I'm so excited to meet you at his birthday party." And then I asked her about what kind of cake her son liked. I expected an energetic answer about chocolate or carrot or red velvet, but instead my question was met with cold silence.

What I didn't know then, when I made that phone call, was that Jason was abandoned by his mother when he was two years old. She left Georgia and moved to Florida. She told family and friends that she had to escape since his father was so terrible and abusive. But if he was so terrible and abusive, how could she leave her small child alone with him?

Some mothers have been known to summon the strength to lift cars off their babies. Others have fled from war-torn countries with nothing but rags on their backs to offer a safer life to their young. Some mothers perjure themselves and give false alibis in court, preventing their criminal children from being locked up, endangering the lives of others to keep their own offspring free. This innate determination to protect one's own and the irrational, unconditional love of a mother for her child are what fuels the continuation of the human race. Plenty of mothers endure abusive relationships and traumatic divorces and ugly custody battles to ensure they get to raise their own children. So what kind of mother leaves without taking her son with her? A bad mother. Maybe a mentally ill mother. Maybe a narcissist. Perhaps even a sociopath.

So Jason was raised by a stern single dad who could sometimes be cruel. There were rules and expectations and chores, and there was yelling, and the occasional spanking, and a few times the belt was taken out, and in a small percentage of those times the metal buckle end was used. His father was certainly not perfect. And like so many teenage boys, Jason grew to hate him. Not because he was evil, but because he was there.

Since Gertrude wasn't there, to get frustrated, or yell, or have a meltdown, or say an unkind word, or embarrass him in front of his friends, or make a mistake, or spank him, or hit him with a leather belt, in Jason's mind she became a saint. The perfect mother. The enormous affront of her abandoning him was too much for his young emotions to dissect, so instead he focused on the positive little things. Like the sound of her voice on the phone that became so familiar as they chatted over the years. Or the little gifts she would sometimes mail, like a baseball cap or a toy car. Or the birthday cards he would get that always started out with "Dear Son" and ended with "Love, Mom." He cherished those cards and as a boy would run his hand over the words *Son* and *Mom* again and again to make sure they were real.

Gertrude was able to be maternal to a point, from seven hundred miles away, on her own terms. And Jason clung to these maternal gestures like an undernourished flower planted in the shade of a much bigger tree desperately clinging to the smallest sliver of sunlight. Gertrude was the villain. It was so clear. But since she wasn't the one in the trenches raising him, for a long time in Jason's mind she was the hero.

Jason said he was going to explain everything to me, about his mom, about how she left when he was little. And how then, senior year of high school, when he turned eighteen, he punched his dad in the face and his dad punched him back and then kicked him out of the house, yelling, "You can come home when you apologize!"

But Jason never apologized. And he never went home. Instead he moved in with his high school girlfriend, Cindy. They had been dating for two years and it was pretty serious. Living at her house with her folks was okay for a couple of weeks, but her parents wouldn't let him stay forever. Not unless he and Cindy got married. This was the type of small town where people grew up, married each other young, hung around, got local jobs, and had kids of their own, who then started the cycle all over again. So Cindy's parents wanting a ring on her finger from a mall jewelry store paid for in installments by her high school boyfriend was not out of the ordinary. They would welcome their son-in-law into their home with open arms, but not a young man who was merely their teenage daughter's boyfriend.

The wrinkle was, Jason wasn't sure he wanted to get married at eighteen. Having a chronic illness was a curse for all the obvious reasons, but it was also a blessing. It forced him to do research about his health, be an advocate for himself, learn how to ask doctors intelligent questions, and investigate different types of food and exercise. It made him more worldly than the average small-town Georgia kid, and although he held no judgment about those who stayed, he had a sneaking suspicion that his future could hold more than working at the AutoZone in the next town over.

He loved Cindy deeply in that teenage "I might die without you" way, but marrying her seemed like a big decision to have to make under such extreme circumstances. So he turned to the comforting voice of his mother. He called her and filled her in. She didn't like the idea of Jason getting married one bit, but she took great delight in learning he finally had a major falling-out with his father and hated him as much as she did.

By never being there, she had won. And now that Jason was eighteen and self-sufficient, a man so to speak, she welcomed him into her life and into her home with open arms. He said goodbye to a teary Cindy. She tried to give him back his high school ring, which she proudly wore on her wedding ring finger with a Band-Aid wrapped around the back since it was way too big for her, but he told her to keep it. As a token to remember him by. But she threw it at him and screamed, "I don't want to remember you!"

He had a sheen of tears in his eyes when he told me about this next part. About how Cindy then immediately regretted throwing the ring and she ran and searched for it in the grass, trying to find where it had landed. The yellow center stone glimmered in the sun, giving her a clue. She picked it back up and held it to her heart and sobbed.

Jason took a Greyhound bus to Fort Lauderdale. He moved in with his mother, became a Florida resident, got his GED instead of finishing out his senior year at a whole new high school, and because of a talent for taking photographs, he got into Florida State University the following semester. He visited his mother on holidays and long weekends, and after he graduated, he moved to Miami to be closer to her, and ever since then she had been an enormous part of his life. Him happy to make up for lost time. Her maybe assuaging her guilt for abandoning him in the first place. Or maybe enjoying being needed by someone not quite as needy as a toddler would have been.

He was going to tell me all this soon, before I met her at his party, but was stalling because he didn't want me to hear about all his childhood baggage and overanalyze him. Some therapists spend entire careers asking, "How do you feel about your mother?" I did think it was an important question. But I also practiced a more in-the-moment approach. We all have childhood trauma in one form or another. We can dwell on it in therapy, which sometimes unlocks the key to healing and moving forward. But often talking about the current situation is a faster way into change and betterment. Once the milk is spoiled, it has to be thrown out. So throw it out! No need to wallow in the putrid smell of bad childhoods. But when I got on the phone that day, I had no idea how much baggage there was to be unpacked.

I would later understand that I was met with a cold silence because Gertrude abandoned Jason when he was two years old and thus didn't know the answer to my simple question. She was taken aback and defensive. Like I had asked her about the cake on purpose to call her out, to show how little she knew about her own son, to prove what a terrible mother she had been. She was paranoid that I was out to expose her.

Then she was angry that I was thoughtful enough to have even had the idea to order him a special cake in the first place. Instead of being happy her son was dating an attentive girl, she twisted it around and made it about herself. Classic narcissist behavior. She was so self-absorbed she thought all my actions were in direct relation to her. She was embarrassed she herself hadn't thought of getting him a sugar-free cake of some sort and that his new troublemaking girlfriend was in essence putting a mirror up to show what a horrible, selfish person she had been and still was.

She spat out, "If you're trying to make me look bad, it won't work."

"I'm just trying to get a cake."

"Don't get smart with me."

"I'm not 'getting smart.' I'm just stating the actual situation."

Her anger melted into embarrassment, and the embarrassment quickly turned into shame. And that shame, because it was not addressed in a healthy manner, was regurgitated into an outpouring of hatred. Toward me.

At the birthday party Gertrude played it off with a cool calmness. She gave me a hug that was so icy I felt the contrivance burrow through the fabric of my Grecian dress, past my gold bikini, and into my skin and my muscle and even deep into my bones. But to an onlooker the embrace would have appeared perfectly friendly. She was an attractive lady with medium-length dark brown hair, turquoise earrings with a necklace to match, and an appealing figure. She seemed totally normal, and that was her greatest asset. Her normalcy made my reactions to her seem like I was the crazy one.

Experts in the field of domestic violence have created two categories for abusers: "pit bulls" and "cobras." The pit bull (and I apologize since I don't like the idea of propagating the negative image of the pit bull breed since they can be wonderful and there are no bad dogs, only bad owners) is loud, out-of-control, sloppy, aggressive, passionate, and hotheaded. Like a pit bull dog keeps his strong jaws locked once he has his prey in his mouth, once a pit bull abuser latches onto a prize or target, it's hard for them to let go. However, once they do finally lose their grip and the thing they are grasping escapes from them, they will quickly move on to something else they might want. Pit bulls don't linger or ruminate or remember. If an abused wife can get away from her pit bull husband, she'll be all right. Assuming she doesn't continue her own cycle and fall for another pit bull.

The cobra abuser is much scarier. They are sly and smart and quiet. Their intelligence overrides their emotion, and they constantly calibrate their actions. When the cops arrive on the scene, cobras are respectful and levelheaded. They will apologize to the officers for the miscommunication, the misunderstanding, and calmly show all is well. To the untrained eye, they are good citizens. Cobras abuse in a systematic, manipulative, and clever way. They know how and where to hit without leaving bruises, and have the control to do so. They also know that creating fear in others is invisible. And once a cobra has their eyes on you, they will never let you go. They will stalk their prey, even if it means their own demise, until that prey is dead. To survive, a person abused by a cobra has to flee, change identity, never stay in one place for too long, or the cobra ex will eventually resurface.

In my professional opinion, Gertrude was a cobra. When I first tried to discuss this with Jason, a couple weeks after his birthday, he defended her completely. She was young back then, didn't know how to be a mother. She left him, but she always loved him. She talked to him on the phone and sent him gifts. There was nothing abusive about it! Of course I knew these calls and gifts were her way of never really letting him go. Her way of selfishly leaving him, yet keeping him on a long leash just in case she wanted to yank him back one day. A very cobra thing to do. To cut all ties forever would have been healthier for him. But Gertrude didn't care about Jason's emotional well-being.

When I pushed on and mentioned this, Jason was quick to point out that his mother has been there for him every single day for the past ten years, and that isn't something to take lightly. Then he threw some of my own therapy back at me: "Like you always say, there's no point in regrets or guilt. So why would I punish her for what she did then when our relationship now is amazing?"

Hearing this made me deeply sad for him because it was a textbook response from an abused and neglected child desperate to be loved by the one person who doesn't have the capacity to love. But I wouldn't do to Jason what that therapist Gloria did to me, and try to convince him that he was a victim. I couldn't force him to see anything. I would just have to hope that with some time he would see that his mother was toxic and realize he was strong enough to not need her.

After much discussion with the baker I had hired, I had ended up ordering Jason a light and airy dark chocolate chip angel food cake sweetened with applesauce. Everyone at the party loved it except for Gertrude. She only took one bite and in her charming Southern accent said it was a pity that I had spent so much money on something that tasted like cardboard. Of course she beamed at everyone else, and only whispered this to me. Even though it was eighty-nine degrees and sunny, I felt a chill as I realized I was now officially in the crosshairs of a cobra. I knew as long as I stayed in Jason's life, my own would be under siege.

CHAPTER 25

GABRIELLE

AFTER I WAS LICENSED, IT WAS TIME FOR ME TO GET MY VERY own office. I chose a space in a high-rise on Biscayne Boulevard, near the Venetian Causeway, with a gorgeous view of the bay. The rent was affordable, as long as I quickly got clients and kept them. I was willing to bet on myself. The office had an old black overstuffed chair, for the therapist, and a plump merlot-colored love seat, for the patient. There was no coffee table creating a barrier between the two, which I liked. It seemed more intimate. Small side tables were perched near the chair and the love seat. For the tissue boxes.

The sunlight coming from the large window was so bright and gorgeous I knew I would only need to use the overhead lights for late-night sessions. I had already learned my lesson about not bringing in beloved personal items, such as my lamp. I placed a blooming orchid on one of the side tables. I sat in my new old chair, looking at the empty love seat that would soon be filled with all sorts of people, and I was happy.

My first new client was Gabrielle R. She came to me for post-traumatic stress disorder. She was twenty-two, had also grown up on Miami Beach, had gone to college in the Northeast and then returned back here to set up her adult life, hoping to be a professional writer, currently paying her bills by bartending. She was extremely pale, had black hair, and wore deep bloodred lipstick and matching nail polish. She told me that she was sensitive to the sun, basically allergic, so she had to stay away from the beach during the day, but she loved all things Miami otherwise. Especially the nightlife, when only the moon was out and she could frolic in tank tops and miniskirts and expose her porcelain skin. Instead of just looking like a pasty loser in junior high, she opted to turn her paleness into a lifestyle and went full goth. As she talked, I thought of Hannah's clothing line, Vampire in the Sun, and told Gabrielle all about it. She was excited to check it out. This was all the easy getting-to-know-each-other banter before the real therapy began. Unlike in police interrogations, in therapy there is small talk.

A month earlier, while she was on a first date with a guy named Derrick Roberts, a man with a gun came into the Thai restaurant Gabrielle had chosen and shot up the place. Her date dove on top of her to shield her from any bullets, and it worked. She was unharmed, physically. Derrick was shot three times in the back, bled out all over her, and died within seconds.

Gabrielle explained to me how she usually maintained a no-dating-customers policy, but Derrick had been charming and confident yet not cocky. He had a commanding jawline, and his lips seemed to be asking to be kissed. He never drank too much, and he was quick to help ward off unwanted advances from the men who did. So after several weeks of seeing him sit in her section, Gabrielle had asked him out. And after a moment of hesitation, he had said yes.

She has reviewed that moment of hesitation on his end over and over and over again. She has relived the decision to go to that Thai restaurant when he had first suggested Italian. She has tortured herself going over every second of her life leading up to the moment that Derrick's body went slack on top of hers.

I started by telling Gabrielle that it was brave and wonderful that she wanted to come to therapy to talk about this terrible trauma, especially so quickly. Just like setting a broken leg in a cast, the sooner a person can set her emotional injury in the right direction, the faster she will heal. And I also said, "It's not your fault that Derrick died. It is the fault of the man who came into that restaurant with a gun and shot him." Gabrielle's eyes glistened with tears. "I know that. Logically. Intellectually. I know that somewhere in the back of my mind. But swirling in the front, pressing against my eyes, emotionally that fact seems like the farthest thing from the truth."

Gabrielle was smart and aware of herself and connected to her feelings in a way that made me hopeful. She was ahead of the game, already able to distinguish logic from emotion. In so many ways, she reminded me of me. I liked her very much, and I was sure we could work through this trauma together. The last thing I ever intended to do was to bring even more trauma into her life. But how was I to know that my own nightmare was only three years away? And that all those who surrounded me would get dragged into my misfortune?

CHAPTER 26

PUSH

WHEN YOU SURF OR SKATEBOARD OR SNOWBOARD, YOUR stance is either "regular," with your left foot in front making your right foot your main source of balance, or "goofy," with your right foot in front making your left foot your main source of balance. If you ask a person who has never done one of these sports before if they are regular or goofy, they won't be able to answer. It's not something you can determine intellectually. The way to tell what you are is to have someone give you a push from behind. Whichever foot automatically steps forward to block your fall is the foot that determines the answer. Your body knows when your mind does not.

I was in love with Jason, there was no question, but had someone asked me if I actively wanted to get married, and many of my friends did, I would hem and haw and overanalyze the institution of marriage and try to reason out the pros and cons. Jason and I hadn't once discussed marriage; we were both happy to date for two years and then move in together. I gave up my cute lavender apartment, and Jason kept his condo as a rental property. We wanted to start our lives joined in a new place, making fresh memories and mingling our books together on shelves. At first Mr. Cat had his doubts about our new, large three-bedroom apartment, but after a week, he got a feel for the place, figured out how to get his little paws into the cabinet latches, and only threw up on our new king-sized bed in protest twice.

I knew the divorce rate was 50 percent, and getting married didn't solve any relationship problems or necessarily mean forever. I had many clients who had been divorced, or were in the middle of divorces, or on the cusp of storming home and demanding a divorce. Also I noticed many people, women especially, thought of marriage as a goal. Something to attain, like getting a promotion. But in order to get that promotion, one has to be attentive and good at the job they have. In terms of a relationship, that entry-level position is dating. And if you don't concentrate on the day-to-day of getting to know someone, and instead keep imagining and longing for the bigger corner office of marriage, you are not going to perform as well at the task at hand. Which is to spend time with your significant other and decide if they bring out the best in you, challenge you in positive ways, but unconditionally love you and support you when you need them to have your back. Wanting to get married for the sake of the title is shortsighted and ends in getting fired. It was important that Jason and I silently agreed on this fact.

Then, one sunset a year into living together, Jason asked if I wanted to go for a walk on the beach. I was exhausted from a full day of clients, but I knew the sight of the ocean and the reds and pinks in the sky would be good for me. I threw on my sneakers and we headed out. Once we were there, Jason got on one knee and proposed. "Ruby Simon, will you marry me?" I looked at him, in a confused daze. It was a scene I had seen so often in movies, it was surreal that it was happening to me. I then noticed a picnic blanket set out, Champagne at the ready. My brain couldn't catch up to the information being funneled in. His question was like a push, and my body reacted with a clear and resounding *Yes!* I didn't have to think about it for a second. I just knew it was the right answer.

Jason put a gorgeous emerald-cut ruby engagement ring with pavé diamonds on my finger. It was so beautiful, so perfectly me. I looked down at him, still on his one knee, in wonderment. Then I stared at my ring again. The vivid red sunset caught the reds of the precious gem. I got down on my knees too and looked into his sky blue eyes that I saw so often I now sometimes took them for granted. The deep blue of the ocean made them look even brighter. In that moment the ocean was like one of his blue shirts, seemingly placed there for the sole purpose of making him shine.

I kissed him, and was filled with love and possibilities and connection. Maybe there was something magic about that piece of paper legally binding us. It was a public expression of commitment. A promise. Maybe I was a romantic after all.

As we sat on the blanket, drank Champagne, and looked at each other through a new, crisper engaged lens, I pictured our wedding. I was well aware that many people put way too much importance on the one specific day and not on the actual marriage. I wasn't naive to this phenomenon and didn't want to become one of those brides-to-be, but now that I'd said "yes," planning our wedding was going to be the most fun and exciting syllabus I'd ever had.

But first Jason wanted to tell his mother he was engaged. He asked me to go with him to Fort Lauderdale and deliver the happy news. To please trust him and give her another chance. I did trust him. Fully. But I did not trust her. I knew that either decision, to go or not to go, would have unpleasant consequences.

CHAPTER 27

KICK

ELLIE WAS PREGNANT. I WAS GOING TO BE AN AUNT! TO A little girl! I couldn't wait to shower her with love and kindness and patience and glittery headbands, if she liked that sort of thing. Ellie had ended up staying in New York City, where she worked as a fundraising consultant for nonprofits. She was great at her job. As organized and efficient as I, but with a relentless yet light touch needed to gracefully and constantly ask people for money. She married Spencer Jack, a chef who catered one of her charity events. They bonded over their love of sourdough bread. Spencer was a little bit freaked out about being a good dad. But I told him it was no different from being a good chef. I said, "Raising a kid is just like cooking. There isn't always an exact recipe. You only need two ingredients for sure. Love and structure. And the rest is to taste. The kid is becoming bratty? Take away a toy and add a chore. The kid is lonely and misunderstood? Add in some more hugs and words of support." Of course

I was saying this only having studied parental psychology. I had zero boots-on-the-ground experience raising a child.

While I was FaceTiming with Ellie, having my morning coffee as Jason had his morning Diet Coke, Ellie doubled over in pain. Spencer rushed into the frame, worried. But when she looked up, I could see she wasn't afraid. She was inspired.

Ellie smiled. "I just felt the baby kick! For the first time. Holy shit, she is strong!"

Even though babies kick billions of times every day inside millions of mothers-to-be, it was like a miracle to all four of us. I got off FaceTime and turned to Jason. The idea of Ellie's kicking baby sucked me into a centrifuge of love, momentarily spun out all my raggedy baggage and left my center filled with tenderness. Even though all my training taught me that cobras couldn't be changed, I wanted to try and repair my relationship with Gertrude. To claw my way out of the horrible cliché of not getting along with my soon-to-be mother-in-law. So I told Jason I would go with him to tell Gertrude that we were engaged.

The first five minutes of our visit seemed to go well enough. Gertrude's subdivision house was exactly as I had pictured. A small two-story, built in the early nineties, with a manicured lawn, which, aside from her many ceramic frog decorations, had an exterior that looked exactly like every other dwelling in the area, including a doormat that cheerily read, "Welcome." Inside was neat and tidy, with frog figurines thoughtfully perched on every surface from the side tables to the windowsills. There must have been over a thousand frogs of one sort or another in there. The frog lamp Jason had given his mother was prominently displayed in the breakfast nook.

Bland prints of Anne Geddes babies in flowerbeds and Thomas Kinkade cottages lined the beige walls of the downstairs areas. I lingered too long at one of the baby pictures, thinking about all the conservative male politicians who rail against homosexuals and then get caught having sex with men in bathrooms. Those who feel guilty about their own behavior are often the ones who protest the loudest about that same behavior in others. Like this woman who abandoned her own toddler but now had a house full of photos of happy boisterous babies in Easter baskets.

Evil people are often very intelligent. It's how they survive and thrive in society undetected. Gertrude watched me as I stared at the large print of the smiling baby boy surrounded by pastel-dyed eggs, like she was reading my thoughts. The irony being she didn't want her own thoughts to be read.

She said, "You better not be trying to get into my brain, little missy."

But I was already in there. Deep. Judging her. Judging what kind of repugnant person abandons her own son and then manipulates him for the rest of his adult life.

I knew Gertrude had hated all of Jason's girlfriends, including his high school sweetheart, Cindy, who she felt wasn't good enough for him, even though she barely knew Jason himself and had never even met the young lady. But I realized as I stood in her living room that she was especially scared of me not because I was "the one" for Jason, the one he actually was going to marry, but because I was a psychologist. She feared I could see what lurked inside her and that I would use my skill to diagnose her and uncover her bottomless pit of wretchedness. She was right. But in order to keep the peace and try to mend and not tear apart this precarious relationship, I turned toward her and lied to quell her worries.

"I'm not trying to get into your brain. Therapy doesn't quite work like that. I'm not like an FBI profiler. I have to talk to people to get to know them, to then be able to help them. And only if they want to be helped."

"I don't need your help."

"Well, perfect, then. Because I'm off the clock." I smiled.

But she couldn't just stop there.

"As far as I can tell, therapy doesn't work at all, for anyone. Whining about things incessantly makes people weaker. Not stronger. Where I come from, the past is the past. Move forward, already, is what I say."

I listened, and said, "Moving forward is healthy. I agree. But without a solid foundation, everything crumbles eventually."

She wasn't sure if that was a threat or just the plain truth. She retreated into her breakfast nook to organize her thoughts and plan her retaliation.

Gertrude had not yet offered us anything to eat or drink. Jason planned on sitting her down and giving her the good news, but she noticed my engagement ring immediately. So within seconds the information had been received. And now we were all sort of at a loss for what to do next. So Jason asked if I wanted something, and I mentioned coffee might be nice. He poured himself some diet soda, which Gertrude had liters of in her fridge, and started to make me coffee in her standard drip pot. Since Jason didn't drink coffee, making it did not come naturally to him. Gertrude didn't offer to help, so I stepped in and said I would make a nice fresh pot for us. I told her I liked mine really strong. She snapped back with, "So do I." But I knew by the shade of light brown water left in the pot from earlier that her Georgia idea of strong was not the same thing as my Miami raised-on-Cuban-coffee idea of strong.

I used three scoops of her grocery-store-bought, already-ground beans, keeping in mind not to overdo it. I truly wanted to make this woman happy. As the coffee dripped into the pot, I wondered about the theory that we pick mates who are just like our parents. Oedipus and Electra complexes urging us to continue the cycles of our childhoods. Did that mean that somewhere in the depths of Jason's unconscious he thought I was similar to his mother? I might be way more cobra than pit bull, but I was nothing like Gertrude. I was loyal to those I loved and wanted them to be happy on their own terms, not mine. I was also in touch with my flaws, had spent hundreds of hours discussing and dissecting my own strengths and weaknesses, motivations, and feelings. I was not perfect, certainly, but I was aware of myself. Gertrude, it seemed, was so locked in her own denial that she wasn't aware of anything but her need to remain unaware.

But then I remembered how after my first big fight with Roman, the one about me enjoying when others knew my name when I didn't know theirs, he later put his make-amends note in my textbook, in the narcissist section. I always assumed he was admitting that he was a narcissist, flaring obliques and all. But maybe he was poking fun at the fact that I was the narcissist. Which would put me a step closer to Gertrude. Who now sat in her dining room area with Jason, who was dutifully saying that the next time he came over he would fix the creak in the back screen door.

I found mugs in the cabinet above the coffee maker, and brought in two cups of hot coffee. I put one in front of Gertrude, asking if she wanted anything else. Sugar? Cream? Not that I knew where any of that was. It was odd that I was playing hostess in her home, but it was another way to put me on edge, while she maintained control.

She said no, she liked her coffee black. She took a sip and then spit it back into the cup. I thought maybe it was too hot, so I took a sip of my own, to test it. It was the perfect temperature.

She looked at me and calmly said, "You did this on purpose."

I looked at her. "Excuse me?"

Jason jumped in, "Mom?"

Gertrude said, "She made this coffee so strong it's undrinkable. Just to prove some sort of point."

I sighed. Sadly not surprised by her paranoid outburst.

Jason said, "Mom. I don't see what point that could possibly be."

Jason was trying. I knew that. But the intense love I felt for him was draining from me. If my devotion to him was oxygen and I wore a space suit that had a rip in it, my low-levels warning siren would be blaring. The feeling that Jason and I were on the same team was also plummeting, so I quickly regrouped my insides for my own self-preservation. I felt like I was in enemy territory, the hundreds of frogs inching forward to attack me, their buggy eyes turning from kitschy to menacing. I needed to get out of Gertrude's house immediately. I stood up from the table.

"Jason, can I speak with you privately?"

I wanted to tell him this was a big mistake, coming here to his mother's house. She hated me and that was that, but I wouldn't stick around and be accused of making coffee too strong on purpose, especially when I made it weaker than I normally would have to appease her! But I didn't have a chance to say any of those things, because Gertrude wouldn't accept me speaking to Jason privately. She gently turned to her son as he was about to stand and said to him, "I won't have her turning you against me. If she wants to say anything in my house, she can say it to my face."

Sure, there were many things I wanted to say to her face. I wanted to call her a big cunt with bad taste in art, to accuse her of being a horrible mother, a despicable, manipulative, damaged snake of a person. I wanted to take a coffee mug and break it against the table and use a shard of thick mass-produced ceramic to cut open her jugular.

But my training in dealing with the mentally ill kept me calm, and I knew nothing I screamed at her would make me feel any better in the long run, and it would only give her proof that I was the problem. She could report back to her friends that I had the nerve to call her a cunt in her own home, in front of Jason and her frogs! I refused to give her any more ammunition to use against me.

So all I said was, "Gertrude, this visit clearly isn't working out. I'm going to leave now. Goodbye."

I grabbed my purse, which I had left near the front door in the living room. She was delighted to see me going, and she stood to slam the door behind me. But she didn't expect Jason to also stand and start to leave with me.

She spat out, "And where are you going?"

"Mother, your behavior is not okay. We can talk about it another time, but right now I'm leaving with Ruby."

And with that the love level in my tank bolted up past the emergency low mark and the warning sirens in my head quieted. I think I must have smiled at Jason. And my smile pushed Gertrude over the edge. "Then get out!" she screamed. "Get out!" And she kicked me. Right in the shin. Jason was shocked. I was stunned. Mostly that the cobra in her had turned a little pit bull.

Jason and I walked out together, hand in hand. The frog door knocker slapped against the wood as we shut the door. Jason would never see his mother again. I, however, would not be so lucky.

"He was a handsome man," Detective Keith Jackson casually remarked while glancing at the photo of Jason.

"Yes, he was," I said.

"Who did he take after?"

"Excuse me?"

Detective Jackson waxed on. "I look exactly like my mother. No offense to her. And my sister, if you can believe it, looks like our father. I'm just wondering, did Jason take after his mom, Gertrude? Same-shaped face, or ears? Lots of hereditary markers in the ears."

I had been thinking about Gertrude seconds before, but her name coming out of the detective's mouth was even more jarring than hearing desk-duty guy mention my veterinarian.

"What?" I answered reflexively.

The detective tried again. "You have met Gertrude Hollander, haven't you?"

"Yes. Of course I have," I said.

Detective Jackson nodded, as if to confirm I was correct. He sat still for a moment, and was in no hurry to flip over the fourth photo. He made it clear with his body language that we were going to stay on the topic of Jason, and his mother, for a while. And I made it clear with my body language, as best I could, that because I had nothing to hide, that was just fine by me. I even smiled a little. Because I could tell the giant strong detective was now getting chilly himself, since the air-conditioning never stopped blowing. I remembered reading somewhere that the reason women always seem cold is because most office buildings, museums, theaters, and the like have temperature controls designed to keep a man who weighs about 170 pounds, wearing a full suit, comfortable. Leaving women to fend for themselves with small space heaters and shawls. I took comfort in knowing that this interview was breaking the detective down, just as much as it was rubbing me raw.

CHAPTER 28

LOVE

ONCE WE WERE ENGAGED, JASON TOLD ME HE WANTED TO get a dog. He grew up with dogs and missed having them around. And he always enjoyed seeing dogs at weddings. Bringing the rings to the altar, wearing bow ties, sitting with the wedding party making staged photos seem a little more candid. But I worried about Mr. Cat.

I asked, "What if they don't get along?"

"We will make sure that they do."

"But what if they don't?"

"I promise Mr. Cat will be okay."

And I worried about other things too. Like, "I've never had a dog, I have no idea what to do."

"I'll teach you."

"But . . ."

"But what?"

The real "but" I would save for my next session with Alisha.

I knew she would be able to pull out of me my true aversion to getting a dog.

While sitting on her couch, I finally got to it: "But what if I don't have enough love to share with Mr. Cat and Jason and a dog? I'm happy just the way we are."

Alisha reminded me that my favorite Ellie quality, one I often talked about, was her belief that joy brought more joy, and there was no finite amount. Alisha said there was only so much time in the day, so if I was worried about making my schedule work with dog walks and vet visits and such, that was a reasonable concern. But if I'm open to it, my capacity for love is limitless. So fearing I would run out of love was not a reasonable reason to not get a dog.

Jason and I went to a no-kill shelter, figuring by rescuing a dog from there, we were saving two lives: the one we rescued and the one that would fill the space of the one we rescued. A small fawn boxer weighing in at forty pounds, every rib showing, that the shelter had named Star, caught my eye. They said she was about three years old, but it was hard to tell for sure. She had the kindest eyes, and when they brought her out of her crate to say hello, her little nub of a cropped tail wiggled with glee. She nuzzled up to Jason and me and trotted by our sides, as if to say, *I'm already yours.* And she was. We filled out the paperwork and proudly walked her out of the shelter.

We immediately drove to the veterinarian, Dr. Hamilton. He was able to fit us in and gave "Star" a once-over. Heart and lungs and eyes and ears looked and sounded good, and the shelter had already spayed her. She desperately needed a flea bath, a regular bath, a teeth cleaning, and about fifteen more pounds. The vet said, based on her general condition, that she was probably used by a backyard breeder to push out puppies, way more litters than her little body would have liked, and then they abandoned her when she could no longer get pregnant. He punctuated all this with, "I could kill those people." I probably could too, if given the chance. I just nodded in agreement.

After all shots and baths were given, the receptionist who had thought the name Mr. Cat was meta asked what we were going to name her. Mrs. Dog seemed too preposterous. And neither of us loved the name Star. As if on cue, our little boxer dog pushed her newly clean and soft snub-nosed face into a box of toys for sale and pulled out a stuffed kangaroo.

"Kangaroo?" Jason asked. It was adorable and perfect.

"Yes!" I turned to the receptionist. "Add the toy to our bill, please."

She smiled at us. "The toy is on the house."

As I lay in bed, snuggled into contortions with Jason and Kangaroo and Mr. Cat, I felt a deep contentment. I was at peace, happier than ever before, because not only did I have a fiancé and a cat and a dog that I profoundly loved, I also had the knowledge that I could love and love and love and never again have to worry that I would use it all up. In these moments in bed, I knew this was the meaning of life, and I let the constantly running to-do list in my head briefly fall away. Invitation fonts, color schemes, and signature cocktail decisions could wait until tomorrow.

Ten months after the proposal, Jason and I got married on the beach in Key West. Kangaroo wore a lavender collar that matched the sash on my dress; our wedding cake was composed of tiered single-serving key-lime-pie tartlets since key lime pie, I would eventually find out, was Jason's favorite of all desserts. The top tier was made with sugar-free pie filling just for him.

We did not invite Gertrude. After the blowup about the strong coffee, he suggested they go to family therapy or speak to a pastor of some sort, if that made her more comfortable, to work out the very old, deep, unhealthy patterns in their mother-son relationship. Gertrude refused. So Jason took a stand and cut her out of his life. He survived childhood without her; he could certainly survive adulthood without her as well, especially now that he was going to therapy regularly on his own and had a lot more coping tools in his own toolbox.

Our wedding felt like a warm bath filled to the brim with bubbles of jubilance. Everywhere we looked, there was someone we loved, watching us vow to love each other. Ellie and Spencer and their baby girl, Molly. My parents. Jason's father was not there because he had died from a heart attack two months earlier, but he had been invited. Thanks to therapy and breaking away from the belief that his mother was a saint and his father a demon, Jason had reconnected with him and they both made amends before the end.

Ameena and her wife, happy to have a vacation, left their twin sons in Chicago. After dating a series of men, all inappropriate matches for her, according to her parents, Ameena had tapped into her true desires and started dating women. Her parents were convinced she was doing it just to punish them. They severed all ties with her and she with them. Then, a couple years later, she fell in love with a nice Hindu Indian girl named Padma. If only Padma had been a man, her parents would have finally been happy! A year later Padma and Ameena had twin boys. Ameena carried them. And couldn't believe after having to grow up with little twin brothers she now had twin sons. But she let the absurd coincidence wash over her with poise. Once there were bouncing babies in the picture, sons no less, Ameena's parents apologized, put aside their old-world beliefs, and embraced her and her wife and their beautiful children.

Benita from the bird sanctuary was there with her equally panda-like husband. I wanted to invite Alisha, but I knew that wasn't okay since she was my therapist. Dr. Don attended and generously gave us all ten of the dinner plates on our registry. Jason's closest friends and colleagues made the trip, as did Amy, Erika, Sharon, and Hannah. Although I sat them at separate tables, since over the years squabbles and perceived slights had put them all at odds, by the end of the night the four girls found their way to sit together, leaving past issues behind. The happiness and love felt at our wedding was contagious, and so strong that it seemed it would never wane. But it did. It all slipped away. The Grim Reaper in our midst.

CHAPTER 29

DEATH

THREE MONTHS AFTER THE WEDDING, JASON AND I WERE on our usual morning walk with Kangaroo when all of a sudden she collapsed. Her soft, wiggly little body crumpled, and she fell face-first onto the sidewalk. Jason sprinted back to our place to get the car; I threw myself on the ground and held her limp head in my lap and called Dr. Hamilton's office to say we would be racing over.

We rushed her into the animal hospital, but her magical spirit had already left her stout brown package of a body. Dr. Hamilton couldn't be sure without an autopsy but felt fairly certain she had had a heart attack. These things do happen, especially with boxers, and perhaps there is comfort in knowing she went quickly and painlessly, and she had a wonderful life with us, and that's all there was to say, really.

We left the vet without her. I silently sobbed in the car, not able to get enough air into or out of my lungs to make a sound. A deep grief swallowed me up. Kangaroo had been my shadow for the past year. She was such a sweet, well-behaved dog, bringing everyone who saw her so much joy, that I brought her to my office most days. I stacked my few clients who were allergic to dogs on the same day, so on all other days I could parade her in and let her shine her light. She was nicknamed Buddha Dog because of her centered, loving presence. She had a way of looking at you like she understood the pain and suffering of the world and that it would all be okay.

I had never before felt such grief. Like frozen tar stuck to my insides that wouldn't move or flow or pass through me. I spoke to Alisha at length about my thick grief and how lucky I was that this was the first time in my life I was feeling such an intense loss. When my grandparents had died, I was sad, sure, but they had never followed me around all day, every day. They didn't depend on me for exercise and food and affection and look up at me with big brown eyes and wag their happy stub every time I entered a room. They were not a part of the daily minutiae of my life, trotting by my side. So when they died, it wasn't as impactful to me as when Kangaroo died. Her death made me so conscious and grateful that I had never had to suffer that deep grief before.

I knew, despite the sadness, that I was lucky, as Dr. Hamilton had said, that she went like she did. Suddenly and painlessly. Rather than from a long, drawn-out disease that left us with the horrendous decision of when to "put her to sleep." Another death euphemism created by people in denial. Instead of putting our beloved pets to death, we tell ourselves it's an eternal sleep, crossing the rainbow. While I organized every last plushy dog toy into a giant pile, I thought about the people I had killed. Putting them to sleep was an easy decision. One I made within seconds. And so I concentrated on the idea that I was lucky that sweet little Kangaroo went quickly in her own time. And it wasn't on me to decide the moment and the place.

Alisha compassionately said, "Ruby, you keep focusing on how and why you are lucky. And that's wonderful, to be grateful for the things you have. But right now, you need to focus on the grief. If you don't, it will remain stuck. That tar, as you call it, will keep hardening and be much more difficult to ever clear from your system. So let's talk about it. Let's get that tar boiling and bubbling up and moving around. How are you feeling inside? How do you feel right now?"

I sobbed out, "I feel like I have way too much time every single day. And it's filled with nothing but a bottomless void of sorrow."

I grabbed a tissue from the table, wiped my eyes, and explained. Every morning I used to spend several minutes watching Kangaroo stretch and wiggle her butt, excited for the brand-new day. I would cuddle with her and let her lick my face and then watch her lick Jason's face. Then watch her attempt to lick Mr. Cat, who would begrudgingly allow it. I would then let Kangaroo out, take her on her walk, feed her, and watch her butt wiggle some more when she heard the jingle of me grabbing my car keys. Half of all my conversations with Jason revolved around Kangaroo. "Such a good girl today!" "Do you want to give her carrots or should I?" "Look at that cuteness!" I would glance in my rear-view mirror to make sure she was still in the back seat of my car, happily sniffing the humid air as we drove over the causeway. Then there was an evening walk, dinner, one more yard break, and nighttime snuggling. But not before she would make several circles around on her blanket, to get it just so, and then sink into it with a sigh. Then I would watch her paws twitch in the night, and I could only assume she was dreaming about running through fields of flowers. All that time I devoted to her every day was still there, but she was not.

I had to tell my clients that Kangaroo had died since they were used to her always being at my office. I was dreading it. I almost wished I had never brought her in so I wouldn't now be tasked with reliving her death over and over, telling everyone, passing along heartache to others, to the very people I was supposed to be lifting up and helping. But behind the tar, I knew that the joy Kangaroo had brought me and everyone else she came into contact with overrode the current sadness.

I also knew I had to use this loss to help my patients, guide the session toward their own feelings of grief in their own lives. I had to remain professional and not melt down. I was able to do that with everyone except for Gabrielle. Kangaroo had taken to her in a very specific way. Her nubby tail would start wiggling about five minutes before Gabrielle would click on the light letting me know that she had arrived and was in the waiting room. Which meant Kangaroo could smell her and feel her presence in the building lobby, in the elevator, in the hall, well before Gabrielle alerted me with the flicker of the light switch.

Once Gabrielle got settled on the love seat, she would pat the area next to her, inviting Kangaroo up. And Kangaroo would jump her boxer body up there and do her two or three little circles in the small space still available on the couch, and then curl up in a ball, her head resting on Gabrielle's lap. And they would stay like that for the full fifty minutes. Kangaroo would leave a layer of caramel fur on Gabrielle's black Vampire in the Sun clothes. She was now one of Hannah's biggest customers. Gabrielle kept a roll of tape in her punk cross-body messenger bag so she could pull off the fur before venturing back into the public world again.

The little light in my office turned on, and I knew Gabrielle was in the waiting room. There was no Kangaroo to wiggle. I opened the door to let Gabrielle in, and I broke down into sobs. Gabrielle noticed immediately that Kangaroo was not there and she realized what had happened. She hugged me and started sobbing too. We both wailed into the other's shoulder, still standing in the door frame. We both needed to grieve and release the tar. I knew that by crying with Gabrielle I had crossed a line professionally, but there was no stopping it. My emotions couldn't wait for the fifty minutes to be over and the door to swing closed, like projectile vomit won't wait for the toilet lid to be opened.

The other person deeply saddened by Kangaroo's death was Jesula. Ever since my Kremlin clubbing days, I loosely kept in touch with the nice lady who made sure the coed bathroom was always so tidy. And when Jason and I bought a house together during our engagement, I reached out to her to see if she would like to come twice a week to clean. She was delighted. It was much easier work than her other part-time job as a janitor at a sports bar in Aventura and a great way to make an extra two days of income. So she came every Monday and every Friday. She loved having Kangaroo in the house while she worked. Mr. Cat would hide in a closet every time, like he had never seen the woman before in his life, but Kangaroo followed her from room to room, keeping her company as she tidied up, giving her licks when she bent down for this or that. Jesula was so irritated when I took Kangaroo to work with me and away from her that I again rearranged my entire client schedule so that the dog-allergy people and non-animal-lovers all came in on Mondays and Fridays. That way Kangaroo would be home with Jesula, and everyone would be happy.

Jason always told me Kangaroo was a special dog. Since she

was my first one, I had nothing to compare her to, but I understood. Many dogs were adorable and eager to please and well trained and loving, but Kangaroo had a wisdom to her, like she was enlightened. When Mr. Cat would stubbornly stand in front of Kangaroo's food dish, she would wait patiently. She would never growl or nudge Mr. Cat out of the way. She would just sit, with no agenda or time frame, like Siddhartha under the tree. She would wait and wait until eventually Mr. Cat himself would get bored with his power trip and wander off of his own volition.

Once Kangaroo was dead and gone, no longer patiently waiting, Mr. Cat also felt the loss. He wandered the new house, a bright two-story Mediterranean, and looked for Kangaroo. Mr. Cat would lie in all of Kangaroo's favorite spots, and sit in the living room nook, where her dog bed once was. Mr. Cat was also lonely and depressed. His best friend, aside from me, had just vanished one day. I tried to explain to Mr. Cat, while holding him over my shoulder and deep into my hair, patting his rump, that Kangaroo had died quickly without pain and we were all very sad, but he needed no explanation. He knew his friend was gone and that a darkness had descended on our happy home.

We all grieve differently. There is no right or wrong way. I wanted to immediately get rid of everything that reminded me of Kangaroo. Get it out of the house. Donate it all to an animal shelter, so the visuals of her absence didn't blind me. Her basket of toys and containers of treats and myriad collars and matching leashes seemed to be in every corner and on every counter, reminding me of their uselessness.

Jesula was horrified. At first she judged me for the perceived precision and coldness with which I grieved. She refused to let me part with all of Kangaroo's stuff so quickly, and she clung to the soft purple dog blanket and canister of peanut butter treats.

But she understood it was ultimately my choice. And when she saw the sadness in my face, she was reminded of what I hoped she always knew. That I wasn't cold. And that I was so distraught I couldn't handle moving forward in any other way. I watched as Jesula quietly took Kangaroo's favorite blanket and favorite toy out of the donate pile. She brought them home with her so she could grieve in her own way, with soft, faintly doggie-smelling physical reminders.

Jason was so shut down he didn't have it in him to argue with me. But he insisted on keeping Kangaroo's cheery yellow collar and heart-shaped stainless steel tag, which he hung on the corner of his bedroom dresser mirror. So he could see it doubly. Once as it was, and once in the reflection.

And we all forged ahead in our own ways. I knew that no matter how we individually coped, processing and time were what we all needed. What I didn't know then was that my beloved dog's death was only the tip of the grief iceberg.

A couple months after Kangaroo died, I found Mr. Cat hunched under a chair in the dining room. He had never been under this particular chair before, and even though I knew he was still sad and lonely without his doggie friend, it seemed odd. Even depressed, he wanted to be in bed curled up with me and not all alone in the least-frequented room in the house. I called to him to come out from under there, but he refused. I reached for him, and when I touched his flank, he hissed and tensed, clearly in terrible pain.

Rushing Mr. Cat to the animal hospital brought back all the terrible trauma of rushing the lifeless Kangaroo to the same place just months earlier. How could I possibly handle Mr. Cat's dying too? After many tests Dr. Hamilton concluded that Mr. Cat had severe pancreatitis that brought on diabetes. His blood sugar was dangerously high. He was given insulin and an IV drip of antibiotics and painkillers. After three days in the kitty emergency room, he was out of the woods and was going to be just fine as long as I kept his eating regulated and administered two shots of insulin a day to the scruff of his neck. Mr. Cat could live another ten years, no problem. Maybe even fifteen!

Had I not spent the past several years with Jason, the diagnosis of diabetes and the idea of having to give Mr. Cat shots of insulin would have overwhelmed me. I've never been great with needles and often faint when I get shots. That I had braved getting my ears pierced at the mall was a miracle, but vanity beat out fear. Yet now, because of Jason, I understood diabetes, and I knew I could manage and handle Mr. Cat's every need. And all of a sudden Jason and Mr. Cat had something in common, the same chronic life-threatening disease. And because of this Jason felt more bonded to Mr. Cat than ever before. Both their vials of insulin were kept in the fridge, clearly labeled, side by side. A friendship newly forged.

Jason once explained to me that a healthy pancreas is like a full tank of gas in a car. It doles out insulin all day long. A little or a lot, working with the body to keep everything moving along evenly. Exercise, a stomach bug, an extra slice of pizza, these are things a healthy person doesn't think about twice. Like with a full tank, you can drive fast or slow, long distances or short, and the gas will be used as needed. But when your pancreas doesn't work at all, and no insulin is being created and given, you have to constantly guess how much you will need. So it would be like filling up your gas tank ten times a day with only specific amounts necessary to get you from point A to point B. Sometimes you might underestimate and run out of gas; other times you might overestimate and have too much gas. Any slight traffic delay, use of extra energy for your windshield wipers to push off heavy rains, or flat tire could throw off your gas estimations completely. That dance to survive was Jason's daily life.

And now it was my responsibility to make sure Mr. Cat did the same dance. I had to give him his daily insulin shots and ensure that he ate measured meals. It was a delicate balance, because if I gave him too much insulin, his blood sugar would plummet, and if I didn't catch it in time and quickly feed him high-sugar treats, he would die.

This severe low that leads to death is most likely to happen when a diabetic is asleep, when the diabetic is not conscious enough to feel the warning signs of a low blood sugar. The tremors and sweat and nausea go unnoticed, and the diabetic continues to sleep peacefully. This is so common it actually has a name, "dead in bed."

CHAPTER 30

HUMAN

WHAT I WANTED TO EXPLAIN TO DETECTIVE JACKSON, BUT didn't because I was savvy enough to know saying less would benefit me more while in this "informative, unofficial, friendly" interrogation, was that within just over one year I planned a wedding, got married, bought a house, moved into the house, turned thirty, and endured Kangaroo's death and Mr. Cat's near-fatal illness. And throughout all that I had a thriving full-time psychology practice. I was doing my best to cope with it all, but I was tired and stressed out. Or, as I learned in my own therapy, I was stressing myself out.

I knew based on several studies that happy moments in life can be just as physically taxing as unhappy moments. For instance, a wedding is a wonderful, joyous occasion, but the buildup and the planning and the anticipation and the emotional implications and the life changes are still processed in the body as stress, which spikes adrenaline and cortisol. The same can be said for buying a house and moving and doing well at a job. All these things are positive, but can leave a fingerprint of exhaustion, especially when large life events happen all at once, which they often do.

My mother's yoga teacher forwarded me an email about a study being done on stress and telomeres. The scientists and researchers who created the study needed one hundred type A women for one week of enforced relaxation at a resort hotel and spa in Key Largo. The whole thing sounded like some sort of time-share ploy. An all-expenses-paid week of lounging by a pool and getting pedicures? Jason encouraged me to call. I didn't want to.

He asked, "What's the downside?"

"The downside," I said, "is that I get tricked into this thing and then stuck in a six-hour lecture in a dark hotel conference room about the joys and financial gains of buying a vacation property."

Jason gave me a look. He saw through to the real reason I wasn't calling. My alien knew me too well. So I called.

The woman who answered seemed on the up-and-up and gave me a quick preliminary interview. No, I was not on any antidepressants. No, I was not suicidal. Yes, I considered myself type A. Yes, I worked full-time. Yes, I was highly organized. Oh, you want an example? Hmmm. I only use one pen until that one pen runs out. Then I throw it away, and use another pen. And all my pens are purple. Pilot Precise V5 Extra Fine Rolling Ball. Because purple is my favorite color, and I like my notes to have a cohesive look and . . . What's that? Ah. I'm cleared for a second interview. Great.

I hung up the phone, terrified of taking a week off to do absolutely nothing. Jason could see me gulp down the horror of forced relaxation, but reminded me I was always encouraging my patients to take care of themselves and to explore things they were afraid of because that's when growth happens. And for me, doing this insane thing like taking a vacation was both of those.

Not to mention I would also be helping science. Telomeres, until recently thought of as useless strands connected to the tips of our mitochondria, were the new marker of life expectancy and health and aging. The longer the telomere, the better off the person. Scientists were buzzing about them. And this was an opportunity to be a part of a cutting-edge study—certainly the type A person in me would feel calmed by that notion. My idleness was actually helping further the understanding of the human body.

After an in-person interview and a blood test, I was accepted into the study. But I still wasn't sure if I wanted to officially sign up. Alisha thought this was going to be the very best thing I had ever done for myself because it was an opportunity to stand up to my fear of stillness. She said she was very proud of me for considering it, and would be even prouder to see me take this on. Hearing these words from her made me well up. I was reminded of my report card on Roman's parents' fridge. Which made me well up even more. Of course Alisha noticed. "I see some tears in your eyes. Let's explore that." My emotions were close enough to the surface at this point in my life, because of being in therapy and being a psychologist, that I could answer with clear precision. "The tears are happy. Because you're proud of me. But then the tears make me ashamed. Because if you're proud of me, it also means you can be disappointed in me. And how could I live with that?"

My last attempt at not committing to the study was the parking. Yeah, they were paying for a gorgeous hotel room on the beach for a full week, plus all my meals and various fun activities and fascinating lectures, but, I told Jason, "if they don't cover the cost of parking, then forget it! I'm not going!" So I called, ready to be irate, and the nice lady told me of course the study covered all parking fees. I wouldn't have to spend a dime. There would be absolutely nothing there that would add stress, physically, financially, or otherwise, to my life. Damn it. I had no other excuses to give to avoid confronting my fear of relaxing. I cleared out my workweek, kissed Mr. Cat and Jason goodbye, and drove to Key Largo to rest for seven days. And to my dismay I was not given any kind of schedule prior to or after my arrival. No syllabus!

There were rules, however. We were allowed to check in with family once every evening, but general use of cell phones and laptops was prohibited. All distractions of work and family and the world were stripped away. We were left with just pampering and our own thoughts. Because they had carefully chosen women who would never allow themselves a weeklong vacation for any other reason, we were all a bundle of nerves. Twitchy even. Uncomfortably smiling at one another as we piled into the bright and breezy hotel conference room lanai.

They gave us each a full physical and again took our blood when we arrived. To get an official baseline. Then the organizer of the study gave us each a piece of paper. A cup of pens stood on each table. The paper had only one sentence: "I am a _____." We were supposed to fill in the blank with our very first thought.

I am a murderer.

That was my first thought. And I was shocked that I thought of myself in this way. Why did that word pop into my brain instead of a thousand other words? There was no way I was going to write that down. So I wrote down my second thought.

I am a <u>psychologist</u>.

The first three days there were the hardest. I was going through major stimulation withdrawal. The lectures on sleep and nutrition and anxiety were interesting. And the healthful Ayurvedic meals were delicious. And I did enjoy my long day swims in the ocean and night swims in the Olympic-sized resort pool. But there was no hustle or bustle, nothing looming that I had to achieve, nothing for me to worry about. It was torture. My dreams were even more vivid and anxiety-ridden than usual. No more salt nightmares, but other things. Like trying to drive a moving car from the back seat, my leg almost reaching the brake but inches shy of it, my hands almost touching the steering wheel but my arms not quite long enough, watching as the car nearly crashed over and over again.

On the fourth day it seemed all the study subjects arrived at our greatest fear at the same time. Life was going on just fine at home without us. Our jobs, our families, our pets and children and plants, were all chugging along okay. This made us all collectively feel unnecessary, which at first was upsetting and then was freeing. *How can things be okay without me overseeing every detail?* Which brings up the next thought: *Maybe I don't need to be so concerned about every detail?* And that was the wake-up call. The moment when our type A selves sort of melted into the pool chairs and lecture seats. I inhaled and exhaled deeply. Was this what they meant by relaxing?

We got another piece of paper. This time it had five blank lines after "I am a _____." We were instructed to quickly fill in every line with a different thought, the first five original thoughts that popped into our heads. But we were not to use the same

word we used on day one. "And don't overthink it!" the organizer said. I filled in:

I am a <u>wife</u>.
I am a <u>sister</u>.
I am a <u>daughter</u>.
I am a <u>Miamian</u>.
I am a <u>Yalie</u>.

On the morning of the seventh day, the scientists conducting
the study again gave us a physical and took our blood. I was officially test subject number forty-seven. I would forever be in a
telomere study database. The researchers were looking for markers, to see if with just one week of relaxing, the body could produce more telomerase, an important goo that clung to the end of
the telomeres, protecting them from further shortening. Those
results would not be made known to us for a very long time. But
I had a hunch about them already. And right before we left our
hotel spa haven of relaxation and comfort, we were given one last
piece of paper. Again it had one line on it, to fill in with our very
first thought: "I am a _____."

I pulled my car out of the hotel garage, my free parking
voucher in hand. It wasn't until I was on the highway heading
north toward Miami Beach that the weight of what I had written hit me. "I am a <u>human</u>."

CHAPTER 31

BEEP

DETECTIVE JACKSON KEPT HIS EYES ON THE PHOTO OF Jason. He tapped his finger on it, over Jason's chest, almost like he was trying to bring his heartbeat back. Thump, thump. Tap, tap. If only it were that easy. I would give almost anything to rest my head on his beating chest one more time. Detective Jackson said again, "Handsome guy." I nodded. Even on this pathetic excuse for paper stock, Jason's cute nose and high cheekbones and symmetrical jaw shone through. The detective added, "You two made a nice-looking couple." I nodded again, but he wasn't even looking at me. Not then. A beat later he looked up and asked, "Want to tell me what happened the night he died? What really happened? Fill in a few details?" I kept my voice even and said, "It's all in the autopsy report."

Coming home from the telomere study a human had changed me. I arrived at the house so calm and serene that it freaked Jason out. He worried they had drugged me. Once I explained my epiphany, he was thrilled. I didn't know how long it would last, but being a human was pretty amazing. I could allow myself a spectrum of feelings, I could have triumphs and failures, I could make others proud and disappointed, I could have love and grief and fear, and no matter what, right or wrong, I was still a human. That was the constant, and it was incredibly comforting. Such a painfully obvious concept, but for me it took being pulled out of my patterns and into a scientific study to find it.

I relaxed for seven days and experienced three consecutive nights of sleeping so soundly that I didn't remember my dreams at all for the first time in my life. The night I got home, I fell into a deep sleep. Mr. Cat snuggled on my right shoulder. Jason snuggled to my left. And in the early hours of the morning, my mind drifted to when I was really little and my mother would plop me in the bathtub and leave me to my own devices. This wasn't totally irresponsible because I had always been a good swimmer and she asked that I yell out "Beep" every few moments so she could hear me in the other room and know I was safe and sound. Every once in a while, just to make sure she was paying attention and that she cared about me, I would purposefully withhold my beep and count how many seconds it would take her to realize. And just when I decided she had forgotten all about me, she would yell, "Where's the beep!?" And I would happily "beep" back. I dreamily thought about this as I started to hear an actual beep noise. But this beep wasn't the laughing beep of a child in a bathtub. It was shrill and demanding. It was relentless and urgent. I popped open my eyes.

Jason wore a continuous glucose monitor, to alert him if his blood sugar went dangerously high or dangerously low. If he dipped under a fifty, it would beep loudly. This was designed to prevent "dead in bed." If he went low in the night, the beep should wake him up so he could quickly eat the sugar goo he kept on his bedside table. But Jason was an incredibly sound sleeper. He always fell asleep within moments of his head hitting his pillow and slept deeply all night. I usually lay there, my mind racing and sorting things, reviewing and planning. I would fall asleep eventually, but it took me a while to unwind and drift off. And when I finally fell asleep, I slept lightly.

For years I had been woken up nightly by Mr. Cat's antics. And once I started dating Jason, I was woken up countless times by his glucose monitor's beep. Once it woke me up, I would wake him up. He would be startled and groggy. I would say, "Jason. You're beeping." He would say, "Okay." And then sometimes fall back asleep without reacting, without reaching to his bedside table and eating sugar because he was low. So I would wake him up again. "You're still beeping!" And sometimes I would be a little grumpy about the whole thing. And he would get upset that I thought it was so cute when Mr. Cat woke me up ten times a night, but one little beep and I was all bossy. And I would say, "I'm sorry. I don't mean to be bossy. But you have to take care of yourself and make it stop beeping!" And he would adjust his insulin intake on his pump and open a sugary goo packet and suck down the contents and his blood sugar would reach a safe number and the beeping would stop. And then in the morning he wouldn't remember any of it, and I would have to show him on his monitor that it had in fact gone off and had been beeping. This went on the entire time we were together.

But this time was different. When my eyes popped open, I noticed that Mr. Cat was in the middle of our bed, and he was screaming meows at me. His meows were in between each beep. Since I was so deeply relaxed from my telomere week, it took a few moments for my brain to click in. I thought, *Mr. Cat always sleeps to my right. He is never in the middle. Why is he in the middle?*

Why is he meowing? And the glucose monitor kept beeping. It was as loud as it could get. As usual, Jason was sleeping right through it.

I said, "Jason. You're beeping."

I waited a second, but Jason didn't stir. So I nudged his shoulder.

"Jason, wake up. You're beeping!"

Still nothing. I started to understand. I shot up and frantically turned to him, my heart thumping in my throat. I screamed.

"Jason! Jason! Get up!"

He was cold and lifeless. Mr. Cat had stopped meowing now that I was awake and aware of the situation. I grabbed my cell and called 9-1-1 while I raced to Jason's side of the bed and ripped open a sugar packet. I slathered it into Jason's mouth, hoping some of the lime-green goo would reach his bloodstream in time and revive his still heart. A wave of déjà vu passed through me. Like I'd done this before. Been here before. But I knew I hadn't. Time slowed as I waited for the emergency operator to answer, and a tiny memory came through like radio static. As I desperately rubbed sugar onto Jason's gums, to bring him back to life, I saw a flash of Duncan's mother doing the same thing to herself with wisps of cocaine in the club bathroom.

I poured another packet of goo into Jason's mouth, this one a cherry red. And then another. Tangerine. I could tell by the sickening slack of his head when I grabbed his shoulders and shook him that he was already dead. But I still had to keep trying. I knew it wasn't rational. I grabbed a fourth packet. Grape. And was told by the emergency operator that an ambulance was on the way.

CHAPTER 32

WIDOW

FOR THE NEXT COUPLE OF WEEKS I WAS IN A COMPLETE daze. I woke up each morning because that's what people who are alive do. My parents came over every day to check on me, and try to make me eat something. Ellie flew down immediately, even though she was in the middle of her own marital issues. There was a funeral, exactly the way Jason laid out in his will. Once his body was returned to me, which took a week because, as I was told by the authorities, an autopsy is always preformed when a relatively young person dies at home, I had him cremated. And invited all his close friends to join me on a boat and celebrate his life and watch his ashes gracefully drop into the Atlantic, where they would become one with the ocean. He would spend eternity in his favorite place. This brought me zero comfort.

I already knew how and why Jason died. But an official-looking letter arrived in the mail. The coroner concluded that there was no foul play. No poison or alcohol or drugs found in Jason's body. Jason tragically died in his sleep because of dangerously low blood sugar, substantiated by his glucose monitor stats. Jason became a statistic. Another type 1 diabetic dead in bed.

A few days later ABC local news did a moving human-interest story on type 1 diabetes and honored Jason, their beloved employee, by showing his picture and adding information about where people can donate to fund research to find a cure for the deadly disease. No one warned me this would be on television. Or maybe someone did call and leave a message, during those first few days of widowed fog. But I definitely wasn't ready to interact with people outside my inner circle.

After the news story aired, flowers started arriving from acquaintances and colleagues I hadn't spoken to in years. I knew they all meant well, but every time the doorbell rang Mr. Cat would run into the closet to hide and I would be forced out of bed, to handle the delivery with a modicum of composure. One day after the bell rang, I looked out the peephole and saw a bouquet of lilies floating in midair. Lilies are highly toxic to cats. Jason knew this, of course, I thought sadly, but the sender clearly did not. So I yelled, "Just leave them outside the door. Thank you!" It was a relief to not have to see another person face-to-face. I don't know how I didn't think of this solution sooner. The lilies, and all the other flowers that came after, could stay outside, get burned by the sun, and decay even faster.

The doorbell rang again, and I called out, "Just leave them outside the door. Thank you!" I heard a deep voice respond. "I'm looking for a Ruby Simon. This is Detective Keith Jackson."

I dragged myself over and looked out the peephole. Sure enough, I did not see flowers. I saw a badge. I opened the door to a very tall man in slacks and a button-down short-sleeve shirt. I smiled, a little.

The man asked, "Are you Ruby Simon?"

"I am."

He said, "Sorry to barge in on you. Is now an okay time to talk for a moment?"

Now was not an okay time to talk, but I felt like I might never have an okay time to talk for the rest of my life. So I shrugged, sure. And let him in. I couldn't imagine what he wanted to talk about, but it occurred to me that maybe one of my patients was in some sort of trouble. That happened from time to time. Especially when I was working at juvie. I would, of course, need to respectfully tell this towering detective that I could not divulge any information because of doctor-patient confidentiality, and remind him that even with a warrant it can be tricky.

I asked, "Can I get you anything? I have fresh orange juice."

"That's very kind. No, thank you."

He was extremely polite, almost sheepish. As he glanced around the living room, I wondered when he would get to the point. I was too depleted to wait while standing, so I walked into the kitchen and sat on a stool at the island. He followed me in and had three other stools to choose from. He choose the one closest to me. His knees hit the top of the counter, but he didn't shift.

He said, "I'm here to tie up some loose ends regarding Mr. Hollander's death."

I was confused. I had no idea there were loose ends. I searched back in my brain to make sense of what the detective was saying.

"You mean Jason's father? In Georgia? He died a little over a year ago. I might have his death certificate in a file if you need it?"

"No. I mean Jason Hollander. Your late husband."

I stared at him. Still at a loss.

He said, "Let me start by offering my condolences. My grandpa had type 2 diabetes. He had his foot amputated toward the end." I had heard a variation of this dozens of times. People often tried to connect in the most misguided ways. I said, "It's a terrible disease."

"Know what?" he said. "I will take a small glass of that fresh orange juice. If you don't mind."

At this point I was happy to have a chore, so I got up and poured the juice into a good glass. One from our wedding registry. As I handed it to him, I saw his eyes dart over the nearly empty kitchen counter. And land on a half-filled bookshelf in the vestibule.

"Did Jason live here with you?"

"Of course. Yes."

My brain was still searching, trying to be helpful. I asked, "Are the loose ends about his address? Because he also owned a condo that we use as an investment property."

Detective Jackson chugged his juice in what seemed one large sip, and gingerly placed the glass on the island. He gave me a nod of thanks, pressed himself up off his stool, and walked back into the living room, toward the front door, as if this strange, vague visit was perfectly normal. I followed him. Still baffled.

Before he reached the knob, he turned to me and asked, "Where's all Jason's stuff? This house seems half empty."

It was a reasonable question. I would learn soon enough that many of Detective Keith Jackson's questions were reasonable. And I could have given him a whole lecture about how we all grieve differently. About how the day Jason died, I removed every item of his, from cookbooks to flip-flops to surf wax, in a frenzy because the sight of it all made me sick with sadness. I could tell him I did the same exact thing when our cherished dog died. And how me wanting every physical shred of Jason gone didn't make me an unloving person. And how even my housekeeper, Jesula, understood this. She helped me pack up all of Jason's things. But I felt this intimate answer was none of Detective Keith Jackson's damn business. So I merely said, "I'm kind of a neat freak."

Detective Jackson stayed standing still. So still that Mr. Cat actually ventured out from the closet, wandered toward us, unafraid, and wove his body in figure eights around the long legs of the stranger in our house. It was remarkable. Mr. Cat usually hated everyone.

I was so thrown by the whole visit, so off my game, I asked, "Is there more you want to talk about?"

Detective Jackson bent over and gave Mr. Cat a nice pat on the side. He said, "No rush on my end. Will you be in town for a while?"

"Absolutely. I'm not going anywhere."

"That's good to hear."

As he walked out, I thought about the morning that Richard Vale's body was discovered. I woke up to a scream. And assumed, correctly, that Hannah's mother had found her husband dead on the kitchen floor. The police arrived. And chatted with a few neighbors, who popped out to see what was going on. They all mentioned the Vales fought a lot. Screamed at each other, threw things sometimes. I knew that the spouse is always the first suspect when someone dies, and for a moment that morning, I worried that Mrs. Vale would be in trouble for what I had done. Killing Richard sat fine with me, but having her get punished for it would not be okay. So I was uneasy for a bit. But after a quick interview with her, it seemed, based on the detective's expertise, that the wife didn't want the husband dead. She was sobbing all morning. And it wasn't just tears that poured out of her; it was snot too. Any good cop knows that people can train themselves to cry, but no one can fake snot. If honest-to-goodness snot comes out of a nose, it's a sign that the person is in fact keening and is probably not the killer.

Then I thought about my own reaction when the ambulance and police came for Jason. I was crying, wasn't I? Sobbing like a new young widow should be sobbing? But thinking back to that horrific early morning, I remember feeling so dry. It was more like I was heaving. Screaming. Hyperventilating. All which can be acted out. Did I have any big wet tears? Did my face show any signs of snot at all? I don't think it did. I was in shock—that's why my brain was arid. Or maybe, because of the things I'd done, I no longer had the ability to react to trauma within a range of normal human behavior. I hoped to God no one else noticed my lack of flowing mucus.

By the time Detective Jackson pulled out of my driveway, I felt a sinking panic in my gut. I tried to will myself into believing I was just being paranoid. And then I googled him. I scrolled through police websites and read articles and learned that Keith Jackson was not in the "tying up loose ends" division, but rather he was in the homicide division. He had a clean record, no complaints. And was honored by the city of Miami Beach on multiple occasions for his valor and bravery.

I replayed the odd and seemingly pointless visit. His manner was so casual. Too casual. I had taken several undergraduate classes on the criminal mind and graduate school classes on psychological tactics used in law enforcement to profile and catch criminals and lull them into confessing their crimes. Was Detective Jackson's friendly meandering a way to get invited into my house without any just cause? A way to keep me, a grieving widow, off guard? But I had nothing to be guarded about. Jason died of natural causes. Everyone knew that already.

I rinsed out the orange juice glass with scalding water and

then put it in the dishwasher. I didn't want any of that man lingering. I paced around the kitchen island, around the living room, around the completely empty room that was once Jason's office. Homicide detective meant murder. Did I get away with it three times, just to later be accused of murdering someone I truly loved and didn't kill?

A rush of adrenaline shot through me, and I was sure I could feel my telomeres shortening under the strain. I didn't know what to do next. Or how to act. I needed advice. I needed help. I took some deep breaths, finally calmed myself down, and stopped sharking through the house. I made a decision, and once it was made, I felt better immediately. I picked up my phone and called one of the best and brightest criminal defense attorneys in the county. He was currently living in Washington, DC, and he owed me a big fucking favor.

CHAPTER 33

LAWYER

ROMAN GOT ON THE PHONE IMMEDIATELY. IT ONLY TOOK A few minutes for us to move past the awkwardness and fall back into the ease and depth of our old friendship. At this point in life I was older and wiser and had long ago forgiven him his now silly-seeming college trespasses. But I'd never told him he had been forgiven, so it had been a decade since we had spoken.

After my meeting with the dean, the chair, and the professor, Roman had been cleared of all cheating charges. I later found a note hidden in one of my textbooks. It had three words on it. "I owe you." Roman graduated at the top of our class and went on to Yale Law School. He was courted by tons of corporate firms offering him enormous starting salaries, but he declined them all. He knew the exact path he wanted to take and never deviated. He clerked with a judge who was notoriously tough on crime and known for doling out maximum sentences. Then he worked in the district attorney's office, then honed his skills at the public defender's office, and then joined a small but prominent firm defending the rich and guilty. Where he quickly made partner.

"What do I need to know?" Roman asked me over the phone.

"I didn't kill my husband."

He said, "I actually don't need to know that. I need to know why, after an autopsy concluded your husband died of a disease he has had since childhood, a homicide detective is sniffing around, thinking you did kill him."

I answered truthfully. "I don't know."

He hated that answer. He wanted to hear something definitive. By the time we got off the phone, Roman's assistant had booked him a first-class seat on the next flight to Miami.

Six hours later Roman marched through my door. He hugged me and squeezed me tight, and I could feel his washboard abs pressing against me. He was still square-jawed, ridiculously fit, and had a head of thick wavy hair controlled by just a little product. Now that he was a full-grown man, his underbite gave him added gravitas. I hugged him back, hard. He smelled the same. Like cedar. I didn't know until that moment how much I had truly missed him all these years. He put his hands on my shoulders and looked at me, eye to eye.

"Hey, I'm sorry," he said.

I brushed his apology aside. "Bygones. I shouldn't have made such a big deal about it for so long. We were young."

"No, Ruby. I mean I'm sorry about your husband."

"Oh." This felt like a stab to my heart. For a split second I was lost in the cedar smell and the happy memories of college and youthful folly. But reality was still there, waiting to be acknowledged. My husband was dead. I said, "Thank you."

Roman set up a makeshift war room in Jason's empty office. He made it clear to me that if he was going to make all this go away, he needed to know everything. Absolutely everything. I looked at him, at a loss. "I don't know what everything is! You're going to have to ask me very specific questions. Give me some guidelines about what exactly you mean by everything."

Roman started with the basics.

"Have you ever cheated on Jason?"

"No!"

"Emotionally? Online? Texting? Anything?"

"No."

"That's good. Did he ever cheat on you?"

"No! I mean, not that I know of."

"Okay. I'll look into it."

Before I could respond to this and defend Jason's honor, Roman kept going.

"Do you have money problems? Debt? Gambling issues?"

"No."

"Did he?"

"No."

"Did Jason's death leave you better off than you were when he was alive?"

"Of course not. What the fuck?"

I knew Roman hadn't gotten married yet. His plan was always to play around until he turned forty. Then settle down with the right one. He was so confident it would work like that, I didn't question his life syllabus. But I needed him to understand that my marriage was real.

"I loved Jason. I really did."

"Right, I'm not implying you didn't. I mean, are you financially better off with him dead?"

I had to think. "I guess. Technically."

I told Roman that when Jason and I bought our house

together, our accountant advised we each get life insurance. In case something were to happen to one of us, that insurance would help the other cover the mortgage on a single income. I didn't like the idea of life insurance. Roman nodded. He remembered my father once saying, "It's better to be worth more alive than dead." And I was, and Jason was, but Jason felt it was important to listen to the accountant's advice, so I went along with his wishes. Because he had type 1 diabetes, his yearly quote was extremely high. But we signed up anyway. If he were to die, his policy would pay me out $300,000. And because my life insurance was so inexpensive comparatively, since I didn't have a pre-existing condition, if I died, he would receive $600,000. These numbers might seem like a lot, but to cover a mortgage on a house in Miami Beach, they weren't.

Jason also still owned his condo, which he continued to use as a rental property. This was great additional income for us. And when Jason's father died, he left everything to Jason. Roman asked about the details of Jason's early life, which propelled me into memories of going to the funeral in Morrow, Georgia. I told Roman how surreal it was for Jason to be there again, having not been back since he had left at age eighteen. Cindy, his high school sweetheart, came to the funeral to pay her respects. We learned that after Jason left town, she married one of his friends who consoled her in his absence. They had four children together. He worked at the local hardware store, and she managed a diner. She seemed like a happy person. She loved Georgia and never wanted to leave. I had a flash of judgment: How sad to live such a small life. But quickly realized ultimately I too had stayed in my own hometown. I wasn't so different from Cindy.

At the gathering after the funeral, Cindy returned Jason's class ring. She had kept it all those years thinking Jason might eventually want it back to pass onto his future son someday. Jason and I went through his father's house. There wasn't much there of value, but Jason kept a few sentimental things. A toolbox, his father's military trunk. He was touched to see his father still had photographs of him as a boy lined up on the dusty mantel. Proof that even in those years they were estranged, his father wanted to see his face every day. Jason sold the house and the five acres it sat on. Between that and the money his frugal father had squirreled away, Jason inherited a little over $200,000.

So when Jason died, I got $300,000 in life insurance, a condo worth about $400,000, and $200,000 recently acquired from his father's estate.

Roman said, "That's almost a million dollars."

"Yeah, I guess so. I'm not really focusing on money right now."

Roman looked at me sternly. "That's motive."

"Not to me."

Roman began a new line of questioning. "Did Jason have any enemies?"

"I don't think so."

"Is it possible someone did kill him and made it look like he died of natural causes?"

"I mean, technically, yes. But no. How? We were in bed together all night."

"Okay." Roman paused. "Do you have any enemies?"

"I don't think so. No."

It seemed the questions were now over. And the lecture was starting. Roman said if Detective Jackson were to ever show up at my house again, not to let him in. Unless, of course, he has a warrant. This all felt too real too quickly. "A warrant? Why would he have a warrant?" Roman ignored me and kept going.

"Do not say another word to him without your lawyer present. Your lawyer being me. If he calls, send it to voicemail. If he 'accidentally' runs into you on the street, say the word *lawyer* and nothing else. Understand?" Yes, I understood. And the severity of my situation was slowly starting to become clear. But, Roman mused, it could be helpful to go into the station together the next day, seem cooperative, answer some easy questions, try to find out what the police knew, get ahead of some things so we wouldn't be blindsided later if an arrest came.

I gasped. "An arrest?" I was blindsided the moment Roman said the word. It made me woozy. Like I was standing on a precipice and I just noticed I was wearing stilettos and the ground was dangerously uneven. I didn't sleep at all that night. I was too nervous, steeling myself for battle the next day. That morning I had my coffee. Threw on some actual clothes and grabbed my purse. I drove to pick up Roman at his hotel, and we headed for the police station on Collins Avenue. Roman reminded me to say as little as possible. This was a fishing expedition. On both sides.

CHAPTER 34

CLUTTER

I WANTED TO PUT ON A FRESH LAYER OF LIP GLOSS. NOT because I cared about my appearance in front of Detective Jackson, but because I thought it might at least keep my lips warm. I reached back for my purse and pulled out my burnt-plum-blossom gloss. As I applied a quick coat, I was aware of the small space. Aware that my elbow nearly grazed the stiff broad shoulders only a few inches to my left. They belonged to Roman, who was quietly sitting next to me, on his own thin metal chair.

This whole time Roman had been expressionless and still, taking it all in, listening and looking and learning, assessing the situation, formulating a plan. He had barely made a peep, because making too much noise can scare away the fish. So his voice rang clear and loud when he did all of a sudden speak.

Roman asked me if I would like his jacket. Since the room was so cold. He was wearing a serious Washington, DC, navy blue suit. I said, "Yes, thank you." He slid his bespoke silk-lined thin wool jacket off and passed it to me. I draped it around my shoulders. And immediately felt more comfortable. Like I had a new layer of armor. Detective Jackson, also clearly chilly, used this exchange to his advantage. He leaned a long arm over to the door handle and opened it a bit. He yelled out, "Can someone turn the air off in here?" He closed the door and crossed his legs the other way. Flashing an inch of skin on his other ankle. And we all heard the air click off.

Then, with no fanfare, the detective moved on to the final photo. It was easy to forget there was a fourth photo still face-down on the table, because what and who could be more devastating than seeing a smiling, living, breathing Jason? Detective Jackson turned the last photo over. I saw thin dishwater-brown hair and a pointy nose. It was a DMV picture of the Witch, Evelyn W.

Roman glanced at it, like he had for the first three. His face continued to give nothing away. My face, however, was starting to show a range of emotions from exhausted to irate to confused. Yes, Evelyn W. was dead. But why did the detective think that had anything to do with me? I was beginning to regret the decision to come in here and chat. And was starting to spin out. One second feeling confident, the next feeling disoriented, the next wanting to furiously defend myself, which would only make me seem more guilty. And I couldn't begin to imagine what Roman must be thinking. Four dead people.

It was so odd to me that Detective Jackson revealed the photos in this order. Building up to Jason, the most recent death and clearly the most personal death, and then crescendoing to Evelyn W. As much as I wanted to be a cool customer, I was now rattled. And I knew it was not some mistake or random decision of the detective's; it was a tactic. If this was his way of throwing me off balance, he had fully succeeded. I was agitated and uneasy. I was definitely not pleased to see Evelyn W.'s odious face, but it was him ending the twisted, warped game show on someone so seemingly inconsequential that worried me most.

It was true that I was volunteering at juvie when Dr. Don called me to tell me that, ding dong, the Witch was dead. However, it was not true that this was the first time I learned she was dead. I had already known that fact for a solid hour before he called.

After the lamp debacle, the Witch came back for therapy, since she had no shame and she needed to finish her court-ordered hours. Dr. Don had no choice but to finish up her sessions. He couldn't tell me about them, but I was certain she was still arriving as usual, screaming at someone on her cell phone, and storming out as usual, screaming at someone else on her cell phone. I knew her usual therapy schedule and how many mandated hours she had left. So on the day of her last session, I decided to drive over, park in the lot across the street, briefly linger, and watch the Witch's skeletal frame march out of Dr. Don's building. I saw her staring at her phone and heard her mumbling "Stupid bitch" to someone in her orbit who had to endure her abuse. I followed her to the crosswalk. At any moment she could have lifted her face from her phone screen and noticed that I was standing near her, but she didn't. It was pouring rain, so fewer people were out. But a smattering of folks huddled under umbrellas waiting for the light to change. The Witch flipped up the hood of her raincoat to keep her already limp hair dry.

A large grocery store chain delivery truck clanged toward us. I had no desire to push her in front of the eighteen-wheeler. That would have been murder. With witnesses everywhere. I wanted something more subtle. I wanted her own behavior to be her demise. If my plan worked, wonderful. If it didn't, I would let it go, hoping to never see the Witch again. But I had to at least try to fully remove her rotten soul from this planet. I had to try and give karma a push in the right direction.

The timing had to be just right. A few seconds before the truck was going to drive past us, I stood shoulder to shoulder with the Witch. I then stepped off the curb, into the street. She sensed the movement forward and stepped off the curb as well, never once taking her eyes off her cell phone. I quickly stepped back, onto the safety of the curb. It wasn't until she heard a deafening honk and screeching of overtaxed brakes that she looked up. Horror on her face as she saw she was standing in the middle of the street, the truck's shiny wet metal grille just inches from her witchy nose. Evelyn W. was truly present for maybe the first time in her life. Present in the moment right before she got hit, broken, smushed, dragged, and killed. I looked away. I didn't need to see the final carnage. I walked back to my parked car, contented, feeling as though I had done a good deed, and went to my internship bettering the lives of juvenile delinquents.

The truck driver was cleared of all wrongdoing. Witnesses stated that the woman just stepped right into oncoming traffic, not paying attention at all. There was no way the driver could have stopped in time. Especially with the streets being slick from the rain.

"Do you know this woman?" Detective Jackson asked.

To deny I did would have been asinine. "Yes. And to say anything further would break doctor-patient confidentiality."

Detective Jackson accepted this response way too easily. He moved his gaze away from Evelyn W.'s photo and placed his massive hand again on Jason's photo. Thump, thump. Tap, tap. I realized then that like a game show, the wheel spun with possibilities, but there was really only one place for it to land and actually matter. The Witch was merely a distraction. The tactic of ending on her was to make me dizzy, then loop back to the real prize, which was Jason.

The detective said, "I've been married over twenty years. Not to the same woman, but it all adds up. So I know it can be a frustrating institution. Day in and day out." He looked right at me, eyeballs to eyeballs. I often do this when I'm in a session. To connect and to filter out the white lies and self-sabotage and self-aggrandizing. So I looked right back, sure not to glance away or flutter my lashes too much.

He continued, "I'm sure you had a nice wedding. They always feel so optimistic."

"Yes, we did."

"Why was your mother-in-law not invited?"

"Jason did not want her there."

"Fair enough. She was also not welcome at his funeral, is that right?"

I couldn't piece together why any of this was of consequence. And then I remembered his tactics. These were all fake questions. More meaningless, prizeless stops on the wheel. I looked at the detective calmly. Hiding the fury behind my auburn eyes.

And then he said, "Tell me, Ruby Simon, did you ever wish your husband was dead?"

Roman spoke again, crisp and clear. "We are happy to cooperate, but I don't think that is an appropriate question for my client. We'll be going now."

What an idiotic question. Of course I had wished for Jason to be dead. Every now and again. What wife hasn't had that fantasy creep in? I liked the countertops of the kitchen to be totally free of clutter, but he liked to have the blender, the toaster, his protein powder, various water bottles, a canister of cooking utensils, the spice rack, everything and anything we might possibly use at some point in our lives out all the time. I knew this about him from the minute I first stepped into his condo and looked at his kitchen. So it wasn't a surprise to me, but it was grating. Clutter, clutter everywhere.

In the time between Jason immediately falling asleep at night and the twenty minutes to an hour it would take me to drift off, my mind raced with scenarios. I would sometimes imagine him dying, in some vague way, painlessly and quickly, of course, and how I would immediately clean the kitchen counters and clear out his side of the closet and have so much more space and I would keep things perfectly tidy. And no more shoes by the door. The thought of that alone soothed me like mint tea with honey.

The antique marble-topped dresser on my side of the bedroom had exactly nothing on it. The sparseness pleased me, knowing everything was put away. In its place. The dresser on Jason's side of the bedroom had important items on it like test strips and packets of sugar goo. But it was also cluttered with books he pretended to want to read, baseball caps, random quarters, single socks, and old paper receipts dredged out of jean pockets. He was a grown man; he had the right to have his side of the bedroom just as he wanted it. I knew this. Because of years of therapy, because of practicing being rational, and because Ellie told me in no uncertain terms not to micromanage him. Alisha too encouraged me not to oversee and control Jason's space. My way was not right, and his way was not wrong. We were merely different. Which is what makes marriage so beautiful. Loving another person not for their sameness, but for the oppositeness.

At times Jason and I compromised to the point that we were both unhappy. That is marriage. He wanted black square tiles for the kitchen backsplash. I wanted lavender mosaic tiles. So we got white subway tiles. And we both vaguely didn't like them. I always thought the Julia Tuttle Causeway was fastest. He liked MacArthur. So we often found ourselves taking Venetian.

Sometimes I wanted to come home from a long day of work and hide. But Jason could read my every facial expression and emotion. He wanted to talk, to demand I open up more, to share real feelings all the time. Like his refusal to ask the typical first-date questions, he refused to make end-of-day idle chatter. But sometimes that was all I had left in me after hours of counseling others. Sometimes I just wanted to be left alone. I wanted to sit and watch stupid TV shows. I wanted him to go away. And some-times that wanting-him-to-go-away feeling would hop toward, *Maybe he'll die and then I won't have to deal with him at all anymore.* I knew I had to work on just telling him that I needed some space for a few hours. He would understand. But I would have to say it in a kind and loving way so as not to hurt his feelings, and that alone took energy. And sometimes I didn't have enough left.

On occasion we would fight. He thought I was distant. I thought he was needy. He would get mad and yell. I would get mad and give him the silent treatment. One day I was so furious I stormed into a different room and gave him the finger through the wall. It was immature of me. But it felt good. *Fuck you, Ja-son! Fuck you!* We made up twenty minutes later. Laughing about how silly we were. We said "I love you" to each other and kissed and went about our mostly happy marriage.

I knew I annoyed the hell out of him at times. Constantly wanting to plan, never letting anything go. I'm sure in the depths of Jason's mind he thought about strangling me from time to time. Mostly to stop me from nagging or back seat driving or grumbling while passive-aggressively tossing his sandy flip-flops outside the back door. An occasional fantasy about a spouse dying is normal and common. It's not a threat; it's flippant frustration. A natural symptom of two imperfect people living together while attempting to maintain a personal sense of style and space and budget and a sex life. But there is no way I was going to admit any of this. To anyone.

Especially not to Detective Keith Jackson. Who was now stretching. He reached his arms over his head, and pushed his legs straight out against the bolted-down table. He wanted to convey he was so comfortable and confident that he didn't feel the need to protect his innards.

Roman stood up. The chair scraped across the cement floor. It was time to go. But it was ten seconds too late. Because I lost my guile. Detective Jackson's insinuations about me and Jason were too much for me to handle with grace. I stood up quickly, my chair flinging back, almost toppling over, and I said in a cold huff, "I'm sorry your marriages weren't successful, Detective, but don't put your shit on me. I'm not perfect. But I loved my husband."

Roman guided me out of the room before I could say another word. His jacket was slipping off my shoulders, and he caught it before it fell. As we walked out, Detective Jackson opened his arms wide; his wingspan looked impressive inside the small room, his middle fingers almost able to touch each wall. He said, "Thanks so much for coming in."

CHAPTER 35

ELEPHANT

I GLANCED AT THE CLOCK IN MY CAR AS I SLID INTO THE
driver's seat. The leather was warm from being drenched in the
Miami sun, and it felt good on the backs of my legs. A familiar
creature comfort. It seemed like I was inside that police station
for hours. Days. A lifetime even. But in actuality, it was only
twenty-four minutes.

Roman waited until I shut my car door before yelling at me.
"What the fuck, Ruby! Seriously. What the fuck!? I told you to
tell me everything. And you told me that you did tell me everything! Then that guy with his fucking folder and photos." Roman paused, but his anger didn't diminish. "I do not like to be
blindsided."

And so there it was. The three big elephants in the room of
my mind, Duncan, Richard, and Evelyn, who had been quietly
snorting around, had finally stomped and reared and stampeded
out. I couldn't look at Roman. I was too embarrassed. I said,
"I'm sorry. I didn't think those other people were a part of the

everything. They are totally unrelated to Jason." Roman looked at me as I continued to look down. He asked, "But are they totally unrelated to you?" I couldn't say they were. So I shook my head no. In a softer voice Roman said, "Well, this is a lesson for me. Next time I interview a client suspected of murder, I will explicitly ask if any other people have died right in front of them."

He had a right to be mad at me. And I hated it. He had heard details about some of the elephants in that twenty-four minutes, but I felt I had to explain, again. "Duncan drowned. I was in the ocean at the same time. We were kids. Richard died when I was having a sleepover with my friend. And Evelyn, she got hit by a truck. I happened to be on the corner. That's all." After I said this last part, I did wonder out loud how Detective Jackson knew I was there when Evelyn was hit. It was common knowledge I was in the ocean when Duncan died. And the detective pieced together the Richard part of it all because I was on record as driving his car that night. But Evelyn? No one knew I was within arm's reach of her when she was mowed down.

I started my car. And finally glanced over at Roman before I backed out of the police station parking lot. He looked worried. I realized I'd never seen him actually look truly worried before. My heart sank. He must think I'm evil. I asked, "Do you hate me?"

He was offended by the question. "No, I don't hate you! I just wish I'd had some of this information sooner. I need a minute, to figure out how to keep you safe." A swell of relief hit me. He wasn't worried that I might be a serial killer. He was worried that he might actually lose a case. My case. He wanted to keep me out of harm's way. And out of prison. And if anyone could keep me out of jail, it would be him. As I drove us back to my house, I could almost hear the wheels in his brilliant brain turning.

He asked, "Are there any other bodies you need to tell me about?"

I answered, "I didn't kill Jason."

He said, "That's not what I asked. Are there. Any other. Bodies. I need. To know. About?"

I pulled into my driveway. I could answer this one honestly. "No."

Roman hired a private investigator, someone out of DC who he trusted. He flew him down to Miami and put him on the clock to dig into how Detective Jackson knew I was on the curb when Evelyn W. met her rainy demise. All of this was pro bono, of course. Roman was happy to take care of it, no matter how long it might drag on. Which could be months or even years. He told me not to worry about paying him a cent since without my little lie he wouldn't have a career in the first place.

I wanted my parents to know he was back in my life. They had always liked him. They felt he was my equal in intelligence and fortitude, and enjoyed when he would come home with me during spring breaks, and never learn his lesson about sunscreen and get a wicked sunburn every single time. But I worried if I told them, if he saw them for dinner, I would have to explain to them how he had resurfaced. And I definitely didn't want them to know that there were people out in the world who believed I murdered Jason. It was too awful a thought to put into their heads. And I didn't want them to worry about me, and imagine detectives coming into my house and judging me for my half-filled bookshelves and sparse kitchen counters. I could have lied, said that I reached out to Roman in my grief. Simple as that. But I just couldn't deal with a new lie. I was already juggling so many thoughts and secrets that I had to keep hidden away for my own self-preservation. I couldn't handle another one. Roman was just too big a part of my past to make up a story about why he was back in my present. So I kept him to myself.

As Roman packed his suitcase to return to DC, placing his running shoes in their own neat compartment, he paused and turned to me. He asked, "If this hadn't happened, with Jason and with the cops, do you think you would have reached out to me? Like, ever?"

I knew my answer immediately because I had thought about it for years. I said, "No. But here's what I imagined would've happened. I would have seen you at our twentieth college re-union. We would both be forty-one. And we would both still look amazing."

"Duh."

"We would be coy for the first hour, and downplay the in-tense bond we once had. Then stop the charade and sit together. You would meet Jason there, and like him, and respect him. And toss me a look of approval. I pictured you newly married. Your wife would be younger but not embarrassingly so. Maybe thirty-four. Pretty and smart and the kind of woman who does cardio every morning, even when on vacation. Your wife would chat with Jason about her skin-care line, or some such thing, and he would talk about his news-cameraman background, while we re-paired old wounds and caught up on the past two decades."

"Wow. Specific."

"But instead here you are now. At pretty much the worst time in my life. You'll never get to meet Jason, or give me that look of approval."

As I said this, my eyelashes fluttered to stop the tears. Roman pulled me in for a hug, and this human connection broke my thin eyelid dam. He held me, and I sobbed onto his expensive tailored dress shirt. Once I finished my bout of crying, he told me there was nothing else for me to do now but wait for information. I was to try and stay calm, and was not to talk to anyone about anything involving any of this. In other words, I couldn't let any more elephants get free.

Through a cruel twist of events, Roman was once again the most important person in my life and it felt like my fate hung on his divine shoulders. He left Miami, traveled back to his office, and promised to return at a moment's notice. I was to keep him apprised and try to get back to my normal life. Except now, normal life was as a working widow being doggedly investigated for one, if not four, murders.

CHAPTER 36

FURY

THE SUN ROSE THE NEXT DAY. AND AGAIN. AND AGAIN. EACH morning I blinked at the light streaming in from the bottom of the bedroom curtains. It looked like a thick rod of gold. Another day that I woke up in my own home, and not in a prison cell. With each sunrise I worried Detective Jackson was an inch closer to wrongfully imprisoning me for killing the man I loved. I reminded myself never to relax into my pillow, and that just because I hadn't heard a word from him didn't mean he wasn't putting together an airtight case against me. So I stared and stared at the rod of gold until it crept its way up and disappeared.

I had been on sick leave for a month, and it was time for me to try and pull myself together and get in my car and drive to work. I didn't want to tell my patients my husband had died, and because I had kept my last name, there was no way that they could connect him to me even if they had seen that lovely human-interest story on the local news. His death was a part of my life that was too personal to share with them. It would swing the therapy-session pendulum my way, allowing the patients to skirt their own issues. Kangaroo's dying was different. Since everyone knew her because she was always in the office with me, I had to tell them why she vanished. But my patients didn't know Jason, so they didn't need to know that he was no longer on this earth. I continued to wear my engagement and wedding rings, not ready to answer questions, not ready to see and feel my naked finger, and definitely not ready to let go of the idea that I was still committed to someone.

That first day back, I pulled into my office parking spot, put my car in park, got out, and forgot to turn the engine off. Normal rote actions were lost on me. I listened to my clients and nodded and asked the usual questions and got through it all until lunch. I stared at my unopened raspberry yogurt. That night I brushed my teeth and was so distracted by my thoughts that I put the toothpaste back where my hairbrush goes. I replayed the chain of events leading up to Jason's death. Over and over. If I hadn't gone to that relaxation retreat, I wouldn't have slept through the beep. Why did I go to that stupid fucking thing? I knew I shouldn't have gone. I should have listened to my own inner voice. My fear of relaxing lived within me for a reason. Anxiety and stress were necessary tools for survival. My vigilance had always kept me and the ones I loved safe. And then I let myself be lulled into dropping my guard, all for science. Tricked into finding serenity. Manipulated into thinking that being a human was anything more than pure and simple weakness and mediocrity. And now what did I have? A dead husband.

In our past therapy sessions, I urged Gabrielle to stop replaying all her decisions leading up to that night at the Thai restaurant when her date, Derrick, was killed while protecting her from gunshots. I told her it wasn't her fault. I believed that. And yet I blamed myself and couldn't stop replaying my own decisions up until the moment I poured grape sugar goo into Jason's cold mouth. I was angry. Extremely angry. Furious, actually. I was awash with vicious, searing hot sparks burrowing into and flying forth from my every pore. Fury should be the step in the grieving process, and not milquetoast anger.

As I raged to Alisha about my fury, about how life is often so unfair, she pointed out that my emotions were a positive sign. "Ruby, call it anger or call it fury, but this is healthy. You're moving into the second stage. It means you've moved past denial. Your grief is making its way through you. It's not stuck."

I snapped back, "Don't tell me it's positive. This is your fault! Why am I even talking to you anymore? You encouraged me to go to that stupid study! If I hadn't gone, I would have heard the beep. I would have woken up like always. And Jason would still be alive!"

She listened to me lash out and I watched her face. Her brow furrowed just a little. She was concerned but not hurt. She didn't take anything I was saying personally. Which spoke to how professional she was. Which made me more furious. So I said, "Why am I even still here? Sitting on this couch. What's the point of any of it?! I'm leaving." I thought about standing up and storming out. I meant to do it, but my body knew I was bluffing and stayed put. I couldn't find the strength in my thigh muscles to raise me up.

Alisha leaned forward. "I believe you're still here talking to me because you know Jason's death is not my fault. Nor is it your fault."

I shook my head and huffed back into the cushions, like a horse rearing up against a stormy wind. I was so tired of talking and listening and feeling. But Alisha was not tired of being the best therapist I would ever know. "Ruby. I would like to talk about your belief that your heightened awareness can keep you and the people you love safe from harm. That the workings of the world lie on your shoulders. You are willingly taking a stance that Atlas was forced to take as the ultimate punishment—the world on your shoulders. You do not deserve to be punished. And you are not a Titan. As you know, you are a human."

I didn't say anything. I couldn't think of anything to say. Because I felt my little hands wrap around Duncan's ankle. And I tasted peanuts and cheap milk chocolate on the roof of my mouth. And I heard fat raindrops plop as I lured Evelyn into the street. Proof my vigilance alone could protect me and those I love and make the world a happier place.

Alisha continued, "That belief is a distorted thought. Tragedy and sorrow are a part of life. We can't prevent them. No matter how smart or strong or brave or vigilant we are. We can only control our reactions to grief . . . Ruby? Where are you? Are you listening?"

I was barely listening. I had heard enough to know that what Alisha was saying to me about Jason's death was almost the exact same thing I said to Gabrielle about Derrick's death. And it was frustrating and stifling. Because I couldn't yet accept it, but I knew it was correct.

The next day Gabrielle sat across from me. She wore a new tight black catsuit that covered every inch of her pale limbs. Her mouth, in deep red lipstick, opened a little, then closed. She did this so many times she reminded me of a goldfish in duress.

I said, "I sense you want to say something to me. But are holding it in."

She nodded and pursed her red lips. "I went to Hannah's store this morning. Got this new Vampire in the Sun outfit."

I dreaded what was about to come next. "It looks amazing on you."

"Thanks. Um. She mentioned your husband just died. Is that true? Are you okay?"

And my worlds collided again. And the equation of who knew what about my life started to add up. Hannah knew about Duncan, about her dad, of course, and about Jason. Now Gabrielle knew about Jason. My family knew about Duncan and Richard. And Jason. But I never told them about Evelyn W. And some of my colleagues like Dr. Don and, of course, Alisha knew about Evelyn W. dying, and about Jason, but I never told them about Duncan or Richard. Ameena knew about Richard because of her visit to Miami, and she knew about Jason because she was one of my closest friends and I invited her to his funeral. But she did not know about Duncan and Evelyn W. As I shuddered at this math, a new nightmare struck me. Not only might I be hauled off for murdering Jason, but my arrest and, even worse, possible conviction could unearth all my elephants and make them public. Parade them through the streets like the evil circuses I boycotted used to do. My family, friends, colleagues, neighbors, patients, the guy who makes my latte just right at the place down the street, all would know about all four bodies. This thought was so chilling, it briefly pushed out my achy fury that Jason and our life together was gone.

I could see Gabrielle searching my face. Worried that her question had launched me deep into terrible thoughts. Which it had, but not in the way she could imagine.

I answered her. "Yes. My husband died."

The usual next questions were, "How did he die?" And then, "How old was he?" And then, "Do you have kids?" As though having children would make the tragedy even worse because maybe my own loss wasn't quite enough. Before she could ask more questions, to spare both of us the back and forth, I told her about Jason being a type 1 diabetic. That he was way too young to die, and it's horribly sad, but that I'm hanging in there. I was able to remain composed, unlike when I told her Kangaroo had died. I think this was because she was not also sobbing this time. She felt for me, but didn't have her own emotional connection to Jason. She then said, "I feel weird talking about my problems. Stupid things. When you're dealing with all this."

I nodded. "Well, that's a normal feeling. It means you're a conscientious, sympathetic, good person. And that feeling is why I've kept my husband's death from my clients. I wish Hannah hadn't shared it with you, but now that she has, we can talk about it more if you want to. Or we can move on. But please never think of your own problems as stupid. They're just as valid as anyone else's. Especially mine."

I enjoyed being Gabrielle's therapist and felt if we had met on different terms we could have been friends. She was intelligent, had a sense of humor and a healthy appreciation for irony, was willing to look within, and she was a captivating storyteller. After hours and hours of listening to duller people talk about themselves, it was a relief to know Gabrielle would soon be sitting on the love seat, describing her life and her feelings in a way that made what could be tedious facts riveting. I made a point to read all of the articles she wrote and told her so. I was proud of the strides she had made in her career and, more importantly, in her self-growth. As she dug deeper into her emotions, her writing got richer. An unintended upside to our sessions. Therapists, like parents, do have their favorites. They pretend they don't, but it's impossible not to. We are human, after all. And Gabrielle was by far my favorite. I often hoped Alisha, sitting on the other side of things, felt the same way about me.

Because of all this, I decided to open up to Gabrielle. While of course also trying to maintain professional boundaries. I thought she could handle it, just as Alisha believed I could handle the truth about her moving to Miami because of my influence. So I told Gabrielle that I could now personally relate to her anguish. That I too had been replaying my decisions over and over again, and trying not to blame myself for Jason's death. I laid out all my feelings in hopes of bringing the conversation back to her, and focus on her belief that Derrick's death was her fault, and convince her that it wasn't and that she's not alone in this journey. That we were now linked, both struggling with irrational guilt.

Gabrielle had made some strides in therapy, but she still hadn't gone on a date since that lethal night. For an attractive girl in her early twenties who once enjoyed sex and boyfriends, this was an unhealthy choice of avoidance. But when I asked her about it, she gave me her usual answer.

"What's the point? What guy could ever live up to a man I barely knew who literally died for me? Who sacrificed his life while saving mine? 'Oh, thanks for the box of chocolates, Bob, but will you jump in front of a bullet for me? 'Cause Derrick did.'"

Because she barely knew Derrick, it was easy for her to create in her mind a perfect hero without flaws. Similar to how as a child Jason had turned the absent Gertrude into the perfect mother. Derrick became a myth in Gabrielle's memory. And the myth stunted her from connecting to anyone else romantically.

I said, "I think the work we need to do next is for you to stop comparing other men to Derrick. To reframe and try and judge each man on his own merits." But the moment the words came out of my mouth, I felt the weight of that unrealistic task. Gabrielle, smart and quick as always, noticed that I felt it. She responded, "Right. So, you'll just fall in love again and not compare whomever to Jason?"

And this was another problem with patients knowing too much about my life. They could throw things back in my face. I answered, measured, "In time, I will try." And it occurred to me when Roman asked me about my marriage to Jason, I was flooded with memories both good and bad. I loved Jason, but he wasn't perfect. No one is perfect. And an idea formed. A way to help Gabrielle.

I said, "You're stuck because all you really know about Derrick is that he saved your life. Right now in your mind, he has no flaws. But what if you got to know him better, postmortem. Maybe reach out to his parents, or siblings. Did he have siblings?"

She said, "I have no idea. We didn't even get to the 'Do you have any brothers or sisters?' part of the date."

That reminded me of Jason and his alien-like lack of normal first-date questions. I had to hold in my smile. Some memories of him made me so happy. And then I would crash to the present and be miserable because he was now gone. And there would be no new memories made. I focused back on Gabrielle, with a plan of action. I told her to look into Derrick's life. "Contact his family, some of his friends, or coworkers, or even an ex-girlfriend or two. Get to know him through them. I bet you'll discover that while he might have been wonderful in many ways, and he was brave and selfless and he did save your life, he was a three-dimensional person. He must have had some negatives."

This made sense to Gabrielle, and her writer brain immediately saw an article in the making. She would write about her journey to connect with people from Derrick's life, as a catharsis, to try and fall out of love with a man she barely knew.

After she left my office, I felt a little less fury. Alisha was right: I was moving through my stages of grief. And working, seeing my patients, helping others, gave me a sense of purpose and peace during that horribly sad and lonely time. I was an inch closer to acceptance. But Homicide Detective Keith Jackson was not.

CHAPTER 37

EVIDENCE

MY NEIGHBORS PEEKED OUT FROM WINDOWS AND THEIR front doors and walked to their driveways to make sure not to miss a detail of the commotion. They all could definitely hear me scream, "You can't take that! It's for my cat! He needs it!"

The man in the simple white jumpsuit holding the vial of insulin in a plastic bag ignored me and kept walking. Detective Jackson, who was overseeing the whole process, walked over to me and responded, "I'm sorry, we need to take it. It's possible evidence now. Mr. Hollander did die from a low blood sugar. Caused by too much insulin." I wanted to scream some more. *You know he was a type 1 diabetic, you moron!* I also wanted to pound Keith Jackson in his lengthy gut. My quick-twitch muscles took over, and without permission from my brain I actually started to lunge at the giant detective. Roman grabbed my arm, hard, and pulled me back. "Don't," he said. "It's not worth it. And it's not like you to be frantic."

Detective Jackson looked down at me, with a mix of compassion and condescension, and said, "Don't worry about the insulin, I'm sure Dr. Hamilton will be willing to write your cat another prescription." I could see he was trying to get me riled up again. So I could be arrested immediately for assaulting a police officer, or become so flustered I would accidentally admit to something. But with Roman by my side to give me guidance, I refused to take the bait. I swallowed my pride and tried not to make eye contact with my staring and gossiping neighbors. Then I decided I had nothing to be ashamed about. I did not kill my husband. So I pulled my shoulders back and looked my neighbors right in the eyes. To let them know that I had nothing to hide.

Two months had passed since my chat at the police station with Detective Jackson. And as I feared and Roman expected, the detective had been quietly busy at work, pulling together a case against me. Which was now strong enough to get a judge to grant him a search warrant for my house. Roman had anticipated this and started working from Miami full-time for a few weeks so he could make sure to be with me if and when the police came knocking.

While my house continued to be searched, Roman and I sat in my car in the driveway. I kept the engine running so the air conditioner could stay on and keep us cool. Mr. Cat was crammed in his carrier in the back seat. I had to get him contained and out of the house, worried he would be so scared of all the strangers and all the commotion that he would somehow escape, never to be seen again. He was meowing like crazy, furious about the entire situation. I told him, "I know, buddy. I know."

Roman eyed Detective Jackson as he gave orders to others and said to me, "He's convinced you did it, and he's not going to let it go."

"But I didn't do it."

"Well, even if there's no evidence in there, he'll keep trying to find some. I've dealt with guys like him. Good cops who actually care, who work beyond their approved overtime, even when they aren't getting paid. He's trying to prove what he's already certain about. We call people like him true believers. They're relentless."

The irony here was that I usually respected people like that. Since I was one of them. As we waited, I imagined I could hear Roman's watch ticking, but I knew it was one of the really expensive kinds that doesn't make a sound. The ticking was in my head.

I then saw my laptop being walked out in an evidence bag. I pictured some tech person combing through it looking for some sketchy Google search about getting away with murder. They would think I tried to hide something by wiping most of my emails clean. They wouldn't understand that I always keep my computer as tidy as my desk drawer. Deleting anything I deem as clutter. It's not that I was trying to destroy evidence; it's that I am uptight and organized.

I knew the police had already gotten a warrant for my phone records. That was the dig about Dr. Hamilton refilling Mr. Cat's prescription. Now Detective Jackson didn't have to pretend he was in touch with my veterinarian to rattle me, like he had in the interrogation room, because at this point he actually was in touch with him. Other than Ellie and Jason, the number I called and texted most over the past several years belonged to the exceedingly handsome forty-something animal doctor with longish jet-black hair and eyes so dark his pupils were hidden in plain sight. And he had recently gotten a divorce. This was all enough to convince the true believer detective that I was having an affair. Another motive to kill Jason.

Ever since my first appointment with Dr. Hamilton, we had kept in touch. I gave money to his fund to treat stray dogs. He donated to my fund to support continued therapy for juvenile delinquents. We saw each other at least twice a year for Mr. Cat's usual checkups and the occasional cut on a paw or dental cleaning. Once Kangaroo came into the picture, there were many more visits. She needed medicine because she ate three of my makeup-remover wipes and had a stomachache. She needed a few stitches because she sat on a pointy rock and sliced open her thigh. She needed special shampoo because she developed an allergy to down pillows. Between the two pets, it was always something. A rash, a cut, a nose that felt too dry.

And then Kangaroo died, and Dr. Hamilton sent beautiful flowers and a note addressed to both me and Jason, expressing his condolences and his own personal sorrow that she was no longer with us. On the note he included his cell number and told us if we needed anything, we shouldn't hesitate to reach out. So I texted him a thank-you. Then, once Mr. Cat got deathly ill and I was tasked with giving him daily insulin shots and monitoring his eating, I texted Dr. Hamilton a lot more. Sometimes late at night. Mostly about the cat.

Of course Dr. Hamilton, who I at this point in our relationship called Marco, denied an affair as well. He called me immediately when Detective Jackson showed up at his clinic. He explained to the nosy detective that I was a client of his for many years. He was my veterinarian, and over time our acquaintanceship turned into a friendship, but there was absolutely no affair. No photos. No sexting. No witnesses seeing us holding hands under a table at a café. The problem about all this, Roman said, is that you can't prove something *doesn't* exist. And Detective Jackson was certain that I was attracted to Marco. He saved my cat's life, after all. And that kind of skill is very appealing. Sexy. What woman isn't just a little turned on by competence?

The detective couldn't have been more wrong. I did not have an affair. Yet he wasn't stupid either. When I watched Marco in action, handling animals with empathy and confidence, I did have a fantasy or two. He was gentle and strong. Fair yet commanding. I imagined him telling me what to do in bed. "Now turn over." "Now kiss me." "Now open your legs. Good girl."

But similar to thinking about Jason dying every so often, these fantasies about Marco were harmless and healthy. I knew this because it was my job as a psychologist to know. To separate whims from actions. I did not lie to Roman when he asked. I never cheated on Jason. Not once. Not physically or emotionally. The problem was, if he made the right phone calls, Detective Jackson eventually could prove what *did* exist.

More neighbors now stood around, watching. One woman at the end of my block sipped iced coffee while craning her neck, like my life being dismantled was a spectator sport. It occurred to me then that the police would interview everyone on my street, if they hadn't already. And ask the same questions they asked the Vale neighbors the morning Richard was found dead. Did they ever hear any yelling from my house? Or see any physical altercations between me and Jason? Or notice any men other than Jason coming in and out at odd hours? Or women? Perhaps Detective Jackson would even show them all a picture of Marco, hoping to jog their memories.

As I looked around at my once-friendly neighbors who only weeks before were dropping off bagels and condolence cards, I now saw enemies who were excited to think I might be a husband killer. I then caught a glimpse of a lady who looked very familiar. I could see a flash of a turquoise earring. She sat in a parked car, watching my house and all the commotion. But she wasn't a neighbor. And in an instant it became clear. The reason I was being investigated at all. The reason Detective Jackson commented on my mother-in-law not being invited to my wedding, or to her own son's funeral.

I turned to Roman, to revise my previous answer to his question about me having any enemies.

"Roman," I said.

"Yes, Ruby," he said.

"I do have an enemy. A big one. And she is right over there, sitting in that beige car. Her name is Gertrude Hollander. She's Jason's mother."

CHAPTER 38

GOSSIP

I HAD ALWAYS BEEN GOOD AT COMPARTMENTALIZING, BUT now the dividers were being chewed away and I was losing control of the information flow about my personal life. As big and bustling as it might seem, Miami was a small town in some ways. And with the neighbors knowing my house had been raided by the police, I had no choice but to tell my family what was going on. I at least wanted them to hear it from me first. But I dreaded it.

I sat in the den of my childhood home, with my parents and with Roman. There was so much to tell them, and so much to keep from them. The walls had been repainted, and my mother had recently reupholstered the chairs. But the rest was exactly as it had been since I was a small child hearing the wounded cry of Mr. Bird.

I began at the beginning. With Detective Jackson's odd unannounced visit to my house. I was so ashamed to admit to my parents that anyone would suspect me of murdering Jason. My parents were stunned. They sat speechless, hoping for some sort of punch line that never came. As they realized what I was telling them was not a bizarre tasteless prank but reality, their shocked silence morphed into an indignant bluster. They knew, like all parents presume to know, that their child was innocent.

I explained to them that I was now certain my own mother-in-law hated me so much that she went to the police and accused me of killing the man I loved. I suspected Gertrude didn't actually believe that I had done it, but this was her way of getting revenge, because she did blame me for taking Jason from her. So she set the creaky wheels of justice in motion. Reached out to the police to request an inquiry. Roman used his many contacts and confirmed the deceased's mother had been in touch with and interviewed by Miami Beach police detectives the day after Jason's death. And now, on top of that, people from my past were coming out of the woodwork to speak ill of me, some with glee. Like my ex-boyfriend Seth.

Detective Jackson left no stone unturned and found him living in Tampa. Seth was happy to tell the tale of how he proposed to me on our one-year anniversary. And how I said I loved him, but felt way too young to even consider getting married. Way too young to say yes to forever. And as fate would have it, Max from Yale was going to be in Miami for one night before getting on a mind-numbing mandatory family cruise to the Caribbean. Max had his own room in a cheap chain motel near the loading docks. We meant to just go for a drink, but instead we ripped each other's clothes off before I could even register the hideous late-seventies chartreuse curtains.

And when we were done, I felt bad that I had cheated on Seth, but I also felt relieved. This was my way of proving to myself that I was not ready to get married. And that I needed to break up with Seth entirely. It was sad to end it, but a happy thought did creep in between the tears. Sleeping with an ex is not an additional number.

I was sure my version of the story and the version Seth told the detective were very different. To Seth, I was a no-good, cheating, lying, manipulative vixen capable of any misdeed. He would make an excellent character witness for Detective Jackson, whose number one goal was to assassinate my character and put me away for murder.

My mother, desperate to help, asked, "Can we sue that Gertrude woman? For telling the police lies that Ruby killed Jason? It is slander!" Roman answered, "No. Because we can't prove *she* doesn't actually believe Ruby killed her son, so slander is a non-starter. And suing a grieving mother is not a good look. Even if it comes from a grieving widow. That course of action will definitely make Ruby seem like the villain." My mother snapped back, "But she's not a villain! How can we even be having this conversation!? It's outrageous and . . ." She trailed off and sank into a newly upholstered chair, her defeated eyes looked tragically pretty in front of the light green paisley fabric. I knew how she felt. I too was at a loss.

When I had seen Gertrude parked on my street, I asked Roman if I should go on the offensive. Tell the press that she abandoned her son, then manipulated him once he was all grown up, when it was convenient for her. And how she didn't even know what kind of cake he liked! Roman said it would be best if someone else could expose Gertrude's nature. But Jason's father was dead, and his friends never knew the extent of his complicated relationship with her. No one else had witnessed her true essence.

I sat on the arm of the chair and leaned into my mother, just a little. My father, not ready to join the paisley pity party, had a different idea. "Maybe I can ask some old reporter friends to find dirt on this detective. Shut this whole mess down." Roman stopped him there, and assured him, "I already have a private investigator on the case. The top guy in the country. I promise you, Ruby is in good hands, is being taken care of, and it's best for you all to do nothing. So please, just be here to support her, but don't make any calls about it. To anyone. We don't want to fan the flames." My father took this in and patted him on the arm, hard, in that appreciative manly way. "It's good to have you back, Roman."

The flames were being fanned plenty without my parents. My nosy neighbors called their other neighbors, who then called their friends, who then called old friends they hadn't spoken to in years. It was like a pyramid scheme of "Did you hear about Ruby Simon? Yes, her husband, found dead in bed. But clearly the police think she did it! Well, no arrest yet, but they searched her house!"

The blaze crackled and spread in all sorts of directions, including toward Hannah. She called me that week. "Hey, Ruby, can we talk?" Roman had advised me not to talk on the phone about anything at all that could possibly involve Jason or the other three bodies, in case the police were listening. But I didn't want to seem suspicious, in case the police were listening.

"Hey, Hans, I'm actually heading out. Where are you? Maybe I can come by."

"At the shop."

"Oh, perfect. I'll be in the area. I'll stop by."

I walked into her store and was taken with the expansion. I hadn't been there for a while and had no idea Hannah had rented out the spaces on each side of her original area. She'd knocked down some walls and now had an entire room devoted to her own line, Vampire in the Sun. I was so sincerely happy for her, I momentarily forgot my precarious situation.

I exclaimed, "It looks amazing in here!"

"Thanks. Yeah, I'm planning on taking over the whole block if I can. Create my own department-slash-lifestyle store."

As I looked around, Hannah took a step away from me, rather than giving me her usual big hug and "Try this on" greeting. I decided to peruse the racks, casually. But this was an act, because I barely looked at the clothes as they passed through my hands. Hannah kept her distance and folded distressed tees. She said, "So, I was thinking. Remembering, really. And, like, that night. You know. That night my dad died. Did you wake up at all? Or hear anything? Or, like, see my father after we got back?"

Oh, fuck.

I casually took my hand off the clothes and faced her. This conversation deserved attention and respect, even if she couldn't look me in the face.

"No. I just got you and Erika up the stairs and we all sort of passed out."

"Well, you didn't pass out. Exactly. 'Cause you were sober."

"Yeah, but I mean, I fell asleep. I was exhausted. A lot of dancing. And then sugar crash from all the candy. You know."

I could feel the new tension between us growing. So I asked, "What's going on? You okay? You haven't mentioned that night in a long time."

Hannah finished folding the shirts into an expensive little pile. "I guess I'm not okay. 'Cause Detective Jackson came in here to talk to me."

I could now feel myself sinking into the trendy deep-red-stained cement floor. And decided honesty was going to be the best policy. "He thinks I killed Jason. Because Jason's mother went to the police and accused me. You know how he was estranged from her. And she always blamed me for it. But the detective thinks she is credible. So now I'm a suspect in the detective's mind."

Hannah looked miffed. "Oh. I remember my mom had to deal with people thinking she killed my dad. I guess the spouse is always suspected."

"Yeah. It's been really rough."

I waited for some words of comfort. But Hannah didn't give me a peep or expression of sympathy. She moved over to another pile. This time buttery soft leggings. And began refolding.

She said, "Well, the detective guy didn't say a word to me about Jason." She looked up at me. Her blunt bangs framed her eyeliner perfectly. "He wanted to know about the night my father died. He kept asking for details. Like when we got home that night, how drunk I was, and specifically how you acted the next day."

I knew why. But I had to pretend. "Why?"

She had to pretend too. She shrugged. Then said, "I barely remembered this, but I guess my dad had a wound on his head, or something, when he died. The detective kept asking if anything from our kitchen was missing. Like a small knife. Or something that could have made that wound. He even showed me a photo of my dad. Dead. All zoomed in on that head area."

I was truly angry at Detective Jackson for doing this to my friend. "That's horrible!" I said. "What a dick for showing you that."

"He wasn't a dick. He's just trying to get to the truth."

Fuck. Fuck. Fuck.

Hannah continued, "I told him I couldn't remember. It was such a crazy time. But that he could talk to my mom. That she might remember more."

"That's smart."

"I guess I'm smart, sometimes."

"Hannah, you've always been smart."

We stood there. At an impasse of friendship, choices, and lies. Then she said, "Wanna know what's really weird, Ruby?"

I nodded. No longer able to predict where any of this was going.

"The detective didn't ask me anything about Erika that night. Only about you."

I had to keep it together, and said, with the right amount of anger, "Yeah, well, he has it out for me." I knew that neither Hannah nor her mom would ever remember the missing keychain charm at this point. And even if they did, Detective Jackson would never be able to find it. Not in my house, or my car, or my parents' house, or my office. He could get all the warrants he wanted and look and look and look. A few days after Richard Vale died, during my usual scheduled volunteering hours, I buried it with all five bloody flamingo feathers deep in the bird sanctuary. Under trees, among hundreds of other feathers, hidden in damp soil and decaying natural debris.

Hannah looked at me, like she was seeing me clearly for the first time. Her eyes narrowed. She curtly said, "No loitering in the shop, please." I knew that meant I was to leave and never come back. But I felt compelled to show her an act of continuing support. I pulled a black pencil skirt from her own clothing line off a rack, and bought it without trying it on. At this point in my life, fit no longer mattered.

CHAPTER 39

AMMONIA

JASON DYING WAS THE WORST THING THAT HAD EVER happened to me. Then being suspected of killing him added insult to unimaginable injury. It was like Gertrude started a conga line of people who suspected me of murder, and the line kept getting longer. First the well-respected Detective Jackson. Then the faceless judge who issued him those warrants to search my house and cell phone records. Then Hannah Vale. And I knew next in line would be some go-getter prosecutor, excited to sink his teeth into this marital murder and wage a war against me. His job being to get even more people up and dancing, and prove without a reasonable doubt that I was guilty of first-degree murder.

I was sure the detective was using his folder-of-photos game show trick on everyone in the justice system, to rile them up, and showcase that I was some sort of very lazy serial killer. Four deaths in thirty years? Please. If I were a serial killer, I would be way more productive than that. But surprisingly, my being present when Duncan and Richard and Evelyn W. died was not even the most damning thing against me. It was the seemingly meaningless minutiae of my life that would add up to total that I murdered my husband. While I forced myself out of bed every morning and went to work to help other people live their best lives, the police were weaving a web of motives and circumstantial evidence to conclude that I was a cold-blooded killer.

Although all this was technically confidential, Roman had ways of hearing courthouse whispers. He explained to me that what would happen next was the assistant district attorney who took on the case would be discussing my crime in front of a grand jury. This was not a trial to prove I was guilty, but a song and dance to get an indictment, so then Detective Jackson could officially arrest me. And then, a trial. And then life in a maximum security prison. When I was alone, and quiet, and really thought about that possible outcome, I couldn't help but weep into Mr. Cat's fur. Apologizing to him over and over for inevitably having to abandon him.

Roman was telling me about the assistant district attorney and the grand jury while in my kitchen. I sipped a second cup of morning coffee and watched him doing push-ups on the cool Mediterranean-tiled floor as he laid out my future. I was used to him exercising while he spoke. It was a sign he was both revved up and nervous. It also showed how strong his core was, that he could have full legal conversations, breathing deeply, while exerting every muscle in his body. He warned me that the grand jury was the first in what would be a long line of steps.

I was a little miffed. Especially knowing what an amazing lawyer he was. And said, "But maybe they won't indict me? And this will be over?"

He hopped up, his face flush with rushing blood, and walked

over to me. He wanted to make sure what he said next wasn't getting lost in his impeccable pecs.

"A grand jury almost always indicts. It's completely one-sided. The prosecutor calls witnesses, anyone he chooses, and if they refuse, they're in contempt. Then he unfolds his case, manipulating the facts however he wants. And he has a very low burden of proof. There is no defense attorney there to protect you, and no judge to keep the proceedings in order."

"Wait. You mean you won't be there?"

"I can't be there."

I dropped my coffee. The cup clipped the island and chipped. Coffee spilled onto the floor. But I couldn't worry about it just then. I felt faint. Like my life raft had deflated. And I was sinking into the abyss. Deeper and darker. Blotches of black covered my sight until there was nothing but night sky. Roman caught my shoulders before I fell off the island stool. He helped me flop my head in between my knees.

Jesula came in through the front door. She had her own key. And today was one of her cleaning days. There was much less to do now, without Jason, but of course I still wanted to employ her twice a week. She saw Roman, shirtless, a sheen of sweat on his back, standing in the kitchen. And she saw me barely on a stool with my head flopped down. I was unconscious then, but I later worried she had thought she walked in on something untoward, and had lost respect for me.

Roman turned to her and explained, "She just fainted." Jesula rushed over. She knelt under the sink and grabbed some cleaning products. Opened one and sprayed it on the floor beneath me, letting the strong ammonia smell waft up. I could feel my color coming back, my clammy skin return to its normal texture. The black blotches receding. I lifted my head and saw her face. I weakly smiled. "Thank you." She nodded and looked at the spilled coffee. She said, "I'll take care of it. Go lie down."

And without a word Roman gallantly and effortlessly scooped me off the stool and up into his arms. To an onlooker it would have seemed romantic. The start of a fantasy. A steamy sex scene so perfect it only happens to other people. A gesture as elegant as a handsome gentleman seamlessly leaning over at the perfect moment and lighting a cigarette for a beautiful girl at a bar in the 1940s. But that cigarette later causes cancer. And I didn't feel sexy in Roman's arms. I felt like a rag doll. And then, because of the way he was carrying me, I felt like a bride.

"Put me down."

He put me down. Immediately.

"I can make it to the couch myself."

I did make it, and sat in the living room upright. I felt my personality returning to me. My strength and my fury. And I said, "What the fuck? Why can't you be at the grand jury?"

"Because it's not a trial. Or a police interrogation. You won't be there yourself. So, you don't get any advocates. Or have any rights."

This sank in. A man would be saying the worst things about me to a group of well-meaning citizens. While hauling in people from my past. I had never felt so out of control. Roman tried to comfort me. He sat next to me on the couch and nudged me into him. So I rested my weight onto the side of his still-shirtless body.

He said, "We are already ahead of this. Because usually the target of grand juries never even knows there is one happening behind their back."

"Target?"

"Yeah. That's what the defendants are called."

"Doesn't sound very diplomatic."

"It's not. But I know the drill. Just hang in there. And trust me."

I watched Jesula through the doorway as she mopped up the spilled coffee. And I contemplated my options. I really had none. A grand jury would happen. An indictment was bound to come next. And I was now referred to as a target. Trusting Roman and his process would have to be enough.

CHAPTER 40

SMOKE

EVEN THOUGH I WAS NOT ALLOWED TO WATCH THE GRAND jury proceedings, I was able to piece together what was being said and insinuated and then fill in the rest of the blanks with my worst fears. I could do this because unlike a lot of targets, I still had allies among the many witnesses that the assistant district attorney called to the stand. People like Dr. Don and Marco Hamilton and Ellie. If my wedding was heaven, all my favorite people surrounding me in a cocoon of love and support, the grand jury trial was hell. Many of those same people were now being ruthlessly questioned against their own will, and their testimony was being twisted and turned to use against me. And although they were cautioned to keep the content of the questioning confidential, they were outraged to be subpoenaed and dragged in there. And were therefore happy to give me and Roman any advantage they could by giving us every detail they remembered. Roman would use all this information to serve him later. I, however, wanted to know everything they could tell me about the inquisition so I could build up my tolerance to pain.

The first thing that became clear to me was that the ADA, fueled by Detective Jackson's evidence and Gertrude's suspicion, believed that Jason's murder was not a crime of passion, but premeditated first-degree murder. He planned to prove that I was exceptionally capable of executing the whole thing and that Mr. Cat was my accomplice. According to him, once my cat was diagnosed with diabetes, I concocted what I thought was the perfect way to get away with murder. I was well versed with using needles, since I had to give the cat two shots a day. And since I was a "type 3 diabetic," the term for someone who lives with and cares for a type 1, I was also well versed with how insulin affects blood sugar.

The prosecutor believed and planned to convey to the nice folks on the grand jury that I took one of Mr. Cat's extremely thin needles, filled the syringe with insulin from either a backup vial of Jason's or from Mr. Cat's stash, and while Jason was sleeping, I inserted the needle into a place on his body that would be easily missed by the coroner. Probably into a tiny hole from a previous place he had inserted his insulin pump. And because he had been conveniently cremated, under my orders, there was now no chance for the coroner to go over Jason's body again to specifically check for a suspect needle mark.

It was in this manner that I pumped my husband, Jason Hollander, full of insulin. Causing his blood sugar to go dangerously low. His continuous glucose monitor did start beeping a warning, but Jason was already too disoriented to help himself. And I stood by callously and waited until he died. Then I called 9-1-1, shoved some sugar into his mouth once I knew it would do no good, and put on an act and pretended to be upset. Jason's chronic but manageable disease gave me the perfect excuse for his death. Leaving me the freedom to collect his life insurance, as well as his inheritance and condo, and run off with my lover, veterinarian Marco Hamilton. The prosecutor would also make sure to tell the grand jury that the cops who arrived on the scene that early morning did note in their report that I was stunned and in shock but could have been, and this is a quote from the official notes, "merely going through the motions."

Roman assured me that in my actual trial, he would point out that Jason had clearly stated in his own will that he wanted to be cremated, so it was not under my orders at all, but under his. And their entire case against me was ridiculously circumstantial. Not to mention Jason and his mother, the very woman who we have on record calling the police station and first accusing me of his murder, were estranged, and it was her misguided anger that was wasting hardworking taxpayers' money by callously and wrongfully using the justice system for her own petty revenge.

Just when I started to accept the new normal, that every morning while I forged ahead with my life there was a roomful of people listening to nonsense about me, Roman called my cell. He knew I was in session at work, so I knew it must be important. I usually allowed people an extra five or ten minutes in their session, schedule depending, but technically a visit with a psychologist is fifty minutes. So at that mark, I ushered my patient out, planning to call Roman back. And instead was surprised to see him standing in my waiting room. He had never been to my office before. His presence made it look smaller. I remained quiet, saying nothing until he was well inside and I had closed my door. In case there were people in the hallway who could hear us from the waiting room. Because I was an eavesdropper, I assumed everyone else was too.

Roman placed his laptop on a side table and told me to sit down. He pressed play with a heavy finger. I had no idea what I was watching at first, but I saw grainy footage of the busy corner of Forty-First Street and Royal Palm Avenue. It was raining, water drops glided over the security camera that caught the images, obscuring some but not all of the movement below. Then I saw the Witch, looking down at her cell phone. And I knew exactly what I was watching. Something that was not ridiculously circumstantial.

On tape, I saw myself standing near her. Our shoulders close enough for her to sense my forward movement. The whole event played out. Me confidently stepping into the street from the crosswalk while the Witch blindly followed me into the road. Then me quickly hopping back to safety and her getting crunched by a giant truck. The footage wasn't clear enough to read facial expressions, but I remember playing the part, feigning panic and quickly looking away from the carnage.

Before Roman could say a word, I defended myself. "She wasn't looking. It's not my fault . . . Besides, if it is my fault, it's 'implied malice' under the law. Which is much harder to prove than second-degree murder, or manslaughter. Nearly impossible, actually."

Roman's unhappy concern was briefly overshadowed with a look of pride. He was impressed. I told him I did pick up a few things while helping him study for his LSAT. Then my moment of showing off ended, and the hurricane of worry hit me. Roman also got serious again and said, "This footage is how Detective Jackson knew you were on that corner. He knew long before we went into that interrogation room to chat."

My mind raced. "This is bad."

"It's not great."

I asked, "How did you get this?"

"I got it because I know how to do my job. After you wondered aloud how the detective had placed you there, I told the private investigator I had hired to look into every possibility. The PI learned there was a crime-deterrent surveillance camera set up on that block. And that the city had long ago gotten rid of the old footage. But the large grocery store chain, guarding against lawsuits, kept the footage all this time to prove their truck driver was not to blame in case any distant relative of Evelyn W.'s decided to ask for a settlement."

I knew this video might not land me in prison, but if it was leaked to the press, posted online, turned into a gory GIF, it would certainly ruin my life. What people think they know and what people can see with their own eyeballs are two very different things. I would be canceled.

I glanced at Roman. A lump of anxiety in my lungs. "So, what happens now?"

Roman said, "I've made sure the few people at the grocery store chain who had access to this will never let it surface to the public, beyond the police."

"Made sure? How?"

"My firm is very persuasive. And I've also made it clear that if anyone in the police department leaks this to the press, or shows this to anyone outside the investigation, we will sue them and declare a mistrial before they even have a chance to arrest you for Jason's death. My gut tells me Jackson wants to do this the right way. And sending this to the news is not the right way."

I nodded, comforted a little.

Then Roman said, "Let's just hope no more footage, of any kind, surfaces." This felt pointed. And the hurricane around me raged. Before I could let it whisk me away fully, or before I could reach the calm center of the eye, the little light in my office clicked on, signaling my next patient. Other people's problems didn't stop just because mine were overwhelming.

Over the next couple of weeks, I was told "Where there's smoke, there's fire" was the assistant district attorney's favorite phrase. I imagined the ADA informing the grand jurors all about Evelyn W. A woman with some problems, yes, but who was taking the time to work on herself by going to therapy. A woman brave enough to confront her anger issues fifty minutes at a time. Dr. Don, under oath, had to admit that I did call Evelyn W. "the Witch" on numerous occasions. The ADA hammered home that I was her therapist, which made what I did to her even more egregious and obscene and downright evil. I was supposed to be the one to help her, not call her mean names and inch her toward getting horrifically run over by a giant grocery store truck. And of course the ADA would play the video for the grand jury, several times in a row, because people do love a visual aid.

I was sure the prosecutor was telling the grand jury how a little boy, an innocent little seven-year-old named Duncan Reese, drowned tragically and "accidentally" in the ocean. And how I was in the ocean that day too. Yes, I was only five years old. But I was already in the gifted program in my school. Cunning and intelligent, known for eavesdropping and learning grown-up words. And he would explain how that very boy had apparently been bullying my sister, who, by my own admission, I loved more than anything in the world. Protecting one's family was a strong motive for murder, to be sure. When Ellie was called in, she was forced to open old wounds and concede that Duncan Reese had ruthlessly bullied her and yanked a curl from her head and that I was, as everyone already established, in the ocean when he drowned.

"But the ocean is so big!" she yelled to the nameless faces decid-ing my fate. "And Ruby was so little!"

Ellie was then escorted out. Her work was done. But as she left the building, she told me she saw Hannah Vale striding in. Head held high. And I could imagine exactly what would hap-pen next. The ADA would continue, "And speaking of family, Ruby Simon's best friend's father, Richard Vale, also suffered an untimely death while she was in the vicinity. Yes, Mr. Vale was allergic to peanuts, but beyond the horrors of his throat closing up, depriving him of life-sustaining oxygen, there was a little gash on the man's eyebrow, unexplainable at the time of death. However, now looking back at it through a different lens, it speaks to foul play, perhaps a struggle with a homicidal teenage girl who had some sort of pointy object in her hand."

Based on the chilly meeting I recently had with her in her boutique, I knew Hannah would be more than eager to confirm that what the prosecutor was saying was all true. I was sleeping at her house the night her dad died. And she was so drunk she doesn't remember anything. So therefore, technically, anything could have happened. Maybe I wasn't in her bedroom with her the whole time. Maybe I had crept downstairs and murdered her father. My motive? This was a grand jury—a motive was entirely unnecessary. Just an added cherry on top of the sundae.

Then Dr. Marco Hamilton was brought in to serve two pur-poses. He vehemently denied having an affair with me. But just having to be there testifying to our strictly platonic relationship demoralized him and made him seem unsure of what he was say-ing. He was also relentlessly questioned about my ability to un-derstand the use of insulin. He had no choice but to testify to the fact that he did teach me how to administer insulin to Mr. Cat and that I seemed very comfortable and adept with the syringe.

After all this testimony, from all these witnesses, the ADA took a line from Detective Jackson and smartly asked the sixteen impartial strangers on the grand jury how many people had suddenly died within a yard or two of them in their lives. Probably zero. Maybe one, at most.

As Roman and I compared daily notes on what we assumed was said in the closed room, he explained to me that none of this would be admissible in my actual trial, and I would probably not be officially charged with any of the other deaths. But with Gertrude accusing me of killing her son, and Detective Jackson saying the hairs stood up on the back of his neck the first time he met me, the ADA felt the grand jury should be aware that three people in my presence were already dead of supposed freak accidents and now my late husband makes four. Four is beyond a pattern. Four is beyond bad luck or coincidence. Four means I'm at the center of it all, these deaths orbiting around me like the planets around the sun. And so even though there is no concrete evidence, all these deaths should be considered when the grand jury decides if the state has enough evidence to bring me to justice and indict me for murdering Jason Hollander. "Because where there is smoke, there is fire. And around Ruby Simon, there is a hell of a lot of smoke."

CHAPTER 41

CONFESSION

WHEN I SAT DOWN AND QUIETLY AND PRIVATELY TOOK stock, it dawned on me, how mad could I be at my current situation? Detective Jackson wasn't exactly wrong about me. Like when one has a vague toothache and knows something is sick and rotten. He might pick the wrong tooth, but he is correct about the mouth being riddled with cavities and disease. I did have respect for the man, and knew I didn't have a right to be outraged by his accusations, but I still was. Because what hurt me most was that I truly loved Jason. He was a good man who brought out the best in me. And I wanted to have his babies, and I hoped that even though they would grow up in Miami, they would inherit just a hint of his adorable Southern lilt. I wanted to grow old with him, sitting on a beach bench watching the sunset, our dry wrinkled hands entwined.

I felt no weight of guilt pressing down on my chest, shoulders, or heart. Duncan and Richard and Evelyn deserved to die. And part of me would rather everyone knew I killed them, if they would just believe I didn't kill Jason. I was tempted to tell the whole truth. But in moments when a confession was about to seep out, I stopped myself, because I knew it would never work like that. Admitting to killing the other three would only make the case that I killed Jason even stronger. So there was no point in trying to make that imaginary bargain with the world. *Please, punish me for what I have done. And believe I did not do the thing you think I did.* It was not an option.

Plus, Ellie could never know the truth. If I told her I killed Duncan, she would know I did it for her. She would then think that my first kill put me on a lifelong path of being a psycho. She would feel responsible and guilty for all my evil deeds, and that might ruin her life. And the whole point of me killing Duncan in the first place was so that her life would be better. For me to tell her the truth now and destroy her world view, her reality, would be the opposite of what I had set out to do so long ago.

Often, and I knew because I heard about it in sessions, people who revealed hurtful secrets were only trying to release their own pain by handing it off to someone else. Like a hot potato. *Here, quick, take this searing knowledge so I don't have to hold it alone.* This course of action is selfish and does no good, just scalds more people. I was not about to burden anyone else with my demons. Especially Ellie.

I had thought the black hole Kangaroo had left when she died was suffocating, but back then I had Jason, and we got through it together. The hardest part about Jason's not being with me anymore was that I kept wanting to talk to him about my sadness about him being dead, only to remember over and over again that I couldn't talk to him. Ever again. He was gone and would continue to be unreachable. And I would continue to be sad and miss him. It was a circular problem that wouldn't stop churning.

I was lonely. And depressed. And the bed was so big. And my routine was so empty. I no longer had our driving-to-and-from-work check-in phone calls. Or the bickering about what causeway to take, which now was a fond memory, since it had been taken away from me. Or our shorthand about when it was time to graciously leave a dinner party. I would let out a tiny yawn. He would then mention to our hosts that I had a big day the next day. I would then say, "No, but I'm having fun!" And that would set the stage for inching our way out the door. We were a team. I missed him in his entirety.

The feeling of relaxation I adopted and retained from my week in the telomere study had evaporated. I was filled with unease in a purgatory of having no control over my future. No syllabus. And knowing that I was being doggedly investigated by the justice system and could be arrested at any moment distracted me from entirely feeling the weight of Jason's death. So I was handed a sort of moratorium from the full despair of grief, which was replaced by nauseating uncertainty and panic. I knew, however, the sadness and grief were still in there, deeper than I could access, waiting to come out when given a chance. Waiting to take over once my fate was settled. I just hoped that chance would not come when I was serving a life sentence in prison.

CHAPTER 42

STRAW

JESULA STOPPED COMING TO CLEAN MY HOUSE. SHE MISSED one day. I texted her. And called. No response. Then she missed her second day that week, with no explanation. This was very unlike her. I called again and again. It kept going to voicemail. I drove to her apartment to check in on her. I had only been there a few times, but I remembered the brightly painted blue building in Little Haiti. The neighborhood's rent was rising with the water levels on Miami Beach. Rich people moving inward, pushing the lower class out. I knocked. It seemed she wasn't at home. I knew where her son went to junior high school. I thought about trying to reach him. I worried something terrible had happened to her. That afternoon I called Roman. He was back in DC dealing with other cases, but we made sure to talk once a day so he was fully informed. I mentioned Jesula's disappearance and through the phone I could feel his eyes narrow as he paused, like he now knew something.

"Do not try and contact her son. Or her."

"But—"

"Ruby. Give me a day."

In that one day Roman fought to find out if Jesula had been called as a witness to the grand jury, and when it was confirmed she had been, he managed to attain a copy of her testimony through his backdoor channels. He flew to Miami, leaned against a wall of his war room, and slid down so he was sitting on the floor. He liked to stretch out after a flight. He handed me a stack of papers. I sat on the floor across from him. And as I read, I learned sorrow has no bottom.

Far more damning than the Evelyn W. video, or my knowledge of insulin, was Jesula's testimony. What she told them hurt me emotionally, and legally, and the worst part was I hadn't seen it coming. I had known her since I was fifteen years old, and I considered her both my friend as well as a sort of maternal figure.

I'd thought she cared about me. I'd thought she liked me, at the very least. She would often remind me to bring a sweater when I went out, since I got chilled inside movie theaters and malls and especially grocery stores. When she saw I was stressed about work and too busy to eat a proper lunch, she would hand me a banana and a handful of almonds and make sure I finished the small snack before rushing out into the world. She knew about so much of my life, from my party days as a teen, to my sober days, to my breakup with Seth, to my move in with Jason. She knew exactly how I liked my grandmother's tiny antique clocks to be arranged, and when she dusted them, she placed them back just right. And it didn't go only one way. I knew about her extended family still in Haiti. And I helped get her shy, sweet twelve-year-old son into a thriving charter school, which was much better than the barely accredited school he had been attending. Which was also how I would have known how to contact him, should Roman's advice not have stopped me.

But underneath that closeness there was still a divide. There was still my privilege. And when I read her testimony, it hit me. The truth was Jesula cleaned the bathrooms where I shit. Maybe it was never a real friendship. Maybe this was her chance to have power over someone she felt had all the power all along. Perhaps she had resented me this entire time, since the moment I walked into that Kremlin club bathroom and bought lollipops. This realization mortified me. Could I have been so bad at reading people that I invited someone into my home twice a week who secretly hated me?

The tone in her testimony came through clearly. She seemed not reluctant but excited to report to the grand jury, detailing every single fight she had ever overheard between me and Jason. She was in our house for countless days. She saw us getting ready for work in the morning. Saw us grieving over Kangaroo. She heard us talking to each other on the phone while one of us was working late and the other one was pacing in the kitchen. She listened in when we discussed having children someday, and she let me know she would be our nanny if we needed extra help.

She was there for little moments that happen in every marriage, voices raised, frustrations coming to a head. In her testimony, she remembered and recounted every harsh word we had said to each other like she had been taking notes all along, waiting for this moment to help bring me down. She testified to my anger problem, citing that she once saw me give Jason the middle finger. That I stomped into the bedroom all sulky and did it through the bedroom wall. Jesula took only the worst bits and pieces and edited my happy marriage to Jason to create a mosaic of hostility and abuse. Her testimony made it seem like it was probable that I did want to kill my husband. And as type A as I was, that want probably led me to actually do it. In fact, she was happy to report, I was so type A I was accepted into an actual scientific study about goal-oriented people.

All of this was a horrible disfiguring of the facts, like a Picasso painting, but none of it was actually a lie. And then I read on. She had a lot to say about my grieving process. She told the grand jury that when my dog died I hung on to and cherished her every toy. I wouldn't even let Jesula clean the floor because I didn't want all her fur to be swept away forever. The dog's water bowl sat out for months, without being emptied. Eventually the water evaporated. But the dog beds and dog treats and leashes stayed put. None of this was that weird, Jesula explained. Except then, when my husband died, I threw out all his belongings within a day. Closets were emptied. Surfboards given away. His favorite diet soda glasses boxed up and donated. Jesula was horrified by how differently I acted after my dog died versus after my husband died. It was unnatural, she said.

This was an absolute lie. Jesula was there for both deaths. There to see and know that I had the exact same coping mechanism of getting rid of anything that physically reminded me of my dearly departed. She crossed all lines to sabotage me and make sure I seemed guilty of murdering Jason. Simply, if all the prosecutor had before was straws, Jesula was the straw that broke the camel's back. And as Roman predicted, after three weeks of testimony and one day of deliberation, I was indicted for murdering Jason.

CHAPTER 43

CUFFS

GABRIELLE WAS VERY ANGRY WITH ME. I COULD SEE IT ALL over her pale face. She was sitting on the merlot love seat, scowling. Because my suggestion that she track down the friends and family of the man who saved her life turned out to be a very bad one. It seemed there was no record of a Derrick Roberts anywhere. The shooting was reported by the *Miami Herald,* his name was printed, but no funeral information was given, and there were no follow-up articles. The perpetrator apparently was never caught. Derrick had no Facebook page, no Twitter, no Instagram, no online presence at all.

I asked, "Did you check LinkedIn? Even people who never even sign up seem to be on it."

I could see her frustration. She barked, "You think I didn't already think of that? He's not even on LinkedIn!"

Gabrielle told me she dug and dug and couldn't find a record of him anywhere. No driver's license, no birth certificate, no high school transcripts, no insurance. She could never even get to any of his kin or cohorts because it's like he was a ghost before he was a ghost. She asked, desperately, "Did he even exist at all? Was I hallucinating the whole thing? Was he an angel? Am I crazy? Now I'm more obsessed than ever."

This was painful to watch. Our many inroads were being covered up by a blizzard of doubt and lack of facts. She was sliding back to the days when I first met her. I took stock of the situation. We had a lot of work ahead of us, but I knew we could get there. I knew I could help her not feel crazy. Because she wasn't crazy. I was about to say all this when we heard a hostile knock knock knock on my office door. The loud noise made her jump a little since usually this space was serene; the only sound was the occasional whirr of the air conditioner clicking on and off to maintain a perfect seventy-three degrees.

I said to her quietly, "Sorry about this." Then I turned my head toward the door and yelled, "I'm in session!" But I knew who was knocking. No one else would have marched through the waiting room. And I was not sure why I was delaying the inevitable. Knock knock knock again. I was delaying the inevitable because I was scared.

A booming voice came from behind the thin wood door. "Open up or we kick it in."

I wanted to assure Gabrielle that everything would be okay. I wanted to do my job. But I couldn't in this moment. I could only stand and open the door. Two uniformed cops and Detective Jackson walked in. Detective Jackson did the talking.

"Ruby Simon, you are under arrest for the murder of Jason Hollander."

Gabrielle was horrified. She looked at me, confused, then hurt, like I had somehow betrayed her. I could see in her eyes that the mere fact that I was being arrested made her immediately believe I might actually be guilty of the crime.

Her reaction brought my worst fears to the surface. Would anyone believe me when I said I didn't do it? And if I said it confidently and calmly, would I seem more innocent? Or just cold and sociopathic? Should I frantically scream, "I'm innocent!"? Would people believe me then? I knew so much about human behavior, yet I was so used to covering up my lies that I didn't know how to convince everyone around me that this time I was actually telling the truth.

Detective Jackson could easily have arrested me at my house. But he had already turned my neighbors against me. By coming to my office, while I was working, he could also destroy my career. The shorter of the two cops cuffed my hands behind my back. I turned to Gabrielle. Her giant eyes stared at me and tried to dart away at the same time. I needed to speak up. I forced my mouth to work.

"Please, Gabrielle. Call the number on the first page of my notebook by my chair. Roman Miller. Tell him I'm being arrested." She opened her mouth to say something like, "How could you?" Or, "No. I refuse to get involved." But I stopped her. "Please," I repeated. "Please."

CHAPTER 44

JAIL

I DIDN'T SAY A WORD DURING THE DRIVE TO THE POLICE station. I rode with the uniformed officers, not with Detective Jackson. The back of the police car smelled like human sweat and strawberry bubble gum. The seat looked old and worn, but clean. The impotent door handle was scratched up, probably by passengers refusing to believe they were locked in. This was the first time I had ever been in a police car.

When we arrived at the police station, I was handed off to many different people in slightly different apparel, each with a different job. I was patted down thoroughly but not aggressively. My personal effects were placed into a bag. My mugshot was taken. It happened so fast I couldn't think about what expression to make. I ended up looking numb. Then my fingerprints were taken. I knew they were already on file somewhere since I had to have them taken before I worked at the juvenile detention center. I thought about this redundancy in the massive bureaucratic justice system as I gave in and relaxed each digit, and watched all ten be placed in ink and rolled onto paper. I was sure that some departments had laser scanners, but this station felt old-school.

I was then told to sit. At some point a van would be taking me to jail, but there might be a delay. A long, hard wooden bench ran the length of the large open room that sat off the cluttered, bustling bullpen. Several of the fluorescent overhead lights were out, so the space had a dim, serene feel. I sat far to one side of the bench, so I could lean against the corner wall. I no longer had my phone in my possession, so I had no idea how much time I was there. But I was pretty good at gauging time in fifty-minute intervals. I was sure I waited for hours. I could hear employee grumbles and gleaned there was some sort of backlog at the station. Someone didn't show up to work because he was sick and someone else messed something up and things were not moving smoothly. I paid attention to the comings and goings. A meth head was dragged in screaming. A battered girlfriend was begging for her abusive boyfriend to not be detained. A housewife was complaining that her stolen Tesla had still not been found. I listened and I watched.

I heard other things too. It was surreal to be there, arrested for murder, yet sitting quietly like a child outside a principal's office. In a way I was no different from my five-year-old self, eavesdropping. And then something extraordinary happened. Two men in different shades of dark blue suits happened to be on their coffee break. They happened to stroll through the annex I was perched in, and they happened to mention a few key phrases. Like *Thai restaurant.* And *shooting.* And *undercover.* I knew what I'd heard in passing would change Gabrielle's life. And I wanted to get the hell out of there. Get to the next step in the process. Not for my own well-being, but because I desperately needed to talk to her.

I was finally brought to jail in a van that smelled brand-new. I was the only passenger in the back. And again I sat quietly and still. I had a sense I needed to store my energy for what was to come. I was immediately placed in a holding pen. I looked around at the other women, wondering who had been arrested for drugs, or prostitution, or various other victimless crimes. And who, like me, had been arrested for murder.

I was terrified, way more than when I heard Detective Jackson's banging on my office door. Here, in this cement holding pen with actual metal bars lining the only exit, I was a galaxy away from my element. Unsure about the next steps. Stripped of my free will. Trapped with criminals. But then it dawned on me: These women were my peers. Because I was also a criminal. I breathed slowly in and out, to calm my nerves, but the stale air felt ragged and jagged and it kept catching right below my throat.

Three of the women in the pen seemed to already be lifelong friends. I wondered if they in fact were, or if perhaps they had just bonded in the past hour. I wanted to ask them, to join in, but thought better of it. Instead I stayed quiet and kept listening. Doing this had served me well so far. The women talked about how bad traffic has gotten in Miami, with all the new construction. They were normal women living in this world, experiencing traffic like everyone else.

Another woman rocked back and forth in the corner, muttering to herself. I thought for sure she needed mental health care, not jail time. A fifth woman sort of stared at me. And I thought, being in jail wasn't what I'd expected at all. It felt more like waiting at the DMV than waiting in a small cage full of miscreants.

Then the woman who was staring at me stood up. She was a big lady, and her young face showed enough suffering to last a lifetime. She walked over to my side of the cell. I stiffened, and wondered what to do. I had never actually thrown a punch before. Or been punched. I had never been in a physical drag-out fight. For all my killing of people, I had led a very violence-free, peaceful life. She got closer. My heart thumped. Should I block my face? Scream for a guard? Hit her first? *Fuck, fuck, fuck.* I remembered water polo Mikey once telling me about how to punch. To keep my thumb outside my fist so it didn't break on impact. I balled up my hands. I was ready.

Then the hulking woman said, "Miss S.?"

My fear crashed away, and my adrenaline rush ebbed, leaving me depleted. I unballed my fists. When I interned at the juvenile detention center, Joyce Brody didn't want the kids to call me Ruby, since I was sort of an authority figure. But I felt Miss Simon was too formal. So I had everyone call me Miss S.

"Yes."

"It's me. Renee."

"Oh my God, Renee!"

I hugged her. For a long time. When I worked at the detention center, a lot of physical touch was not acceptable for solid, obvious reasons, but I was no longer this girl's therapist and she was no longer a girl. She had gained weight and had grown up since I last saw her, but I recognized her light brown eyes the moment she said her name. And I really needed a hug.

She asked, "What are you doing in here? You volunteering or something?"

"I wish. Sadly, no."

She was so curious about why the hell I was there, I could see her worn face bursting with questions. But she didn't want to ask. I would have been curious too. So I told her.

"My husband died, of a disease, but the cops think I killed him."

"Damn. Hard-core."

"But I didn't kill him. I'm innocent." At that, the three traffic-talking ladies started laughing. One of them said, "We all innocent in here, right, ladies?"

Then a guard came over to the cell. "Cortinez, time to go."

Renee put a gentle hand on my arm, and said, "Hang in there. And look everyone in the eye. You don't want to show any signs of weakness. Got it?"

She gave me a little squeeze of encouragement and walked out with the guard. I smiled a bit—at least I still had the ability to appreciate the irony of the tides as they turned. And I waited for my own name to be called. Having no idea if it would be in minutes, or in days.

CHAPTER 45

WALLS

I HAD SPENT ANOTHER HOUR IN THE HOLDING TANK WHEN Roman came to get me out. Just in time, minutes before I was to be moved into a jail cell to spend the night. At my arraignment that afternoon, I stood before a judge and pleaded not guilty. And Roman argued that I was born and raised in Miami, had deep ties to the community, my parents were still in town, and I ran a successful business. I was clearly not a flight risk. The judge listened, then set my bail at $2 million, double the standard for a homicide case. The city was watching, and so I was to be made an example of and was lucky to have been granted bail at all.

I put my house up as collateral and my parents put their house up as collateral. They didn't for a moment think I'd murdered Jason. They knew me, and they knew if I was unhappy, having an affair or whatever nonsense, I simply would have gotten a divorce. And they knew the idea that I would kill him for money was completely off base. If having money was my end-all mission in life, I would have gone to business school after Yale, and not gotten a doctorate in psychology. It was a wonderful way to make a good living, it was a career I was passionate about, it was fulfilling and challenging, and it certainly didn't scream money-hungry murdering bitch, no matter how Detective Keith Jackson and Gertrude tried to spin it.

Knowing my parents believed I was innocent gave me comfort. And the idea that my childhood home was being used to keep me from spending months in jail while awaiting my trial made all my memories there even more profound. Those walls raised me, and now those walls were still keeping me safe as long as they could. I would never run and let the government take those walls away from my parents. I would stay in my hometown, and face whatever was to come next.

Once my bail was posted, I walked out of jail with Roman by my side, and although this was a huge moment for me, I could only think of Gabrielle. I had to tell her what I had overheard at the police station as soon as possible. As I walked away from the building toward the car Roman had waiting for me, hordes of people with cameras yelled, "Over here!" and, "Ruby, did you do it?" and, "What's your defense?" They snapped photo after photo of me, and the chaos ripped me away from my thoughts about Gabrielle. I didn't know where to look, where to turn. I tried to lean into Roman to use him as a shield, without seeming meek.

I noticed an ABC news van parked up ahead and my stomach flipped. Like a Pavlovian response my brain lit up and I thought, *Jason must be here! I miss him so much. Maybe I can see him soon. He must be one of the men behind the giant news cameras resting on a sturdy shoulder.* Then I remembered, *Of course he's not here. He's dead. I'm here because he's dead.* A ripple of sadness shuddered through me in that second, and I heard *click, click, click.*

Dozens of photographers caught the moment. And that would be the picture that was most shown by my supporters. "Look at her face. You can't fake that kind of sorrow. Clearly Ruby Simon is a grieving widow, being mishandled by the justice system and the gossipmongers."

But there was another side to the coin. The people who were sure I was guilty had their own favorite picture of me, often printed next to headlines that read something like, "Hometown Husband Killer." That picture was also taken outside the jail, several moments after my ripple of sadness smoothed out, and a wry smile passed over my lips. As Roman directed me through the stinging swarm of reporters, he whispered about how ridiculously hot the stenographer was at the bail hearing. His comment was comforting because it reminded me that no matter how bad life got, there were constants I could count on. Like him being a lothario. And so I smiled, a tiny little bit. And it felt nice to allow my mouth to turn upward after months of frowns. But that wry smile was captured on camera and was plastered everywhere to give a visual of the callous husband killer, now out on bail.

Roman apologized profusely for his bad timing with his extremely out-of-vogue objectification of the hot lady, but I knew the rabble would have gotten the shot they wanted one way or another. If it wasn't at that moment, it would have been another moment in which I had the audacity to briefly seem happy or at peace. I didn't blame him.

Just as I got past the densest mash of people outside the jailhouse, and thought I might be safe from any further serious trauma, I heard a voice I recognized. My skin crawled with malice.

"Ruby!"

I looked over, and there, on the outskirts of the crowd,

wearing a modest black mourning dress with one tasteful frog brooch pinned to the neck, was Gertrude. I wanted to rush ahead and dive into my waiting car. She had already stolen so much from me, I did not want to give her another second of my time. But my feet stopped moving. They planted down. My lizard brain would not flee from her. It wanted to fight. I squared my shoulders and stood still. My stillness got the attention of the throng and everyone hushed. It was so quiet for a moment the only sound was the click click click of cameras. All eyes were on the mother and the widow, having a standoff like two cowboys in the center of a dusty town, ready to draw and shoot.

I knew Gertrude wanted me to lash out and seem like a maniac. And that her move would be to seem calm and sane and heartbroken. To look like a saint in front of all this press. So I had to get there first.

I gushed with sincerity and relief, "Oh, Gertrude. I'm so glad you're here! Your support means the world to me. Thank you."

Before she could respond, I ducked my head into my car. Roman got in quickly behind me and shut the door. We drove off. I'm sure a cameraman caught her miffed expression, but I never saw the photo. I did not want to take the time to look for it.

Once I was released on bail, all four of the "deaths in my orbit" were public news, and I was the most salacious and talked-about story in Miami. I pushed the strippers-selling-illegal-exotic-reptiles-in-the-Champagne-room scandal that had been dominating the news to the second page. And no one cared to read about the gang shoot-outs at Miami International Airport anymore. And the story about the mayor getting caught smoking meth with a male prostitute seemed old hat. These other local news stories were exciting, but they didn't elicit much debate, so they faded to the background. My story stayed in the news because I created a city divided. A wall of belief separated those who thought I was a hardworking, caring, loving wife and therapist and those who thought that I was, as one paper dubbed me, "the Purple Widow." A take on the ruthless black widow moniker but substituting in what was clearly my favorite color.

Reporters dredged up hundreds of old photos of me wearing purple clothes. And everything I had ever signed or written in pen was in purple ink. My emails were sent in purple text. And my front door and window trim were painted purple. Jason was so accepting of my love of the hue, he had no issue with it being the accent color on our house.

Gossip traveled and gained speed like it was rolling downhill. "Four dead people and those are only the ones we know about!" "Maybe she's killed hundreds!" "I heard she only uses one pen at a time. Total psycho."

I hoped the Purple Widow sobriquet would go away, but it stuck, and soon every news source in the county adopted it. And Hannah, who never thought for a second that I killed her father until Detective Jackson visited her and all this blew up, was now totally convinced of it. And she gave interviews about me whenever she could, showed photos of us from high school, and used my infamy to propel her own business. She created a Vampire in the Sun T-shirt that read, "Killed by the Purple Widow." The batch sold out in less than an hour, and she was then courted to sell her entire line in department stores nationally. I wasn't even angry. *Good for her*, I thought. *Let her make millions off my misfortune.* Because the truth was, I did kill her disgusting rapist of a father.

Hannah wasn't the only one to profit off my ruinous life. Jason's former place of employment had a leg up because unlike the other news stations, they had insider information. They ran in-depth interviews with the on-camera anchors who had had the pleasure of working with him. And who had also met me at various holiday parties and birthday parties and some who even attended our wedding in Key West.

"Were you shocked to hear this development that Ruby Simon was a suspect in Jason's death?"

"Did you feel like she was a cold-blooded killer? Excuse me, an 'alleged' cold-blooded killer?"

"Could you sense something was off about her?"

"Did Jason express he felt unsafe in his own home?"

"What signs were there, if any, that Jason was in danger?"

"And what signs can you, the viewer at home, look out for in preventing your own possible murder? Stay tuned until after the weather to find out!"

Gertrude was also interviewed a lot. She came across as reasonable and trustworthy and heartbroken that her only child was dead. When she was pretending to be nervous about saying too much, she would fidget with her necklace, a gold chain with a small gold frog charm. Her face and voice and existence filled me with so much rage that I thought about driving to her house and stabbing her to death. With a blade so small it would take hundreds of thrusts and cause her maximum pain before she expired. And then sitting in the bloodbath and waiting for Detective Jackson to arrive and haul me off to jail again. I thought witnessing her last gasp might be worth a life in prison, behind steel bars and inside concrete walls. Just put me away for killing her, and forget you ever accused me of killing her son.

But I would not drive over to murder her. Because I thought of Ellie and my adorable niece. I thought of my parents, who believed in my innocence and goodness. And I knew that I couldn't shatter all that. So instead of stabbing Gertrude to death, I turned off her sanctimonious interviews.

Photos of my wedding surfaced, although I never gave anyone permission to release them, and it seemed nothing about my marriage was private anymore. I was losing Jason all over again because I was losing what remained of our intimacy to a city devouring my story. The news station Jason had worked for was now running trashy segments about my drug-fueled youth, when just months before they were running conscientious type-1-diabetes-awareness campaigns.

And slowly a city divided seemed not so divided anymore. The wall got chipped away and broken down and became a pile of rubble. The city finally united in what they deemed my clear guilt. Because in the end it was more fun for the public to hate me than to believe me. And the good citizens of Miami wanted to see me pay for my many sins. "The electric chair for the Purple Widow!" I was not allowed to travel, as part of my bail agreement, so I was stuck staying in the city I dearly loved as it turned against me. I couldn't go to my favorite corner coffee shop without encountering angry stares. I couldn't go to the beach without being surrounded by untrusting lifeguards. I couldn't step outside my house without hearing spiteful whispers from my purple door. I was stuck inside my own walls.

Most of my clients stopped seeing me. And the few who kept coming didn't want to talk about their own issues. Instead they just wanted to ask me questions about all the allegations. "Did you do it?" "Any of it?" "What was it like being in jail?" "Come on. You sort of enjoy all the attention, right?"

I kept calling Gabrielle, but she was still avoiding me. Even though I made it clear in my messages that I understood why she no longer wanted to see me as a therapist and I was not trying to convince her otherwise. I pleaded with her. "I need to tell you something. I'd rather not leave it on your voicemail. Please, just give me five minutes to talk." But she still didn't call me back.

Within one week of my arrest, I had to give up on trying to maintain any normalcy in my life, and I closed down my therapy practice. The other tenants in my office building complained about the constant news crews camped outside hoping to catch a glimpse or a sound bite from the Purple Widow. They also complained about working alongside a serial killer. I saw the building manager skulking about in her wedge heels, near the elevators, trying to gather up her courage. She finally lightly tapped on my office door and apologetically asked me to give up my lease.

"I will issue you a refund, of course. And pay for any inconvenience this might cause. Reimburse you for your business cards that have this address on them. Anything like that. Anything you want."

She seemed so frightened of me, like I might murder her too, right then and there. It was heartbreaking. I told her I completely understood her position and I gave up my office without a fight. I didn't want my drama and deeds to bring down any more of the innocent bystanders in my life.

I took my diplomas off the walls. I left the merlot-colored trash can I had bought. It matched the love seat so nicely I felt it would be a pity to break up the pair. The next tenant would be in need of a trash can anyway. I debated about the orchid. I had been putting a fresh one in the office every few months. I found they were a perfect focal point if a patient was starting to have a panic attack. I would ask them to stare at the flower. "Describe the color." "Describe the shape of the petals." "What does the stem look like?" And after a few minutes of being in the moment with the flower, the person's amorphous generalized panic would always fade away.

I sat in the love seat and looked at the orchid. The color was grape purple. The kind of shade that is striking on a flower but not quite right for clothes or upholstery. The five petals fanned out, like two elephant ears on top of a plane propeller. The stem was bright green and thin and elegant.

I burst into tears. My body curdled with violent sobs. And the snot came out. Finally. It felt like all the tar from all the grief from my entire life, and maybe even past lives if they existed, was shaken free. And it flowed. I allowed it to flow. I curled up in the fetal position and wailed. I felt the tears drip down my face and saw them darken the merlot-colored fabric of the love seat. I then sank down to the floor, like the closer I could get to the earth, the more comforted I would feel. I pictured falling through all the other office floors until I landed in a heap of wet rubble. With bay water lapping at my broken body and spirit.

Was I being punished? Did Jason die because I was evil and did not deserve to be happy? I asked the orchid these questions. It stared back at me, open and purple and silent. And in the silence I found my answer. Jason died because he had a terrible disease. He died because his pancreas didn't work. There was nothing more to it and nothing less. Just like Gabrielle was not responsible for Derrick's death, I was not responsible for Jason's. I couldn't let the public's perception of me erode my belief in myself. I stood up. And walked out for the final time. I left the orchid where it sat.

CHAPTER 46

OMISSION

I KNEW THE MOMENT I WALKED IN THAT SOMETHING WAS wrong. More wrong than the obvious facts that my husband was dead, my career was destroyed, my city loathed me, and I was awaiting my murder trial that was months away. Out on bail, I had nothing to do but wait. Roman was doing his job, preparing to prove my innocence. My only job was to carry on as best I could. I sat down, unsure what was going to happen next.

Alisha said, "I've been thinking a lot about you. Reviewing our years together. And I need to know, when we discussed your salt nightmares, why is it you never mentioned being in the ocean as a child with a young boy who drowned?"

Alisha lived in the same city as me, so of course she had seen the newspapers and the television coverage. Of course she had heard the gossip. Of course, as my longtime therapist, she was contacted by Detective Jackson. And of course she told him that she could not reveal any information about me. Not that she had any to reveal that would have helped his case anyway. And of course she had learned about the other three dead bodies in my wake. I knew she was smart enough to know that I was too smart to not have made the possible salt connection in my own mind. Salty ocean water, boy dying, nightmares about salt. So I couldn't feign surprise and say, "Oh! I never thought about it that way!" Especially since she was well aware that I loved thinking about everything in many different ways. She knew delving into the human psyche to uncover all sorts of hidden subconscious hints into what makes a person tick was both my profession and my favorite hobby.

"I didn't want to talk about it," was my response.

"Why?"

I couldn't tell her that I had grabbed Duncan's ankle and held him under the salty ocean water until he stopped flopping. I couldn't tell her way back when I was a freshman in college, and I still couldn't tell her now. If I admitted it, it could be her duty to report me. Murder is one of the few things doctor-patient confidentiality does not cover, especially if the doctor believes the patient might murder again. Even though I was only five years old. Even though it was over twenty-five years ago. Murder, like death, had no time limit.

I reviewed my options. I could lie and say it was all too painful to talk about, so when I uncovered the slug connection and my nightmares went away, I felt there was no reason to revisit the horror of that sunny day. Or I could say I was ashamed that I was so happy when Duncan died, since he had bullied my sister. But the problem with having been in therapy for so many years with the same therapist and having been honest about so many other things was that Alisha would know these were lies. I certainly hadn't felt ashamed about being happy when Evelyn W. had died. So it wouldn't track that I was ashamed about Duncan. And the idea that I wouldn't talk about something painful also didn't fit. Since I did openly discuss so many other painful topics.

Alisha watched me as I sifted through all this. And she wasn't going to back down. She asked, "Why did you never tell me your friend's father died when you were sleeping over?" Her question reminded me of how shocked Ameena was to learn of this fact.

Again, I couldn't brush it off by saying I didn't think to discuss it since it held no importance, when I had spent plenty of hours telling Alisha everything else about my childhood and my childhood friends. She knew about when I found a rhinestone in a sandbox and was certain it was a magical gem. It was then that I learned the word *talisman* and looked it up in the giant dictionary. She knew about when I lent Erika my favorite jeans and then she got her period for the first time and started crying and I told her it was okay and we washed the blood out together in her kitchen sink. I even told Alisha about Hannah's store and how cool it was that gothy Gabrielle was one of her biggest clients. So it absolutely would make no sense that I would never think to mention to Alisha that Hannah's father died a horrible death twelve carpeted steps below where I was sleeping.

Alisha knew that by omitting these giant events in my life, I was clearly hiding something. And the only something it could be was my guilt. Not emotional guilt necessarily, but criminal guilt. And for Alisha, these other two deaths coming to light put a new sheen on Evelyn W. walking out into the street in front of a truck. As Roman promised, the video had not leaked, so the impact of people actually seeing me lead Evelyn to her death was not an issue. But the detail that I had been there on that curb when she got struck did get out. I was so shortsighted to not have seen this problem heading my way. To not realize that once my life compartments were destroyed, Alisha would want to know what the fuck I had been hiding.

I looked at her and all I could say was, "I didn't kill Jason."

She said, "I believe you."

This was a huge relief. I believed that she did believe me. She had heard me talk about my intense bond with him for years. How his influence had morphed me into the type of person who would buy a silly souvenir at a tourist gift shop so I would have a tangible item to connect with a memory. Yeah, maybe then I would put that token in a labeled box stored neatly in a closet, but I would own it and that counted for personal growth. She knew that sex between me and Jason seemed to matter every single time. That our intimacy and passion kept growing. She knew I loved him deeply. Yet there was still tension in the air. I wished it would go away.

She then said, "But, Ruby, I think you had a hand in the other three deaths. I don't know exactly how or why, but I no longer trust you. And because I don't trust you, I can no longer in good faith advise you. And because I can no longer advise you, it would be unethical of me to continue to be your therapist." She did not follow that up with, "And how does that make you feel?" She let it hang in the air, like a single shelf bound by indestructible wall brackets. Had she asked, I would have said it made me feel abandoned. It made me feel alone. After thirteen years of sitting on her couch, she was breaking up with me.

Until that moment I had thought Alisha was the best therapist I would ever know. But I would not give up on someone the way she had given up on me. I vowed to be a better therapist than her. I vowed to reach Gabrielle and tell her what I needed to tell her, even if she didn't want to listen. She had now blocked my number. Making it abundantly clear that she no longer wanted to see me or hear from me ever again. She thought I was dangerous. So, I had no choice but to track her down and meet her in person.

CHAPTER 47

ABSOLUTION

THE HUMAN BRAIN TRIES TO FIND CONNECTIONS. ALWAYS and constantly. We strive to create order in chaos by linking together cause and effect in our search for meaning. This is called fate by some. Science, religion, superstition, or karma by others. I understood this about the human condition from a clinical standpoint, yet couldn't untangle my own need to piece together the events of my life in search of a master plan. I knew logically that one event had nothing to do with another, yet when I laid it out linearly, I was sure my entire journey up until this point was designed for the purpose of giving Gabrielle closure. When I thought in those terms, I could calm the gnawing uncertainty in my mind and body. I could worry less about my unknown future because my present mission was so clear.

I knew Gabrielle's schedule pretty well because, similarly to how I discussed my daily minutiae with Alisha, Gabrielle discussed hers with me. For about a year she had been able to fully support herself writing, so she no longer bartended. She usually worked from her one-bedroom apartment on Fourteenth Street and Ocean Drive. I did know her exact address but felt showing up at her home would definitely seem too aggressive on my part. I needed to see her in a public setting, so she wouldn't feel as threatened.

So I went to drag queen bingo at the Standard hotel on the Venetian Causeway. It was a retro space, filled with modern tastemakers. The event was held every Monday night, and Gabrielle was a regular. It started at seven and finished at ten. So I got there at 6:45 to be sure not to miss her. I wore a baseball cap pulled way down, paid my twenty dollars, and hoped no one would recognize me. I sat down with my bingo card and played so I would fit in. Glancing up every so often to look for her. I hit bingo but did not raise my hand. I didn't need the added attention. Gabrielle never showed up.

I had to wait another whole week to try and see her again, and I kept myself mostly at home cocooned with Mr. Cat, giving him the new insulin that hadn't been seized as evidence and letting him indulge in the running faucet. I had dinner with my parents several times. Not out. Always in. Away from strangers and now-unfriendly friends.

That next Monday night I went back to bingo. Gabrielle walked in with two friends at ten minutes to seven. Based on her descriptions in therapy, I knew immediately who these friends were. The tall one with the blunt bangs was Lola, and she had just had an abortion because she had slept with two different guys in the same week and couldn't handle having a baby without knowing who the father was during the pregnancy. Gabrielle thought this was a bullshit reason and wanted Lola to just admit she was having an abortion because she didn't want a baby at all, which was totally okay. I had gently reminded Gabrielle not to be judgmental since no one could really know what Lola was going through except for Lola. The shorter girl with a blond pixie cut was Kat and she probably had a drinking problem, although Gabrielle wasn't sure if it was something she should address with her or not. I asked Gabrielle if the situation was in reverse, and it was Gabrielle with the possible drinking problem, would she want Kat to mention it to her? Gabrielle said, "Yes. That's what friends are for. To look out for each other." And so there was her answer.

I didn't want to wait for Gabrielle to spot me first because I didn't want her to feel like I was lurking. So I walked right up to her, again wearing my baseball cap pulled low. She seemed confused and disoriented. Then embarrassed. Like when you're a kid and you randomly see one of your teachers out in public and not in the classroom. Seeing your therapist in public has the same effect. Therapists are people too and it's extremely weird to think about. They have wants and needs and allergies and cars and different outfits. Thinking about it too much is enough to make a person dizzy.

Usually if a therapist sees a patient out and about, they might make eye contact in acknowledgment and then ignore the patient. Therapists don't want to overstep their boundaries, so they leave it up to the patient to make the first move. Maybe the patient says, "Hello." Maybe they give a quick smile and a wave. Maybe they avoid the entire thing, dart out of the vicinity, and then talk about it incessantly in their next session. Some people overdo it and yell out, "Ha! That's my therapist! Oh my God, this is so weird!" One of these four responses usually happens. But this was not a usual circumstance.

Gabrielle quickly processed how odd it was to run into me there; then I saw a look of paranoia sweep over her face. It occurred to her that I knew everything about her and her two friends. She willed me with her eyes to please not say anything about anything. To please not sabotage her life by exploiting all her secrets at drag queen bingo. Of course I would never. Besides the obvious fact that it would be absolutely unethical and cruel, I could lose my license over that sort of behavior. I might have been accused of murder, but I still had my license and a strong sense of professional ethics. Then I saw a new expression on her face. Her paranoia turned into fear. I wanted to put my hand on her arm, to comfort her. But I stopped just shy, not wanting to seem physically threatening in any way. So instead I seemed awkward as I jerked my arm back down.

"Gabrielle, I just need five minutes."

Even after all these years of being her therapist, I couldn't predict her behavior for sure. It wasn't an exact science. She might scream. Or run. Or punch me in the face like I almost did to Renee. She looked around the crowded hotel lobby, decorated in high-end plastic furniture and neon kitsch, filled with aging drag queens and young hipsters wearing rompers, and she weighed her options.

I caught her searching eyes and said, "I promise you. After I tell you what I need to tell you, I will leave you alone forever."

This was clearly what she wanted most, and she wanted it to start as soon as possible. She turned to her friends. "I'll be back in five minutes. If I'm not, get security. And the real police."

Ouch. But I understood.

I inched her into a corner of the main lobby, where it was sort of private. And I explained. "When I was little, like a tiny child, I loved to eavesdrop, to gain insight into a world much larger than my own. And I was really good at it. I sort of melted into the scenery and I heard all sorts of things I wasn't supposed to hear and I almost never got caught listening in."

"What the fuck are you trying to say?"

"When I got arrested, I had to wait at the police station for hours. People came in and out. Conversations were had. I sat quietly, watching the ruckus of criminals struggling against cops, drug addicts going through withdrawal, all types of screaming to no one in particular that life wasn't fair. And soon enough no one even noticed I was still sitting there."

"And?"

"I overheard a couple detectives talking about the undercover Fed who was gunned down at a Thai restaurant several years back. And that the intel he got before he was found out and killed was enough to finally put away the boss of a drug-trafficking ring that spanned from Havana all the way to Montreal."

She stared at me, trying to understand.

"Derrick was an undercover FBI agent. That's why you could never find his family or friends. That's why there is no trace of him. That wasn't his real name."

Gabrielle turned even whiter than normal. Then a heat rose to her face, and I could see patches of red crawling up her neck and onto her cheeks.

"Here is the most important part," I said. "That man with the gun went to that restaurant *specifically* to kill Derrick. It wasn't random. *He* was the target because his cover had somehow been blown. So he didn't die for you, or because of you. He was going to be killed anyway. Italian or Thai. It was *him* who put *you* in harm's way that night. Not the other way around. Do you understand?"

She kept looking at me blankly. Her mind was desperately trying to rewrite a story she had etched in stone so long ago.

"I'm sure that's why he hesitated when you first asked him out. The hesitation was about his own life, his own secrets. Could he and should he let someone in? It had nothing to do with you. Do you hear me? What I'm saying to you, Gabrielle, is you are absolved. Date other men. Be open to love. Live your life! Let go of this weight that should never have been on your shoulders."

She started to weep. I could feel her releasing years of guilt and tension. It was such a natural reaction for me to hug her, so I did. And she wept on my shoulder. Just like I wept on hers when Kangaroo died.

"Thank you," she said.

I felt a little lighter. I had helped her. I had done my job. In a way she was an extension of me. And doing right by her lifted me up. But before I got too attached to the notion that her absolution had anything to do with my own, Lola and Kat rushed over. Lola yelled, "It's been five minutes!" They saw that Gabrielle was crying and assumed I was to blame. They knew exactly who I was. Lola hissed, "If you don't leave now, we're calling the cops!" As I walked out, Gabrielle gave me a tired little nod. I knew she was now free. The only question remaining was, would I ever be free?

CHAPTER 48

DNA

AS PROMISED, BEFORE MY ACTUAL TRIAL WAS UNDER WAY, Roman got to work making sure all the hearsay about the mysterious deaths of Duncan Reese and Richard Vale and Evelyn W. was thrown out. Even if I was in the vicinity, I was never a suspect in any of those deaths, none of which were even considered murders at the crucial point when evidence was at its freshest, witnesses were at their sharpest, and the police were at their most motivated to solve the cases. On top of that, those other "crimes" didn't establish any kind of modus operandi. It wasn't like I had gone around shooting people up with insulin for years and had finally been caught doing it to my own husband. Therefore, those three other deaths had nothing whatsoever to do with the indictment at hand.

Roman told me that the judge listened to him, and agreed that any mention of the other deaths just served as a character assassination, which was inadmissible in trial. How they were going to find an impartial jury who hadn't already seen all the news about

Duncan Reese and Richard Vale and Evelyn W. was a different problem. But Roman kept telling me, one thing at a time. This pace was especially difficult for me, since I always wanted to get the syllabus over with. But the justice system could not be rushed. And so my anxiety of not knowing what would happen to me next had to be handled. Benita let me visit the birds after hours. So I would be alone, away from judging eyes, able to live in the moment of each wing twitch and feather ruffle. We never discussed it, but I got the sense that she believed someone so caring to animals could never kill a human. Unless they deserved it.

With the background noise stripped away, all the assistant district attorney had was the fact that my husband died of complications from low blood sugar, I had access to insulin and the know-how to use it, and my motives to murder him were threefold. One, money. Two, a probable affair with my veterinarian. Three, and most damning, Jesula's testimony that I was unhappily married. Since she was a regular part of our household, her testimony held a lot of weight. Of all the things I dreaded about my upcoming trial, having to watch her twist my marriage into something ugly and listen to her lies about my anger issues and odd behavior after Jason died was at the top.

My thirty-first birthday came and went. It felt meaningless. The only date that mattered was nine business days away. My trial would begin. While I bided my time, Roman flew back and forth from Miami to DC constantly. He had several ongoing cases. I was one of many, of course, but I knew I was his priority. And at least mingled in with all the tragedy of my entire situation, him being back in my life gave me a glimmer of joy. I could sometimes forget my troubles for a moment or even for an hour. We would jog on the beach together. We would reminisce. We would gossip about people we once both knew.

After one of our long sunset runs, when my thighs ached and my heart pounded so hard my thoughts were mercifully drowned out, Roman turned to me. "Can I tell you something?"

I panted, "Well, yeah. You have to now."

My heart thumped even harder. I was worried and expected the worst. The past year had taught me to always expect the worst, which I hated about my new self. I had turned into a pessimist. Roman saw my expression.

"No, no. It's not bad. It's fun. Kind of. It's stupid. It's about Jake and Melody, from college. They got divorced a few years ago."

Those old wounds seemed so shallow to me, so insignificant and superficial compared to the deep wounds I now faced. Perspective and age could not be rushed.

I said, "I'm not shocked."

He said, "Some leggy pregnant flight attendant showed up at the front door of their Victorian revival, claiming Jake was the father of her unborn baby. He denied, denied, denied. Melody believed him until the woman had the kid, named him Theo, and got a court-ordered DNA test."

"And . . . ?"

"And the DNA was a match to Jake."

"Duh." I took a beat. "But how do you know all this?"

Roman looked sheepish. "Yeah. I'm about to tell you that part. Melody was so furious with him, she wanted all sorts of revenge. So before she officially left him for good, she looked me up and she called me. She said Jake still despised me since I ratted him out in college, and she needed to unleash some rage. Onto my dick."

"She did not say that."

"Well, no. Not a direct quote. But it was implied."

"So . . . ?"

"So I met her in Vegas. And we didn't leave the hotel suite once all weekend."

"Ahhhh. You finally got the girl."

"Are you mad?"

"No, I'm not mad. It's just amazing to me how given enough time life has a way of working itself out."

"I wanted so badly to call you! I almost did, literally from the hotel bathroom. I knew you would appreciate the epilogue. But I got scared."

"Scared of what?"

Roman shrugged. "I guess not knowing if you still hated me was easier than making the call and finding out for sure that you still did."

I understood. "Schrödinger's cat."

"Smarty-pants."

I smiled at Roman. And asked, "Did you ever see her again?"

"Fuck no."

I laughed. My heartbeat was now slow enough to pick up the pace again and race Roman home. Where I would continue to expect the worst.

CHAPTER 49

JESULA

I HAD THREE MORE DAYS OF TRUE FREEDOM AHEAD OF ME. It was pouring rain. Miami had beautiful tropical storms that came through almost every afternoon, raging for an hour and then retreating into the sky without a trace like they had never existed at all. I looked out my window and watched as the billowing clouds slowly crept over my roof. And my doorbell rang. I had installed security cameras since my front yard was often vandalized, and reporters and strangers and haters and curious tourists always lingered outside. But I couldn't imagine who would choose to stand out there in this storm. I looked and saw it was Roman. He wasn't supposed to be back in Miami until tomorrow. And he hadn't called to warn me he was coming sooner. Something very bad must have happened. Something so bad he had to tell me in person. Like cancer.

He was soaked, his wet dress shirt clinging to his abs. One of his curls flopped in front of his eye because it was now straightened with the weight of water. Without a word he grabbed me. He picked me up off the floor and spun me around, and raindrops careened off him and hit everything from my grandmother's tiny clocks to Mr. Cat's fluttering tail. My pathetic-looking sweatpants and faded T-shirt with no bra were now also soaked. Roman set me down.

He said, "Get dressed. We've been summoned to the judge's chambers."

"Why?"

"I'm not sure."

"Then why do you seem happy?"

"I'm just a happy guy. Throw on something." He took inventory of me. "Normal-looking."

Since most clients paid him $1,000 an hour, and I was now curious, I didn't want to waste any time. I threw reputable clothes on my body, grabbed my nice but not too flashy purse, and we headed out my purple door.

The judge's office was extremely masculine. Leather-bound law tomes placed neatly in sturdy bookcases lined one entire wall. The large desk in the center of the small room was burl oak. The throw rug underneath it was drab olive. The desk was covered with enough papers and folders to demonstrate that the judge worked hard, and was arranged in a way that conveyed he respected order. Peeking out from behind a large brass lamp on the corner of the desk was a picture frame. It caught my eye because it was pink, and nothing else in the room was brightly colored. I craned my neck and saw a child's drawing inside the frame. Clearly cherished, it was the only personal item the judge seemed to have in his office. The drawing read, in multicolored bubble letters, "World's Best Grandpa."

The man in fact looked like the world's best grandpa. When I walked into the room and saw him for the first time, I wanted to sit on his lap and tell him what I wished for for Christmas. Which was to have Jason back and to not have to be in that office at all. The judge had a full head of gray hair and twinkling gray eyes that matched in color. We had that in common. I then saw, sitting in the corner in a mismatched chair clearly brought in to provide enough seating for everyone, Jesula.

She looked at me. And I felt like a schoolgirl. Hurt and shunned on the playground. But with life-and-death stakes instead of hopscotch hierarchy. I knew I could handle the judge, especially with Roman by my side, but seeing Jesula made me feel vulnerable. It was hard to keep up my guile. And then I saw a shift as her face turned mournful. She too was feeling vulnerable.

The judge beckoned for Roman and me to sit, and said this was all very irregular. But it was necessary. Jesula had come to see him, and she requested she be able to explain her behavior to me, in a formal setting. Roman and I sat in the two chairs that matched the room. And we both looked toward her.

Jesula's voice was usually smooth and confident, even when it was quiet. But it cracked and sputtered as she said, "Ruby, I'm sorry. I'm sorry."

I wasn't sure what was coming, so I just listened. And she told her story.

"Gertrude Hollander came to my apartment. She found out where I lived because she followed me home from your house one day. About three months ago. I didn't know who she was. Since, why would I? She was very friendly. Said she was Jason's mother and that she wanted to help me. I knew he didn't talk to her, but I thought maybe she had something important to say. So I let her in."

My stomach turned, and I was sure I could feel my telomeres quiver in disgust.

"After a few minutes, I saw she wasn't friendly. She was an enemy. And I understood why Jason didn't talk to her. But then, she offered me ten thousand dollars to exaggerate stories about you. To say you were unhappy with Jason. To say you had a nasty temper. To help convince people that you murdered him." Jesula stopped talking for a moment. Her shame got the best of her, and she needed a breath.

She continued, "I said no way. That I would never lie about you. And that I would never lie in court, to the American government. I kicked her out of my apartment. I thought to call you, but you were under so much stress already. So I was going to keep it secret. But then she came back the next day. I didn't answer my door. But she came back again. And she wouldn't go away. And she threatened to make sure I was deported out of the USA and taken away from my son." Jesula was devastated by the thought of it. "My son!"

I nodded, starting to understand.

"Gertrude told me since I was an illegal immigrant from Haiti that I had no real rights. Unless I did what she wanted, she would make sure I was dragged away and put in a detention camp for years. And I watch the news. I'm not dumb. I know this happens to people, to immigrants, every single day. I couldn't, I couldn't take the chance this would happen to me and my son. So I took her money and I told the lies."

I looked at Roman, unsure what all this would ultimately mean. Behind his solemn expression was a tiny grin. So tiny only someone who knew his face as well as their own could see it.

Jesula continued, "And once I took her money, I couldn't keep coming to your house. I couldn't look at your face and pretend that I wasn't doing a horrible thing to you behind your back. And after you got arrested, I couldn't sleep. I couldn't eat. I could barely live with myself. I took the bribe to protect my son, and our life together, but what kind of mother could I ever be to him knowing my lies caused you, a person who has always been so kind to me, to live the rest of her life in prison?"

Now that she had gotten it all out, she was able to look at me again. "I'm sorry. Please, forgive me. Please." I had already forgiven her. The second I heard the name Gertrude. I knew that woman was evil and cunning and manipulative and intelligent. And could turn good people into her pawns.

"I do forgive you. And I'm sorry that my life brought that woman into yours."

I stood and Jesula stood and we hugged. And the judge watched. And Roman watched. And time stood still. The judge then spoke, and started time again. He let me know that Jesula came to him to tell him everything. That the guilt was driving her mad and so she had to come forward, and she just hoped and prayed that no one would take away her son or deport her. The judge looked at her now, and assured her she would not be deported. And no one would take her son. I believed him. Because he was the world's best grandpa.

Jesula's story was easy for the judge's clerks to confirm. Exactly $10,000 had in fact been taken out of Gertrude's savings account, and later that day Jesula cashed a money order for the same amount. More money than she had ever had at one time in her life. Of course Gertrude denied the whole thing, claiming it was Jesula who approached her, begging for money. Saying she would tell the truth about me to the police, but it would mean losing her job with me, so she needed money to cover lost wages. Gertrude, a grieving mother, was happy to pay for such worthwhile and damning testimony.

Now that I had heard how Gertrude had strong-armed Jesula,

my hurt at her betrayal was replaced by immense gratitude that she had come forward with the truth. My belief in my instincts, in knowing people and reading people correctly, was restored. Jesula did care about me. She was not a resentful enemy all those years. And now everyone involved could see what I already knew. That Gertrude was the real and only bad guy in all of this.

We all left the judge's chambers. I was so elated that Jesula was an ally that I wanted to celebrate. With good food. Fuck it if people stared. They couldn't hurt me any more than I was already hurt. I invited Jesula to join us for lunch, but she declined. She was exhausted from the lies and from the truth.

Roman and I settled into a plastic-cushioned booth at a Cuban restaurant near the courthouse. It was after the rush, so only a few other diners were in the place. They looked and whispered but kept to themselves. And the waitstaff just wanted to get their side work over with and go home. No one hassled me. I ate my entire plate of chicken and plantains and beans and rice in peace. Each bite tasted newly sweet and delicious and energizing. While there, Roman got the official phone call. He took it outside. I watched him pace on the street, through the large restaurant window. It had stopped pouring, and the sun was out. I could tell his shirt had finally fully dried. Roman strode back in, and instead of sitting on his side of the booth, he slid in next to me.

In a very official tone he told me, "Due to recent facts that have come to light about witness tampering, the assistant district attorney has moved to drop the case. The judge will sign off, and the charges against you will disappear. There will be no trial."

I didn't know what to do with all my energy. The nightmare was over. And I was wide-awake. And I wanted to run and run and run. I felt like that first time I tried cocaine. Surging with power and relief. "Let's go for a run." Roman would usually never turn down exercise, but he pointed out we just ate, and he had some work to do. So I would have to turn my energy inward for now.

Roman said there would be an official hearing where the assistant district attorney asked the judge to grant the people's motion to dismiss all charges against me. And it was my legal right to be there, if I wanted to go. But I didn't have to go. Roman would be there representing me. "Fuck yes, I want to go!" I wanted to see that "Where there's smoke, there's fire"–spouting ADA when he admitted he was wrong about me. I had no idea if Detective Jackson would be there, but if he was, I wanted to see his face as all the fruits of his unpaid overtime labor rotted on the vine. I couldn't imagine Gertrude would be there, especially since she was the start of this entire unjust mess, and she had lost. But I wouldn't underestimate her trying to pull one last stunt.

That night I went for a run on the beach by myself. The ocean reminded me of my childhood, and of Jason, and of my life as a whole up to this point. It was so big, and always changing, but also still there.

The next morning, for the first time in months, I left my house with my head held high. I even put on a little lip gloss and eyeliner and flat-ironed my hair. The hearing was very short. Detective Keith Jackson was there, and I noticed he had new pants on, ones that actually fit him. Maybe his most recent wife took him shopping. He looked glum. He listened as the ADA, a balding, wiry middle-aged man with thin metal-rimmed glasses, requested all charges against me be "dismissed in the interest of justice." Ah, justice. I made eye contact with the detective, and I knew he knew he was right about me. At least partially. Those hairs on the back of his neck were probably still standing up. I also saw Jesula there, quietly sitting in the back, watching to make sure all ended well and was made right. I wanted to talk to her afterward, to hug her again, to tell her that it was okay, really. That I 100 percent forgave her. But once the judge officially dropped all charges and said I was free to go, she slipped away before I had a chance.

Gertrude was not there. I kept glancing around the room, checking that she wasn't somehow hiding under a table or behind a curtain. She was sort of haunting me, partially because a few details about the whole bribery story didn't fully sit right. It was nagging at me. Jesula was already a United States citizen. I knew because I had helped her study for the test. And her son was born in Miami. So the threat of her being deported felt off. But I started to second-guess myself. Maybe she didn't pass the citizenship test and was too embarrassed to tell me? Or maybe in this new American climate she didn't trust her fresh citizenship to protect her? Whatever the reason, it was of no matter. She would not be deported. Her son was safe at home. And I would not go to prison.

As I watched the courtroom door close behind Jesula, Roman touched my arm to get my attention. I looked at him and couldn't discern his expression. Then he quietly said, "A video has been leaked."

CHAPTER 50

AUTONOMY

MY BRIEF ELATION DEFLATED. ROMAN HANDED ME HIS PHONE. I was sure Gertrude had somehow gotten hold of the crosswalk video, despite Roman's best efforts to keep it hidden. She would ruin me one way if not the other. But when I looked at the screen, I didn't see grainy wet security camera footage. I saw instead a crisp view of ceramic lawn frogs. And I realized I was looking at the front of Gertrude's house. A man was at her door. He spoke about being a representative of JDRF, an organization that raises money and awareness to find a cure for type 1 diabetes. He asked if perhaps Gertrude, now a bit of a public figure, would want to be a part of the cause? Since her only son had type 1. I could then see Gertrude in her door frame. The camera zoomed in a little—clearly someone was filming from the side of her yard. Gertrude spat, "Why would I support you? My son died of diabetes. So what good are you?" And she shut the door.

It took me a moment to comprehend. Then I got it. Gertrude

just admitted diabetes killed Jason, not me. And it was caught on tape. What were the odds? Who was filming it? When I asked, Roman gave a little shrug. A sly "Who cares?" It was time-stamped and out in the world. And Gertrude's credibility was gone forever. That was the important part. She could haunt me no more.

I called Ellie first. Then my parents. "I'm free!" They were immensely relieved and overjoyed, and now that the insidious pressure was removed, there was room for all the tendrils of their true feelings to spread and slither out. It's classic human nature to lie about worry when the worrying won't be helpful. And then to tell the full truth of the extent of the worry once the danger is over.

For months my family had told me not to panic. "Don't borrow trouble." "You're innocent and justice will prevail." "Roman won't let you down." "Everything is going to be okay." And now that the horror show was officially over, they all said, "Oh, thank God. We thought you were going to prison for life!"

After the hearing, Roman and I drank two bottles of Champagne and danced around my house. I laughed manically because I was both overtired and euphoric. He had his usual hotel room booked at the Soho Beach House, but he stayed with me instead and we curled up in bed together like we used to do at his parents' house. It was the first time anyone had been on Jason's side of the bed since he died almost a year ago. I had bought a new mattress and bedding. It was just too macabre to sleep on the same ones that once held his corpse. But I kept the bed frame. And seeing Roman lie there was surreal. But it felt safe and right. I rested my face against his rock-hard shirtless chest, so aware of his intrinsic attractiveness and yet so aware of the platonic feelings in my core. I tried to match my breath with his, our chests expanding and deflating in time. I looked up at him. He had never asked me if I had done it. Any of it. And he never would.

I fell asleep. Heavy and uninterrupted. My first truly deep sleep since I had missed the beep. When my eyes slowly found their way open, I stretched and looked at the time. I'd been asleep for fifteen hours. I turned toward Jason's side and found I was alone. A little note sat on his pillow. It told me that Roman had taken an early flight back to DC. I was out of danger, so his attention turned back to his life, back to his other clients. His work here was done.

I lay in bed another minute and felt like a little kid when my parents left me at home alone for the first time. That nervous excitement when they pulled out of the driveway, down the street, and out of sight. Like I was finally a grown-up, trusted with the TV and the thermostat and the contents of the fridge. Left alone to make my own decisions, both good and bad. It was exhilarating and scary all at once. It was autonomy.

There was a buzz in my belly. I was completely free and completely alone to do as I pleased. I got out of bed and walked around my empty house. I had a funny little feeling that I had gotten away with something, somehow.

I made coffee and I fed Mr. Cat. And then I sat at the kitchen island. What was I supposed to do now? For the past year my entire focus had been worrying about being accused of killing Jason. It took all my energy, and now that it had been removed, I felt like I was free-falling. As horrific as the worry was, it spread out and filled the void that Jason's death had left. But now that the worry was gone, there was just the void.

I finished my coffee and walked through the empty house again. I rambled to Mr. Cat. I had nowhere to go, nowhere to be. I had no clients, no office, no plans, no local friends, no hope of anonymity or privacy. I had lost the city I loved. I knew the press would be descending upon me soon, once news of my case being dropped reached people's desks. But for now there was a stillness.

I checked my phone and did see the press had already swarmed Gertrude's house. Her accidental admission of my innocence virally spread around town, and even made it all the way up north to Georgia. Where Jason's high school sweetheart, Cindy, was interviewed by the local news and spoke up about him being abandoned and raised without a mother. Gertrude's character was finally being attacked, rightly so, and the best part about it was that my hands were clean.

I noticed the empty bottles of Champagne from the night before, and a sick feeling crept in. I wanted to keep celebrating my exoneration, but Jason was still dead. His closets were still empty. The kitchen countertops were still clean and bare. All my fantasies about having less clutter and more open space seemed so misguided now. Here it was and there was absolutely nothing comforting about it.

I found Mr. Cat inside the primary bedroom closet and stood with him. He circled my ankles a few times and threw his flank against me. Everything was still so quiet. My clothes looked sparse along the rows and rows of wood dowels. Large gaps between each hanger. Like a forest that had been excessively culled. The calm after the storm had arrived, and slowly thoughts of normal daily life breezed through me. I accepted in that moment that my existence as I knew it was over and it would never go back to how it had been. And that I desperately needed a haircut.

CHAPTER 51

LOS ANGELES

THERE CONTINUED TO BE SHOUTS AND WHISPERS THAT maybe the Purple Widow had killed dozens of people over the years. That Jason plus the other three were just the tip of my murdering iceberg. But I knew it was only the three. And because my mind organized things in terms of syllabi, it did occur to me that I had a bit of a schedule. When I was five, when I was sixteen, and when I was twenty-five. About one person every decade. Similar to my number of sex partners, when I thought about that number in a larger context, one murder every ten years seemed extremely reasonable. We all encounter bad people all the time. Backstabbing coworkers. Assholes who litter. Fathers who hit. Mothers who neglect. People who run puppy mills. And on and on. But I was not in the business of killing off every jerk who crossed my path. I was not a homicide slut.

I admitted to myself that the prosecutor was right when he said three was a pattern. So I came to the conclusion that this pattern would become my new rule. One murder every ten years would be the maximum I allowed myself. Like my vow to never sleep with more men than my current age, this rule would give me boundaries and keep me in check. I wouldn't rush into anything. I would take my time. See what opportunities presented themselves. I had about four more years to think on it. To weigh my decisions. And choose wisely.

As I delicately swaddled my cherished lamp in bubble wrap and gingerly placed it into a moving box surrounded by packing peanuts, Detective Jackson came knocking. I knew as long as I was in Miami, he would be watching me. Trying to catch me in some other criminal act. And he was not the only one. So many other people in my hometown still viewed me as an enemy. It was clear, even after my exoneration, that I needed to move. To legally change my name. To dye my hair a color that did not match my eyes. To start over somewhere else so I could have a new life and a new office and a new practice with patients who did not look at me and think, *The Purple Widow.* I taped up the box and grabbed a purple Sharpie and wrote "Fragile" on all four sides. Even with my lasting moniker, I refused to give up my purple pens. I would not let a misinformed public take that harmless joy away from me. And I did not answer the door.

The other reason I wanted to move far away was because although I thought she was too much of a narcissistic coward to ever commit suicide, it did occur to me Gertrude might kill herself in order to frame me. Her one last fuck-you to take me down someday. And if she did try this, I needed an airtight alibi. I needed to be on the other side of the country.

Soon after I was arrested, Ellie found the top of a condom wrapper in Spencer's jean pocket while she was doing the laundry. It was such a textbook mistake, I was sure Spencer wanted to get caught cheating. He was desperate for Ellie to notice him for a moment instead of throwing all her energy and love at their daughter. When she confronted him, he didn't deny any of it. She was stunned at first, but took a step back and then had the wisdom to see that his affair was merely the symptom that brought the diagnosis to light. The marriage had been sick and deteriorating for a while now, and they both had contributed to the illness.

So Ellie, like me, wanted to get out of her established life and start over somewhere entirely new. She told Spencer she hoped to leave New York and take Molly. He could see her summers and holidays and any other time he wanted to visit. What he wanted was to make this divorce as easy and happy as possible for her and Molly, so he supported her out-of-state move.

After much debate, Ellie and I decided on Los Angeles. It was similar enough to Miami that I felt I could be happy there. And it was different enough from New York City that Ellie felt she could also be happy there.

My parents helped me put the house, and Jason's condo, on the market. They helped me pack up my clothes, and my grand-mother's clocks, and my favorite coffee mugs. And they prom-ised to come visit all the time. My leaving would be a good excuse to get them out of their usual routine. Especially since Miami had been no picnic for them the past year either. They had a few people who had stood by them, but the masses dubbed them the Purple Widow Parents.

Within a couple weeks the only thing that remained unpacked was Mr. Cat. The movers loaded all my memories and boxes into the van, and I had hope that maybe one day I could learn to love another city as much as I loved Miami. And maybe one day I could even learn to fall in love with another man, and then eventually excitedly fill half a closet with his belongings, and grow so comfortable with him that in time I would start to daydream about him dying and the closet being gloriously half empty again. Because it is only when one feels truly stable and content that those daydreams are even possible.

CHAPTER 52

LOLLIPOP

I RECEIVED A PACKAGE IN THE MAIL THAT HAD NO RETURN address. My new name and temporary West Coast address were written in clear block letters. I opened it, nervous. Almost no one knew where to find me. Inside the package, wrapped in lavender tissue paper, was one sour apple Blow Pop. This was Jesula's favorite flavor. I knew this because when I went into the Kremlin bathroom for the very first time, I bought a sour apple Blow Pop from Jesula's basket of goodies. In half Creole, half English, she told me that sour apple was also her favorite flavor.

What she didn't expect to then happen was that I bought a second sour apple for full asking price and handed it to her. We clinked the lollipops together like a cheers with wineglasses. She often told me this moment stayed with her forever. Because it was the first moment she felt seen by a stranger, when she was so used to being invisible.

The lollipop must be from her, I thought. But I was confused about why she was sending this to me now. Was it a secret message?

Or a sign? She had avoided me ever since our hug in the judge's office. As I searched for an answer, I also searched the box. And found a note inside that had fallen underneath the sea of tissue. It read, "Ask Roman."

I called him immediately. After a pause, he said he did feel there had been enough time and distance to tell me the whole truth. "What whole truth!?" He wouldn't say over the phone. Leaving me to wonder in my nondescript week-to-week rental apartment until his flight arrived at LAX. He only had an hour to talk. Then had to turn around and go right back to DC. So I met him in baggage claim. It felt fitting.

We sat on a row of plastic airport chairs and watched as travelers impatiently waited for their luggage to spin around on the metal centipede. He explained to me that he set everything up in regard to Jesula and Gertrude. I was stunned, but also, at the same time, not surprised. He left nothing to chance, ever, not even a friendly game of Trivial Pursuit. Not even a college midterm. Why should he have to study for a test when the answers already existed in the world, available for the taking? Why not guarantee success? Maybe this was cheating, but to him, it was also a much better use of his time and a surefire way to win. So of course he never left my own fate up to chance either.

Roman told me that he knew Jesula was on our side from the moment he interviewed her. He interviewed almost everyone who had ever met me, to get a sense of who was truly my friend and who was not on my side. And his instincts about people in this regard were spot-on. He knew how to bring out people's true feelings, and then use those feelings as leverage one way or the other.

It was Jesula, following Roman's instructions to the letter, who did in fact first approach Gertrude for money. Roman used

Gertrude's own evilness against her, knowing that although it was illegal and unethical, she would be more than happy to pay for the testimony that would take me down. Had Gertrude refused to pay and reported this wrongdoing immediately, Roman's plan would not have worked. But in the game of justice, using one person's bad character to your advantage is just as important as using another person's good character.

Money in hand, Jesula then said all those nasty things about me and my marriage to the grand jury, only so she would later be able to take them back. Roman had her build up the strength of the opposition's case so she could then tear it down. He was in control all along, knowing that when Jesula stepped forward and admitted her lies to the judge, the prosecutor's plan of attack would crumble. Roman kept me in the dark about all this because he had to make sure none of it could ever come back on me. Jesula played her role impeccably, knowing it would devastate me in the short term, but was worth it in order to save me in the long run.

Roman confirmed my belief that Jesula was in fact a United States citizen. He made sure of it before he put his plan into action. So that if his plan somehow backfired, she would never actually be in danger of being deported. If she was pressed, her citizenship was something she could easily pretend she was confused about. She could claim Gertrude scared her, telling her lies about poor Black immigrants being shipped away. Jesula was so often overlooked because she was a Haitian maid who spoke English with a thick accent, and she was thrilled to finally have a chance to use this usual disadvantage to her advantage and help me, because I was the one person who had never overlooked her.

Roman told me that package was a sign. Jesula's decision to be the pawn that would save my future all came down to a lollipop. I couldn't believe such a small gesture, so many years ago, would pave the way for her to feel such loyalty. And as Roman spoke, quietly yet still audibly over the din of the hordes of people picking up loads of baggage, I thought about my gesture of covering for him in college. Two people who had never met before had acted together to protect me when I needed it, because I was good to them. It was my kindness that saved me in the long run, not my cunning.

I sent Jesula a package back. No return address. Just a stuffed kangaroo. It was in this way that we communicated secretly for years. I would eventually use some of the money from Jason's life insurance policy, which was paid out to me once all the charges were dropped, to set up a college fund for Jesula's son. By the time he was a senior in high school, there would be enough for a private college education and graduate school if he so chose. If not, it would sit and accrue interest, and once he turned thirty and was mature enough to make good decisions, the money would be his to use as he pleased. I could never overtly thank Jesula for what she had done for me. Roman advised against that, legally. But there were other ways I could show my deep appreciation. Jesula helped to give me a better future; it seemed right that I help give her son a better future to return the favor.

CHAPTER 53

AUNT

I WATCHED MR. CAT LOUNGE IN THE DRY WARMTH OF THE
West Coast sun while my niece, Molly, played pretend under the
shade of the avocado tree. Ellie and I pooled our finances and
together had the money to buy a spacious, airy four-bedroom
house in Santa Monica. I was close enough to the beach to feel
sort of a sense of home. But I would never get used to having the
ocean on the wrong side.

Just like when we were kids, Ellie and I once again slept under the same roof. Sometimes through the walls I could hear her
cry at night, but this time I knew it was healthy and cathartic
and I wasn't worried about her in the long term.

I took the California state licensing boards and passed, so I
could slowly start to rebuild my psychology practice. I liked my
new office. It was three blocks from the Pacific Ocean. And I
didn't need an orchid because right outside the window was a
giant bright pink bougainvillea. I could ask my very first West
Coast patient, Jennifer B., to describe the color, the shape, the

movement of the flowers. And when I wasn't working, I made time for my new hobby, hiking.

As I stood on the edge of a canyon, wearing my trail shoes and long-sleeve wicking top, items I never would have dreamed of owning in Miami, I remembered Alisha telling me that some people are afraid of heights for fear they might fling themselves off into the abyss. I had no desire to do this, but my closeness to the drop did make my hiking partner, Ameena, extremely uncomfortable.

She barked at me like I was one of her sons. "Hey! Too close! Get away from there." I appreciated that she cared, so I stepped back from the precipice.

Ameena was in LA a lot because of conferences. She of course had followed my legal horrors, and never for a second believed any of it, but she couldn't leave her kids and her wife and her job again so soon after taking a full week off to come to my wedding and another full week off to come to Jason's funeral. So she had not seen me in a long time. She was my only friend, other than Roman, who stood by me through it all.

We hiked for at least five miles and covered every topic from hairstyles to reincarnation. She asked if I had considered dating again. I said, "Not yet."

Then she said, sort of wistfully, "I always thought you would end up with him, you know?"

I didn't know. "Him who?"

"Roman."

Oh. I thought about this for a long while. Roman and I talked or texted almost every day. He had been out to visit me in LA three times already. And I had visited him in DC twice. His modern condo was sparsely decorated with Cubist art, blown glass, and sharp furniture. Everything about it said, *Don't get too comfortable here, because you won't be staying long.* We went out to a bar one night, planning on playing wingman for each other, like old times. But we got too caught up in our own conversation to look around for prospects. Roman paraded me around his fancy law firm, which seemed to be made entirely of polished mahogany. I saw a man there, and was certain it was the same man in the video who asked Gertrude to support the JDRF. I didn't ask Roman to confirm because I didn't need to.

I gazed at the skyline that was still so new to me and answered Ameena. "I guess in a weird way I kind of did end up with him."

That afternoon, it was my turn to pick Molly up from preschool. I waited in line with the parents and nannies, inching along as each car lovingly scooped up offspring.

Molly wore a yellow dress with pink stripes that day. She would be hard to miss. I watched the other children bound out of school, full of tales and covered in clumps of clay and swipes of Magic Marker. Then I saw her walking out slowly, slumped. Something was very off. I strapped her into the car seat in the back and asked, "What's wrong, Molly bean?" She shook her head from side to side at first, as if to say, *I don't want to talk about it.* But I was good at this game, since it was my job to get people to talk about exactly what they didn't want to talk about.

By the time we pulled into our driveway I knew all about a little boy named Mason who had been mean to Molly. He called her names, pushed her on the playground, and spit in her hair. Bullying was a hot topic by now. There were school assemblies and public service announcements all about it. The world had gotten better in that way, more aware, but none of this would actually solve the problem.

I looked at Molly and told her, "We can't stop all the bullies, but don't be scared. We can stop being the victim." I saw a flash of strength in her eyes. I knew I wouldn't need to protect Molly in the same way I'd felt I had to protect Ellie. But I could be a good aunt, and give Molly the tools she needed to protect herself. All the while keeping an eye out for my own bullies to slay.

By the time Ellie got home from work that evening, Molly and I were eating our favorite snack, slices of banana with a little honey drizzled on top, and we were giggling together.

ACKNOWLEDGMENTS

THANK YOU:

Josh Turner McGuire. You took a manuscript that was moldering in my laptop and gave me the confidence to dive back in and write a living, breathing novel. You are an incredibly insightful literary manager and a trusted friend.

My editor extraordinaire, Danielle Dieterich. You truly get my voice, and your perceptive guidance elevated this work to heights I could not have achieved without you!

Jess Regel, my literary agent, for taking this on immediately upon reading, believing in it fully, and sharing my passion for murderous antiheroines.

Chad Christopher, my entertainment lawyer, for always having my back.

To my attorney friends, Page Wilkins, Steve Mercer, Sue Mercer, and Allyson Ostrowski, who offered legal advice when I would call them and say, "So if the police thought I killed my husband . . ." and they would say, "Please tell me this is for something you are writing!" And Mike Ferrara, thank you for your legal counsel, but mostly for being a lifelong friend and an indelible muse.

Dr. Stephanie Wells, for talking me through the ins and outs of college cheating. Jennifer Fenten, LMFT, for always being a kind and caring friend, and for walking me through the process of how one becomes a psychologist. Michele Blair and Don Barenfeld, for imparting life-changing wisdom and life-affirming skills fifty minutes at a time.

Randi Barnes, for being my BFF, the angel on my shoulder, and sharing that piña colada with me when I finished my first draft. Lisa Dickey, for all the sage advice about publishing, for truly wanting me to succeed, and for helping me spell the hard words.

Dan Bonventre, for reminding me to write a novel. Page one might not have happened without you. Gabe Lewis, for your generosity in friendship and murderous ideas. Thomas Harris, for always believing I could do it. Ashley Platz, for reading an early draft and supporting me mind and body and soul. Hanna Stanbridge and Chris Martin, for always being there to pick me up when I was at wit's end.

Mother, better known as Susan, for turning me into an avid reader, encouraging me to be an avid writer, and nitpicking to attempted perfection. My siblings, Berns and Chauncey, this is of course a work of fiction, but the loyalty I feel for you certainly helped me imagine.

To all the beloved pets in my life who taught me about unconditional love and unimaginable grief.

My husband, Matt Kay, for supporting me and challenging me and bringing out the best in me. And for loving me when I am at my worst.